Funny [illegible]

"Sweetheart, now th[illegible] place, would you be willing to come up here alone?" Seeing by her expression that she was far from delighted at the prospect, he added quickly, "Or ask Lady Dunnington to come with you, if you'd rather not do it alone."

"Do *what* alone?" she asked, all at sea.

"Have a look about the place. Get someone to show you around, if possible. Ask questions, the sort of questions one might ask if one were hoping to persuade a family member to become a patient."

"Of course, if you wish it, but wouldn't you prefer to ask the questions yourself?"

His gaze slid away from hers, and he suddenly became very interested in the passing scenery. "I—can't."

"Why not?" she asked in growing suspicion.

"Because," he said, "I'm the patient."

THE JOHN PICKETT MYSTERIES:

PICKPOCKET'S APPRENTICE
(prequel novella)

IN MILADY'S CHAMBER

A DEAD BORE

FAMILY PLOT

DINNER MOST DEADLY

WAITING GAME
(Christmas novella)

TOO HOT TO HANDEL

FOR DEADER OR WORSE

MYSTERY LOVES COMPANY

PERIL BY POST

INTO THIN EIRE

BROTHER, CAN YOU SPARE A CRIME?

NOWHERE MAN
(Christmas novella)

Death Can Be Habit-Forming

Another John Pickett Mystery

Sheri Cobb South

DEATH CAN BE HABIT-FORMING

1

Which Finds John Pickett Embarked upon a New Career

"Why can't I go too?"

In answer, John Pickett, formerly of Bow Street, paused in the act of draping a satin-lined cloak of black velvet over his wife's shoulders and looked down into the pleading gaze of his ten-year-old half-brother. "Because you weren't invited," he said with all the impatience of one who has answered the same question too many times already. "It's not a children's party."

"He's quite right, you know," agreed Julia, albeit not without sympathy. "You would be shockingly bored, for none of Mr. Colquhoun's grandchildren are visiting at present."

Christopher Pickett, more familiarly known as Kit, did not seem to consider the dearth of youthful companionship a disadvantage. "Mr. Colquhoun gives me a penny every time he sees me," he informed them in the aggrieved tone of one who is being robbed of great riches.

"Be a good lad for Rogers and Mrs. Applegate, and I'll give you tuppence," promised Pickett.

Julia frowned at him, but merely reminded Kit that Mrs. Applegate had said he might help her with the baking. Not until they had left the house in Curzon Street did she raise any objection, saying, "Really, John, I cannot think it a good idea to pay a child for good behavior. You know what they say about virtue being its own reward. Besides," she added in a more pragmatic vein, "you run the risk of setting a very expensive precedent."

"If we were talking about any other child, I would agree," he said, taking her gloved hand and tucking it into the curve of his arm. "But this is Kit. I have every confidence that any rewards he earns for good behavior will be well within the means of even the most fledgling clerk. Are you quite certain you want to walk? You wouldn't be more comfortable in the carriage?"

If Julia was surprised at the abrupt change of subject, she didn't show it. "*Quite* certain," she assured him, pressing her free hand to the swell of her abdomen. "It isn't as far as all that, and climbing in and out of a carriage is getting more difficult every day." After a tactful pause, she added, "But speaking of clerks, what—or rather, how much—do you intend to tell Mr. Colquhoun?"

"I should say that depends on what, or whether, he asks," Pickett said with a shrug. "It's quite possible the subject won't come up at all."

Julia made no reply, but her silence was apparently answer enough.

"You needn't look at me like that," he said, bristling. "It's nothing to be ashamed of."

She gave his arm a reassuring squeeze. "No. Not at all."

They walked on in companionable silence until, just as their destination came into view, Julia's steps slowed, and she looked up at her husband.

"John—at the risk of sounding like an odiously nagging wife—" She faltered, reluctant to say more.

"What?" he prompted.

"I've been meaning to mention it, but the time never seemed right—"

"What?" he said again. "Sweetheart, you must know you can tell me anything. Is there a problem with Kit?"

"No—well—yes, but only indirectly." She took a deep breath. "John, you need to mind your vowels."

"My wot?" asked Pickett, all at sea.

"Your vowels," she said again, with exaggerated enunciation. "I confess, I had hoped you might influence Kit, rather than the other way 'round."

"Oh," said Pickett, abashed. "I'll try to be more careful. Perhaps not at work, though, or Mr. Ludlow will accuse me of putting on airs."

Julia frowned. "I must say, your new employer sounds perfectly beastly."

"You're not wrong," Pickett admitted. "Still, he gave me a position, so there is that."

"No doubt the best decision he ever made," she declared stoutly. In fact, she suspected her husband's new position was a much greater trial than he let on. But his pride had sustained blows enough over the last few months; if he chose to save face by pretending to be perfectly happy as a counting-house clerk, she would not press for confidences he was not ready to disclose. He would tell her when he was ready. Until then, she could wait.

If Pickett had entertained hopes that his former magistrate would exercise the same forbearance, however, these were destined to be dashed. They were scarcely halfway through the soup course when, having exhausted the subjects of the weather, the latest developments at the Bow Street Public Office, and the challenge of finding a reputable school willing to accept a pupil of Kit's checkered background, Mr. Colquhoun set down his wineglass, turned to Pickett, and said, "Well, John, how goes the private inquiry business?"

"It doesn't," Pickett said in an airy tone, quite as if it didn't matter at all. It was a credible effort, and one which might have deceived anyone less well-acquainted with him than was the man seated at the head of the table—the same man who, a decade earlier, had plucked the fourteen-year-old John Pickett from the rookery of St. Giles. "In fact, I've taken a position as a junior clerk for an importing firm in the City. The pay is not great, and the hours are long, but I have every hope that I may rise in the profession."

"I don't doubt it," was the Scotsman's only reply, and although the words were innocuous enough, there was something in his tone that put Pickett instantly on the defensive.

"The work is not uninteresting," he said quickly. *At least for the first eight hours or so*, he might have added, but did not. "You'd be surprised how many ships arrive in London every day. And their cargo! Tea from the East India Company, of course, but also coffee from Ceylon, saffron from Iran, opium from Turkey—"

"Aye, and more than is entered into any ledger, I'll be bound," Mr. Colquhoun observed cryptically.

Pickett regarded the magistrate with a puzzled frown. "Sir?"

"Not all the opium entering the country is intended for medicinal purposes. Some finds its way into the dens of Limehouse. Some, in a case of carrying coals to Newcastle, is smuggled into China."

"I should think China had enough opium of its own," Pickett objected. "By all accounts, the poppy grows there in abundance." Even after a month of clerking for a firm of importers, Pickett still lacked the magistrate's extensive knowledge of international trade, but he was more than willing to encourage his mentor to expound at length on any subject he desired, if by so doing Pickett might forestall any further interrogation as to his own career choices.

"One would certainly think so," agreed Mr. Colquhoun. "I believe the practice serves to establish a sort of back-door trade with a country that is generally closed to the West. China, in turn, pays for its haul with silver from South America—at least some of which, one must assume, eventually finds its way to your old haunt."

"My old—?"

"The Bank of England's bullion yard," explained the magistrate, with a twinkle in his eye.

Pickett grinned somewhat sheepishly in response. The conversation had come full circle, then, from his new position to the act that had led to his resignation from his old one. And although Mr. Colquhoun had readily believed that he'd acted under duress, breaking into the bank in exchange for Kit's freedom, Pickett could not reconcile it with his conscience to remain with Bow Street—hence his metamorphosis from a principal officer at Bow Street to a very junior clerk in the City.

"But," continued the magistrate, jabbing the air with one forefinger, "You're wrong when you say I would be surprised by the commerce on the Thames. The River Police wasn't formed in a void, you know. Why, ten years ago, almost half a million pounds worth of cargo was stolen every year, and most of it—"

"That's quite enough, Patrick," interrupted his wife, in a weary tone that suggested she had heard his views on the topic more than once. "Julia and I don't intend to sit here listening to you two talk shop all night. For my part, I should like to know how wee Kit is adjusting," she added, turning from her husband to his protégé.

As Pickett recounted a recent incident involving his young half-brother and a squirrel that had recently taken up residence in the back garden, Mr. Colquhoun addressed Julia in an undertone. "He's unhappy, isn't he?"

"Utterly miserable," she agreed. "And he would cut out his tongue before he would admit it."

"I haven't yet named his replacement. I don't suppose he would consider—"

She shook her head. "That's very kind of you, but I'm afraid it wouldn't serve. He is convinced that business with the bank put him completely beyond the pale, and although he has the sweetest temperament of any man I've ever known, he can be amazingly stubborn once his mind is made up." She glanced across the table to make sure her husband's attention was engaged elsewhere, and sighed. "I kept hoping to hear a knock on the door and find that someone wished to engage his services. But the advertisement no longer runs in any of the newspapers—John considered it to be throwing good money after bad—so I fear it seems unlikely now that anyone ever shall."

* * *

Certainly no one had knocked on the door by dawn the next morning, so Pickett arose betimes, made his morning ablutions, and shrugged on the sober black tailcoat that had been the better of the two coats constituting the whole of his wardrobe in the days before his marriage; Mr. Ludlow, it seemed, held no truck with any garment that suggested frivolity, whether worn on his own person or on the persons of his hirelings. It was curious, in a way, Pickett reflected; he'd been a little embarrassed by the fashionable garments Julia had seen fit to bestow upon him, but now that he was forbidden to wear them, he rather missed them.

The walk into the City, the financial heart of London, required a considerably longer time than his daily trek to Bow Street had done, and since he could not bring himself to insist that Cook prepare a full breakfast for him while the sky outside was still dark, he came downstairs to find a cold but hearty repast awaiting him, along with a sleepy-eyed Julia, her dressing gown thrown over her night-rail, seated at the table.

"You don't have to get up when I do," he told her, bending to drop a quick kiss onto her tousled golden hair before seating himself and filling his plate from the selections on offer. "I've told you before."

"Yes, but"—she broke off on a yawn before continuing—"as *I've* told *you* before, if I wait until you come home in the evening, we scarcely see each other at all. Then, too, Kit wants to spend some time with you, so by the time I have you all to myself, it's too late to do anything but collapse into bed. And while I can think of a time not so long ago when that would have seemed a delightful way to spend an evening, I can't say I care much for the current iteration."

It was true. Between his long hours and her pregnancy, to say nothing of the recent addition to their household of a ten-year-old boy, their lives had suddenly and drastically changed. And although she was extremely loth to admit it, those changes had not been unadulterated bliss.

"Speaking of Kit"—Pickett reached into the inside pocket of his coat for his coin purse and extracted a large copper coin—"when he wakes up, will you give him this?"

"Of course." Julia took the coin he offered, and was unsurprised to see a tuppence in the palm of her hand.

"I only wish I could be sure he earned it," he continued darkly. "I suspect Rogers and Mrs. Applegate would swear to his good behavior even if he'd been a perfect hellion. I'm glad he's been accepted into the household, but they don't need to spoil him. And since we're on the subject—sweetheart, is it *normal* for a boy with a room of his own and plenty of toys to play with to want to spend so much time in the kitchen with the servants?"

"Perfectly normal," she assured him. "That is, I can't speak for boys, but I can assure you that Claudia and I did, and we were none the worse for it. The kitchen is always warm, you see, even in the winter, and it smells heavenly! Then, too, the cook will very likely give one currants, and chestnuts, and all the other things one's mama won't allow between meals, and won't be forever reminding one to sit up straight, or take one's elbows off the table, or—"

"Or mind one's vowels," Pickett said, regarding her with a look of limpid innocence.

"Did I hurt your feelings?" asked Julia, conscience-stricken. "I'm sorry; I never meant—"

"You didn't," he assured her. He set down his coffee cup and rose from the table, then took her hand and pulled her to her feet. "Although I feel I should warn you, the only vowels that really interest me are 'U' and 'I'."

" 'O,' Mr. Pickett," she cooed, leaning into his embrace, "what am I to do with you?"

"I'm sure we can think of something," he said, and kissed her lingeringly. At the conclusion of this mutually satisfying exercise, he turned away and picked up a cloth-covered basket containing yet another cold collation, this one intended as a midday meal with which to stave off the pangs of hunger until he returned home for dinner. "Why don't you go back to bed now? After all, you're sleeping for two."

"I think the expression is '*eating* for two,' " she said,

accompanying him to the front door. "I daresay the baby is quite capable of getting plenty of sleep on its own."

"Who said anything about the baby? I meant me." He yawned. "I suppose someday I'll be accustomed to rising before dawn, but today is not that day."

I haven't yet named his replacement. I don't suppose he would consider... The memory of Mr. Colquhoun's words rose unbidden to Julia's mind. "John—" She broke off, unsure how to offer the suggestion in a way that would allow his pride to accept it.

"Yes?" he prompted.

It was no use. He was doing what he thought was right, at a considerable cost to himself. She could not belittle his sacrifice by implying that it was not good enough or, worse, that it was unnecessary—no matter how truthful such a claim would be. She shook her head.

"Never mind. Just—have a good day, and I shall see you tonight."

He regarded her curiously, as if wondering what she had been about to say. "I love you, Julia."

"And I love you." She put up a hand and removed a minuscule speck of lint from his cravat. "So very much."

He opened the door and they stepped out onto the portico, where they kissed once more before he reluctantly released her and set out on the long trudge eastward into the City.

Julia did not return to her bed right away, but stood on the portico and watched him go. His hair, she had noticed, was rather badly in need of a trim, and this, combined with the black tailcoat he'd been wearing when she'd first met him, reminded her forcibly of John Pickett as she'd first known him: young, inexperienced (in more ways than one), and completely in over his head investigating a murder that had set him at odds with both the English aristocracy and the Foreign Office. And yet he'd pulled it off, through sheer dogged determination and keen, if underrated, intelligence.

At what point, she wondered, had she first begun to suspect that the rather gauche, inarticulate young Bow Street Runner who had proven her innocence in the teeth of all opposition was destined to play a much greater rôle in her life? She could not say, any more than she could identify the exact moment that she had fallen in love with him. But love him she did, with a fierceness that was at times almost painful. It seemed a travesty to think that, after all his heroics on her behalf, he should live out the rest of his days endlessly recording figures in a ledger, in thrall to his own unbending sense of honor.

As the distance widened between them, his retreating form grew increasingly blurred and indistinct in the early morning fog, almost as if he were fading away before her eyes. And then the fog swallowed him up, and she saw him no more. Heaving a little sigh, she went back inside and closed the door.

2

In Which Julia Receives an Unexpected Caller

The echoes of St. Michael's church bells tolling the hour had not yet faded as Pickett zigzagged his way down the dark, narrow passage aptly dubbed Crooked Lane and burst through the door of Ludlow & Ludlow, Importers on a swirl of fog, only to discover a tall, cadaverous man wearing an old-fashioned bag wig and a coat of rusty black, standing just inside and rather pointedly regarding the watch in his hand.

"Cutting it a bit close, Mr. Pickett." He snapped the timepiece shut and tucked it into his waistcoat pocket, all the while regarding the new arrival with disfavor.

"I'm sorry, Mr. Ludlow, sir," Pickett said somewhat breathlessly, having drawn up short only just in time to avoid barreling full tilt into his employer. "The fog is rather heavy today, and—"

"I'm not paying you for idle talk about the weather!" barked Mr. Ludlow. "If I want to know about fog, I'll look out the window."

Pickett judged it best not to point out that this tactic was unlikely to prove very informative, given the fact that so little light penetrated the gloomy lane that candles were necessary even on the sunniest of days. "No, sir—er, yes, sir," he stammered, bracing himself instead for the trimming he had no doubt he was about to receive.

"Well?" demanded his employer, his face growing purple beneath his wig. "What are you standing there for? Get to work!"

"Yes, sir," Pickett said again, suppressing a sigh as he made his way past rows of desks, each one occupied by a clerk. A few of his colleagues glanced up in either curiosity or silent sympathy, while others bent fixedly over their work, pretending neither to see nor hear. No one spoke up in his defense, nor did he expect it of them; few men would risk calling Mr. Ludlow's wrath down upon his own head for a stranger's sake. And all of his fellow clerks were indeed still strangers to Pickett, even after several weeks of employment; as he had discovered very early in his tenure, Mr. Ludlow disapproved of fraternization among his staff.

Upon reaching his own desk (third row, nearest the wall opposite the window), Pickett regarded the scarred and ink-stained wooden surface with dismay. The stack of papers awaiting his attention appeared to have grown in the night; he certainly did not remember it being this thick when he'd snuffed his candle and returned his quill to its standish less than twelve hours earlier. As he took his place behind the desk and set the basket containing his lunch on the floor at his feet, he recalled a story he'd once heard as a child, a tale in which a band of elves slipped into a shoemaker's house at night and finished the man's work while he slept. Pickett had a sudden vision of a similar group of nocturnal visitors descending upon the offices of Ludlow & Ludlow, except that instead of doing his work for him, they piled still more atop his desk, cackling fiendishly all the while. Surely there was no other explanation for his acquiring such a backlog overnight.

Heaving a sigh, he reached for the paper on top of the stack, and saw at once the explanation for the sudden deluge. While he had been eating dinner with his former magistrate the previous night, the merchant vessel *Mary Katherine* had docked and her cargo had been off-loaded. Now it was his responsibility to check the ship's bill of lading against the original invoices, ensuring that Ludlow & Ludlow had actually received the goods for which the firm had been charged, then recording the transactions in a large calf-bound ledger.

One thing was certain: the stack of papers was unlikely to shrink of its own accord. He slid the first paper from the top of the pile, then removed the stopper from the bottle of ink, dipped his quill, and began to write.

* * *

While Pickett wrestled with the minutiae of international commerce, Julia sat on a sofa in the drawing room reviewing the brochures from several potential schools in which they might hope to place Kit at the beginning of the Hilary term. Since the Michaelmas term had already been well underway by the time the boy had come to live with them, she and her husband had agreed that Kit might be better served by having some time to adjust to his new circumstances before resuming his frequently-interrupted education.

What neither of them had said was that they might need the extra time to locate a respectable school willing to accept a student of Kit's checkered background.

For her part, Julia was conflicted on the issue. She cherished secret hopes that, should their baby be a boy, he might attend Eton, or at least Harrow, but even if this theoretical boy should be allowed to matriculate there (and they could scrape together sufficient funds with which to send him), any suggestion that so prestigious an institution should accept young Christopher Pickett as a scholar would no doubt be laughed to scorn. Still, she had no desire to sow the seeds of discord by appearing to favor her own child over her young brother-in-law.

And so she turned the newest leaflet over in her hand, pondering the Fountainhead Academy's description of the academic heights to be achieved by the young gentlemen (ages seven to sixteen) who had the felicity of adorning its hallowed halls. Kit, she knew, would have no very high opinion of hallowed halls, nor of the education to be attained there. But the Fountainhead Academy also included among its disciplines such manly arts as riding, marksmanship, and cricket, and these, she was persuaded, might go a long way toward forestalling any envy he might one day feel toward his hypothetical nephew. She set it aside to discuss with her husband upon his return that evening, heaving a sigh at the realization that Kit's needs would dominate their all too brief time together.

She had just picked up the next brochure, this one from The Chesterfield School (a temple of learning apparently so distinguished that even the definite article preceding its name was worthy of capitalization), when she heard a knock on the front door. A moment later, Rogers entered the drawing room.

"Pardon me, your ladyship—er, ma'am," he said, clearing his throat, "but there is a gentleman wishing to speak with the young master."

"Oh?"

From the day Julia's Bow Street Runner had been formally introduced to the staff as her second husband, Rogers had designated Pickett "the young master" to distinguish him from her first husband, who had been "his lordship"; she suspected he would still be "the young master," at least in Rogers's estimation, when he was fifty. It was not the form of address, then, that puzzled her, but something in the butler's facial expression, almost as if he were trying to convey some hidden message—a message, moreover, of far greater significance than the simple announcement of a visitor.

"Oh!" she exclaimed as enlightenment dawned. "Yes! Pray show him in at once!"

A moment later, Mr. Edward Poole was bowing over her hand, a tall fair-haired man in his early thirties, dressed with the casual elegance that bespoke the gentleman of taste and fortune.

"I regret that my husband is at—is not here at present," she said, trying not to betray the depth of that regret. "He will be sorry to have missed you."

"I've come to the right place, then?" he asked uncertainly. "The one advertised in the *Observer* a few weeks ago?"

"Yes"—*in the* Observer, *and the* Times, *and the* Morning Post, *and the*—"that is, if you have need of a—a discreet inquiry, you've come to the right place."

"But at the wrong time, it appears," he said with a note of apology in his voice. "Pray forgive me for the intrusion. I'll trespass no longer on your hospitality—"

"No, no!" Julia said hastily, resisting the urge to fling herself against the front door in order to prevent his leaving. "If you can call again later, I'm sure he would be pleased to discuss the matter with you."

He glanced at the long case clock. "Very well. Shall we say two o'clock? Will he have returned by then, do you suppose?"

Julia reassured him on this head, silently resolving to drag her husband back to Curzon Street by the heels, if necessary, to ensure that he was present to receive the visitor. Mr. Poole made his farewells, and she said all that was proper—at least, she hoped she did; she could never afterwards recall exactly what she'd said. After Rogers had closed the door behind the caller, Julia paced the drawing room floor and forced herself to count slowly to one hundred, ensuring that the unexpected guest was well out of sight before she rang for the footman.

"Andrew," she said when he answered her summons, "have Betsy fetch my bonnet and pelisse, and see that the carriage is brought 'round. I am going out!"

* * *

Pickett, bent over his work, darted a quick glance up at the large clock mounted on the wall, and stifled a groan. Its hands always seemed to move with agonizing slowness, but not today; today the hours had flown by. Now it was already past noon and the stack of invoices on his desk had not dwindled, at least not that he could tell. His progress had not been aided by the fact that the nib of his quill had snapped—twice—obliging him to locate a pen knife and trim what remained into a point fine enough to inscribe numbers and fractions of numbers legibly. Worse, he had been obliged to submit meekly to a condescending lecture on the importance of taking proper care of the tools of one's trade lest just such mishaps occur, resulting in losses to the firm in the form of wasted time, to say nothing of the cost of procuring replacements for those damaged quills.

He glanced down at the untouched basket at his feet. His belly was beginning to complain of his neglect, but he dared not stop to eat until he had more to show for the day's labors.

And yet these were not the last, nor the most distracting, of the interruptions in store. Another disruption occurred when, at twenty minutes past one o'clock, the door opened, admitting the usual cacophony of noises from the street: the cries of street peddlers, the clip-clop of horses' hooves, the creak of wagon wheels, the discordant music of a hurdy-gurdy. Softer and rather nearer at hand (and very likely inaudible to ears less attuned to it) came the sound of a lady's voice, and a moment later the lady herself entered the room. Her fashionable pelisse of blue-gray merino could not conceal the fact that she was in the latter stages of pregnancy, and she scanned the rows of clerks as if searching for one in particular.

"*Julia?*"

She brightened at once as Pickett's stunned exclamation drew her gaze. Almost everyone else turned to stare at Pickett with mingled shock and horror, for their employer held no truck with idle talk—and in Mr. Ludlow's view, *any* talk was idle talk.

The sole exception to this rule was Mr. Ludlow himself, who vehemently objected to this feminine invasion of his temple of commerce. "Now, see here, ma'am—"

"Sweetheart, what brings you here? Is anything wrong?" asked Pickett, abandoning his ledger and hurrying up the aisle to meet her. Seeing Mr. Ludlow's face growing red with barely suppressed fury, he added hastily, "Mr. Ludlow, this is my wife, Julia—Mrs. Pickett, that is." Somewhere at the back of his mind he suspected he'd got it wrong—he rather thought gentlemen should be presented to ladies, rather than the other way 'round—but at the moment, drawing his employer's fire away from his wife appeared to be the more pressing concern, followed by discovering the reason for her unexpected appearance.

"There are to be *no visitors*," Mr. Ludlow sputtered, directing this command more to Pickett than to the visitor herself. "Really, Mr. Pickett, have you no control over your household at all?"

"John, you need to come home," Julia said urgently, acknowledging the infuriated entrepreneur with the most cursory of nods. "A man called, wanting to see you. He will be returning at two, so you see, you must come at once!"

"My good woman, your husband has a job," Mr. Ludlow informed her bluntly. "Although he may not for long, if this is the sort of thing we may expect from him." This last was said with a menacing glare at Pickett which was quite wasted, as its target seemed to be completely oblivious to it.

"Was it about—? Did he want—?" Given his present company, Pickett dared not be more specific. Fortunately, Julia had no difficulty understanding the questions he could not ask.

"Yes! Pray hurry! You will no doubt wish to change your clothes, and perhaps—"

"If you walk out that door, Mr. Pickett," said his employer with terrible calm, "you need not bother walking back in again. Not today, nor any other."

Pickett cast an uncertain glance back at his desk and the unfinished work awaiting his attention, then down at Julia's flushed, eager face, and, finally, at Mr. Ludlow, tight-lipped with fury.

"Yes, sir," he said, then turned and retraced his steps down the aisle to his desk, fully aware that all eyes were upon him.

He stooped to pick up the untouched basket, then strode back up the aisle, took Julia's arm, and walked out the door of Ludlow & Ludlow, Importers without a backward glance.

4

In Which John Pickett Receives a Curious Proposition

"Oh, John! I was never more proud of you!" cried Julia in a choked voice, so far forgetting herself as to throw her arms around him in the middle of Cheapside, to the grinning enjoyment of more than one passerby. "I'm so very *glad!*"

"And I'm glad you're glad," Pickett said, gently disentangling himself from her embrace. "But surely you never walked all this way!"

"No, I took the carriage—and a very clumsy job I made of it! Ah, here it is," she said as the vehicle hove into view, the coachman having walked the horses some little distance up the lane so as not to keep them standing.

The carriage soon drew up alongside them, and Andrew leapt down from his perch at the rear in order to open the door and lower the step. Pickett tenderly handed his very pregnant wife inside, then climbed in and pulled the door closed behind him.

"Now, tell me about this man who came asking for me,"

he said, settling himself on the seat beside her. "Who was he, and what did he—look here, do you mind if I eat? I'm starving!"

"By all means!" Julia waved her hand toward the basket in a gesture that invited him to tuck in.

Having received not merely permission, but encouragement, Pickett folded back the cloth and set to with a will. Belatedly recalling his manners, he mutely held out the basket to her.

She shook her head. "Thank you, but I've already eaten."

"So, about this caller," Pickett said, once his mouth was no longer full, "who was he? Did he leave his name?"

"His name is Poole. Mr. Edward Poole. I should say he is somewhere between thirty and thirty-five years old, and a gentleman, if his clothing was anything to judge by."

But clothing, Pickett might have told her, was *not* anything to judge by; he himself owned garments that anyone would assume to belong to a gentleman, and yet look at him, a junior clerk in the City. Worse, an unemployed junior clerk who had just walked out on the only man in London willing to offer him a position. But maybe—just maybe—that was about to change.

"What does he want me for?" Pickett asked. "Did he say?"

"No, and I didn't inquire. I thought he would very likely wish to explain the matter to you alone, and in private. If you wish, I'll go up to the schoolroom with Kit so you may conduct the interview on your own."

On your own. Before, there had always been Mr.

Colquhoun to whom he could go for advice, or with whom he could share his ideas. He could even call on members of the Foot Patrol, if he expected to be met with resistance. To be sure, Julia was always ready with a listening ear, and perhaps a suggestion (and often a very useful one, at that), but it was unrealistic—yes, and unfair—to expect her to possess the same sort of expertise he might look for in his former Bow Street colleagues. No, however supportive and helpful she might be, he was, for all intents and purposes, on his own.

He looked down at the half-eaten roll in his hand, and put it back into the basket. Suddenly he wasn't so hungry anymore.

* * *

By a quarter to two, there was nothing to do but wait. Pickett had changed his sober black tailcoat for the plum-colored one that, he hoped, would convey the impression of a man who was prosperous and fashionable, yet steady and responsible enough to be entrusted with the most delicate of secrets. For her part, Julia suggested to Kit that the two of them might go upstairs to the schoolroom and try their hands at putting together the dissected map that had thus far defeated him. It soon became apparent, however, that Kit had ideas of his own.

"If we go outside into the back garden," he suggested, "we can listen in by the window."

"Why, Kit, you should be ashamed of yourself!" exclaimed Julia, quite certain she should scold him, but trying her best not to laugh. "What would your brother say?"

Kit pondered this home question for a long moment.

"He'd say we need to stand right up against the wall, so's we can't be seen from the window."

"And the worst thing about it," Julia said much later, when she recounted this story to her grinning husband, "is that I'm very much afraid he was right!"

In the meantime, Julia had tutored Pickett in the niceties of playing host (and, had he but known it, enlisted Rogers's aid in case the young master should require a nudge in the right direction), so that when Mr. Edward Poole knocked on the door at fully ten minutes past two o'clock—by which time Pickett was well on the way to pacing a bald spot in the drawing room carpet—all was in readiness to receive him.

"Mr. Edward Poole," Rogers announced, and a moment later Pickett's first client entered the room.

"Pray forgive my tardiness," Mr. Poole said, offering his hand. "I hope I haven't inconvenienced you."

"Not at all," Pickett assured him with perhaps less than perfect truth, shaking his guest's hand and trying to ignore the butterflies cavorting about in his stomach. "I'm sorry I missed you when you called this morning."

These pleasantries having been exchanged, Pickett knew a moment's panic. What was he supposed to do next? Dimly, he recognized that he ought to discover what, exactly, the man wanted of him, but what then? What if he couldn't deliver what his advertisement had promised? What did he know about making "discreet private inquiries"? What did he really know about investigating at all, his six years at Bow Street notwithstanding?

"*Ahem.*" The sound of Rogers clearing his throat served

to break him out of his paralysis. "If I may make a suggestion, sir, a very excellent sherry was sent over from Berry Brothers just this morning. Shall I decant a bottle?"

"What? Oh! Yes—yes, thank you!" As Rogers departed on this errand, Pickett turned his attention back to his guest. "Won't you sit down, Mr. Poole?"

"Thank you," replied the visitor, regarding Pickett with a somewhat puzzled expression as he sank onto one of the two sofas of straw-colored satin situated at right angles to each other.

No doubt wondering what he's let himself in for, Pickett thought, painfully aware that he was hardly showing to advantage. Seating himself on the adjacent sofa, he said, "I believe my wife said you came in answer to my advertisement in the *Observer*?"

"Yes, although I confess, I was expecting someone rather older."

Someone demonstrating at least a modicum of competence, for starters, Pickett thought. Aloud, he said, "I assure you, I am not without experience. I spent six years with the Bow Street Public Office, and was made a principal officer at the age of three-and-twenty."

Whatever Mr. Poole might have said to this claim was unknown, for at that moment Rogers returned, bearing a silver tray containing a decanter of the promised sherry along with two stemmed glasses and a plate of cakes. Talk was suspended while the butler placed the tray on a small table positioned between the two sofas, then filled both glasses and replaced the decanter on the tray.

"Will there be anything else, sir?" he asked Pickett in a subservient manner calculated to dispel any impression (true or not) that the master of the house took his cues from the butler, rather than the other way 'round.

"No, that will be all, Rogers. Thank you," Pickett added, and Rogers, excellent servant that he was, merely bowed and withdrew, never betraying by so much as the flicker of an eyelid that he recognized the very real gratitude that lay behind the conventional expression—never, at least, until he returned to the servants' domain, where he confided to Mrs. Applegate that the young master was a pleasure to serve, him being always so appreciative of every little thing that was done for him.

Pickett, of course, knew nothing of these very gratifying sentiments, nor would he have had the luxury of dwelling on them even if he had. All too conscious that the next few minutes might well determine the success or failure of his new career, he picked up his glass and waited only long enough to see his guest take a sip before tossing back a gulp sufficient to take the edge off his lacerated nerves. Soon a warm glow filled him, and when Mr. Poole praised the excellence of the sherry, Pickett was able to accept these accolades with all the complaisance of a connoisseur before broaching the subject that had brought the caller to his door.

"Am I to understand, Mr. Poole, that you have some problem for which you require my assistance?" He was rather proud of that phrase; he only hoped Mr. Poole was impressed with his flight of eloquence.

"Er, as a matter of fact, yes," confessed the visitor, and

Pickett was pleased to note that the shoe was now on the other foot: it was Mr. Poole who seemed ill at ease. "It is a rather delicate matter, you see. It—it concerns a lady."

Pickett cocked a knowing eyebrow. "Don't they all?"

Mr. Poole was betrayed into a laugh. "For shame, Mr. Pickett! You forget, I have met your charming wife."

"Oh, but some problems are infinitely worth the having." Having established (he hoped) a rapport with the potential client, he continued. "And this lady—would she by any chance be your own wife?" Mr. Poole was, as Julia had estimated, somewhere between thirty and thirty-five. In other words, a likely age to have a wife—or, perhaps, to find himself embroiled in a dilemma involving someone else's.

"No, I'm afraid I haven't that honor," the visitor said in so wistful a tone that minds far less keen than Pickett's would have recognized that Mr. Poole entertained hopes in that direction. "But her brother was a very dear friend of mine, and I feel I owe it to his memory to take an interest in his sister's wellbeing."

His use of the past tense had initially led Pickett to suppose the two men had fallen out, perhaps over the young woman in question; the mention of "his memory," however, seemed to indicate that the friendship had met quite a different end. "The brother is dead, then." It was a statement, rather than a question.

Edward Poole nodded. "Yes, he died quite recently—September, I believe, or perhaps early October."

"I see." Pickett wished he could take notes, but he'd surrendered his occurrence book when he'd resigned his position at Bow Street. And although he had purchased a small notebook from a stationer's shop, thinking it might serve the same purpose (and never suspecting that its pages would still be blank a month later), Julia had pointed out that anyone with a problem of so sensitive a nature would not take kindly to the idea of its being committed to paper, lest this written record fall into the wrong hands. He had been forced to concede the point, and so was limited to recording the details in his brain—at least until the prospective client had taken his leave, at which point he fully intended to transcribe them in the pristine little notebook lying on the bed upstairs. What Mr. Poole didn't know, Pickett reasoned, wouldn't hurt him.

"Tell me, Mr. Pickett, are you familiar with an establishment called the Larches?"

"No" confessed Pickett, "I can't say that I am."

"It is an asylum for persons in the habit of ingesting opium. Miss—the lady's brother was a resident there when he died."

"He was an opium-eater?"

Mr. Poole shrugged. "It appears his guardians thought so—his aunt and uncle, that is, the sister of his deceased father, and that sister's husband. He is—was—a very young man, you see. He died only a few weeks before reaching his majority." After a pregnant pause, he added, "Now his sister, too, has been admitted to the same establishment."

Pickett frowned thoughtfully. "A family weakness, perhaps?"

It was the wrong thing to say. "I won't believe it!" Mr.

Poole cried indignantly. "Why, I doubt she's ever come in contact with opium in her life, aside from perhaps a drop of laudanum for a toothache or some such thing. No, Mr. Pickett, a weakness there may well be, but you may be sure the fault does *not* lie with the brother and sister!"

"Oh?"

This noncommittal response seemed to strike just the right note to encourage further confidences, for Mr. Poole asked, "Look here, may I trouble you for more of this excellent sherry? Thank you," he said as Pickett refilled his glass. "As I was saying, the parents are both deceased, and now the son has died. In the absence of any other family members, the lady now stands to inherit, upon her twenty-fifth birthday, a considerable sum."

"How old is she now?"

"Twenty-four. She will come into her inheritance in January."

"I see. And exactly what is it that you want me to do?" asked Pickett, judging it time to come to the point.

Mr. Poole took another sip of sherry. "I want you to break into the Larches and spirit the lady away before she meets the same fate as her unfortunate brother."

4

In Which John Pickett Accepts a Commission

Pickett stared at him for a long moment before asking incredulously, "You do realize that what you're asking me to do is illegal?"

"Yes, I suppose it is, but—look here, you are the fellow who broke into the bank and foiled a robbery, aren't you?"

Pickett, stifling a groan, admitted that he was the man. He could not but be grateful to Mr. Colquhoun for intervening, sparing him the humiliation of standing trial, but he wished his magistrate had contrived to do the thing without turning him into a bloody hero. He was not particularly proud of his actions, and yet, when he looked at Kit—bright-eyed, rosy-cheeked, and full of mischief—he could not regret it.

"To be honest," Mr. Poole was saying, "I don't know of any other way to go about it. They won't let me see her," he added morosely, and Pickett, recalling how regretfully the man had admitted that, no, he was not married to the lady, wondered if the Larches had a strict policy against visitors, or if she had not wished to be seen by one who bore all the appearance of a very determined suitor.

"You say the brother was under age, but if his sister is twenty-four, then surely her uncle and aunt couldn't have her committed to such an establishment without her consent," Pickett pointed out. "Perhaps, having seen her brother wrestle with his habit, she chose to go in for a cure before she followed him down the same road."

Mr. Poole shook his head impatiently. "You've got it all wrong, I tell you! She may be of legal age, but until she comes into her inheritance, she is completely in her uncle's power. Of course, if she is deemed unfit," he added darkly. "I'm sure I need not explain that her uncle will continue to administer her inheritance however he sees fit. And if he chooses to line his own pockets at her expense, well, who is there to say him nay?"

Who, indeed? Seized by restlessness, Pickett rose abruptly to his feet and began to pace. Pausing before the hearth, he snatched up the poker and stirred the coals, more from a need to be doing something than from any indication that the fire required tending. In fact, Mr. Poole's words had touched a nerve. It had not been so very long ago that he, too, had been in a very similar state as that gentleman had described, trapped and utterly at the mercy of someone else, someone who had held the power of life and death over him and would not have hesitated to use it, had Pickett not found a way to gain the upper hand. There were few things more terrifying than complete helplessness. Surely it was the moral duty of anyone who knew of a fellow creature in such circumstances to exercise whatever power he possessed on that unfortunate's behalf.

Replacing the poker, he turned back to Mr. Poole with the air of one who has reached a difficult decision.

"Look here," he said, "if I decide to take this on, it will be with the understanding that should I be caught out and criminal charges preferred against me, you will be responsible for any fines or reparations that might be levied, or, if I should be obliged to stand trial, you will pay for a defense counsel of my choosing."

"So you'll do it?" Mr. Poole asked eagerly.

Pickett nodded. "If you find my terms agreeable, yes."

"And what are your terms, pray?"

Pickett leaned one arm against the mantel, bracing himself for the worst. Between the pair of them, Julia and Mr. Colquhoun had decided upon the fees he ought to require, which to him had seemed extortionate. *Oh well, nothing ventured, nothing gained.*

"Ten pounds sterling, payable at once," he said, trying to sound as if this exorbitant sum was really quite reasonable, "plus a per diem charge of two and a half shillings, along with reimbursement for any expenses I may incur. After the matter is successfully concluded—or whenever you choose to withdraw from the agreement, whichever the case may be—I will provide you with an itemized list of any such charges." At least he'd got *something* of value from his mercifully brief employment at Ludlow & Ludlow; if he'd gained nothing else from the experience, there was no denying that he knew his way around an invoice.

"By Gad," exclaimed Mr. Poole in a voice of mingled consternation and respect, "you value your services mighty high!"

"I have reason to," Pickett replied, trying to ignore the butterflies in his belly that argued otherwise. "The Bank of England, remember?"

Mr. Poole gave a philosophical shrug. "Ah well, I like a man who knows his own worth." Setting aside his half-empty glass, he rose to his feet and strode toward Pickett with his hand held out. "Mr. Pickett, you have yourself a bargain!"

* * *

After Mr. Poole had taken his leave some half an hour later, Pickett immediately went upstairs to the bedchamber, where he spent all of twenty minutes filling the pages of his new notebook with any information that might prove useful. Mr. Poole was so careful of the lady's reputation that he had not named any of the persons in question until they had struck a bargain and shaken hands on it; now it behooved Pickett to commit those names to paper before he forgot them. First and foremost was Miss Lydia Bonner, the young woman held at the Larches against her will, and her deceased brother, Mr. Poole's friend Phillip Bonner. The guardians were Mr. and Mrs. Arthur Conway, but it was only with the greatest reluctance that Mr. Poole had made him privy to their identities at all, so fearful was he that Pickett would inadvertently place Miss Bonner in more immediate danger by betraying to these sinister persons his own plans for their niece's rescue. In the end, Pickett was obliged to give his word that he would not approach Miss Bonner's guardians until he had made sure the young lady herself was beyond their reach.

He followed the list of names with his own first impressions of the case, as well as notes to himself on possible lines of inquiry to pursue before making any rescue attempt. Having finished this task, he went up to the schoolroom to emancipate his wife and half-brother.

Kit, at least, did not have to be told twice. He bolted from the room, and the loud thumps coming from the direction of the staircase suggested that he was making the descent at breakneck speed. Pickett realized, somewhat guiltily, that he should have done this as soon as the visitor had gone; at the same time, there was no denying the fact that Kit's forced absence had considerably aided him in the task of recording his thoughts while they were still fresh.

"Sweetheart, would you care to go out for a drive?" Pickett asked Julia, taking her hand and helping her to rise from her place at the low table upon which was assembled a dissected map of Europe—a table that had not been built to accommodate adults, and certainly not adult females in her interesting condition.

"A drive?" Julia echoed in exaggerated surprise at this unexpected invitation. The social niceties having formed no part of her husband's education, the appeal of many of the *ton*'s preferred activities frankly eluded him, and one of the chiefest among these was the idea that one should take a carriage out for no other purpose than to see and be seen. Carriages, so far as he was concerned, were for conveying persons from one point to another, and even then only if the distance was so far as to make walking impractical; the idea that one should make such a journey without having any particular destination in view was, to him, an utterly foreign concept. "My dear John, do you feel quite well?" She laid a hand against his forehead. "Are you perhaps developing a fever of the brain?"

He grinned, but refused to take the bait. "It's not long now until your confinement, so you might as well get out while you can."

"Yes, and it's such a lovely day, isn't it?" She glanced toward the window that looked out over the rear of the house, where gray skies hung over a brown and barren garden. Through the bare limbs of the plane tree, she could see Kit sitting on his haunches on a patch of dead grass and trying to coax a squirrel to sit on his hand. "Where were you planning to go?"

"I thought we might take a turn about Islington," he said with a careless shrug.

Her eyes narrowed in suspicion. "And what is it that you wish to see in Islington?"

"We could have a look at the Angel," he suggested, regarding her with limpid brown eyes. "Although why I should have to drive all the way to Islington for that, when I have you right here at home—"

"John Pickett! If by that remark you mean to imply that I've grown as big as a posting-house—"

He drew her into his arms with a sigh. "No, just your husband making a clumsy attempt at a compliment and putting his foot in it, as usual."

Since she had never really suspected anything else, Julia

readily abandoned her air of ill-usage, and tipped her head back in order to press a quick kiss to his chin. "In all seriousness, John, why this sudden urge to drive to Islington?"

"There's a house there called the Larches. It's an asylum for opium-eaters trying to overcome their habit. I say, do you happen to know of a young woman, age twenty-four, by the name of Bonner?"

Julia cast her mind back. The name was unfamiliar, but then, if this Miss Bonner had made her come-out at eighteen, that would have been six years ago, in the spring of '03, just when she and the late Lord Fieldhurst would have been coming to the end of their honeymoon—in more ways than one—and trying to get out of Paris before the collapse of the short-lived Peace of Amiens. But as she had no intention of spoiling a rare day out with her second husband by dwelling on unhappy memories of her first, she merely shook her head and said, "No, I'm afraid not."

"Mr. Poole believes one of the residents of the Larches—this Miss Bonner—is being held there against her will so that her guardian can keep his hands on her money, which she stands to inherit in two months' time."

"Ugh!" uttered Julia, wrinkling her nose. "And you intend to try and speak to the lady?"

"No—at least, not yet. I only want to have a look at the place." Sensing a lack of enthusiasm on her part, he added quickly, "You need not come with me if you find the idea upsetting."

"No, no," she assured him. "That is, of course I find the idea upsetting—surely anyone of feeling must!—but I have no objection to accompanying you. Only let me fetch a bonnet and pelisse. Oh, and John—" She had already started toward the door, but turned back as a new thought occurred to her.

"What is it, love?"

"Do you want Kit to accompany us?"

He considered the matter for a long moment. "I don't think so," he said at last. "It hasn't been that long since *he* was being held against *his* will, and I don't want to stir up disturbing memories. I suppose I shall have to ask him—I don't want him to feel left out—but I'll do it in such a way that he'll turn it down."

"Oh? And just how, pray, do you intend to do that?"

"Watch and learn," he said, then took her arm and led her out of the schoolroom and down the stairs.

After a pause in their bedchamber to collect warm outer garments, they joined Kit in the small garden behind the house.

"You scared him away," Kit complained, when the squirrel took exception to the newcomers and fled. "I almost had him."

"You might have wished you hadn't," Pickett told him. "They bite, you know."

Kit offered no reply to this, for he had suddenly noticed that they were dressed to go out. "Where are you going?" His voice held a faint note of accusation, as if he suspected them of trying to steal away without him.

"We're just going out for a drive." Pickett stole an arm about Julia's waist and gazed down at her with a singularly fatuous expression on his face. "Care to come along?"

Kit, realizing this question was directed at him, eyed his brother with disfavor. "Will there be any kissing?"

"Really, Kit—" protested Julia.

"Yes, lots of it," Pickett said without hesitation.

Ten minutes later, the carriage set out from Curzon Street bearing only two passengers, these having been informed by Kit in no uncertain terms that he would much prefer to go down to the kitchen and see what Rogers was about than spend even a single minute in a closed carriage with his brother and sister-in-law while the former behaved like a moonling over a girl—even so nice a girl as Julia, he added somewhat sheepishly, giving her a look of rather shamefaced apology. The rebuffed pair accepted this decision with every appearance of somewhat disappointed understanding, but as soon as the vehicle swung left into Piccadilly, Pickett pulled Julia into his arms and kissed her with decision.

"John! In a public thoroughfare?" she protested, yielding to his ardor nonetheless.

"You don't want me to lie to the boy, do you?"

"I think you are quite shameless!" she said with mock severity, straightening the bonnet which he, in his enthusiasm, had knocked askew. "Still, I suppose it is rather pleasant not to be interrupted by gagging noises."

"Yes, I'll have to speak to Rogers about that," Pickett said. "He's old enough to know better."

"*Utterly* shameless!" she scolded, trying not to laugh. "You know very well it isn't Rogers I'm talking about!"

"To tell you the truth," he said, suddenly serious, "I don't mind letting Kit see a bit of how things are between us. He's had only Moll and her culls for his example, and I'd like him to want something better than that for himself. But I'll be more discreet in the future if you like."

"Don't you dare," she said, and returned his kiss with interest.

* * *

Islington, situated just north of Clerkenwell (which was itself situated just north of the City), had been nothing more than a sprawling village along the Great North Road until early in the previous century, when public houses and tea gardens had sprung up to accommodate patrons of the theatre at nearby Sadler's Wells. Rows of terraced houses had soon followed, to the point that the village was now a thriving town of more than ten thousand citizens. Nevertheless, it retained enough of its rural origins that it was still possible to find a large country house set in extensive grounds.

For this was exactly what the Larches was, or had once been, although Pickett, looking at it through the carriage window as they drew abreast of a wide, somewhat rusty scrolled iron gate, thought it unlikely that anyone would mistake it for a prosperous home now. The Georgian house appeared to be intact, at least from the outside, a structure of red brick whose flat, unornamented front was broken only by three rows of sashed windows and the triangular pediment crowning the front portico. Four much smaller windows interrupted the plane of the roof at intervals, suggesting a garret where servants would have been housed. Frowning slightly, Pickett pressed his nose to the carriage window and squinted for a closer look. Were there really bars on the windows of the two middle floors, or had Mr. Poole's claim—a tale that might have sprung from any one of the gothic horror novels currently in vogue—merely planted the idea in his brain? In the next instant, the carriage had rolled on, and with the change in perspective, the illusion was banished, leaving only a rather stark Palladian façade whose woodwork appeared, from this distance, to stand in need of repainting.

As for the park, the name and genius of Capability Brown were alike unknown to Pickett, but even so untrained an eye as his could recognize that the grounds had not always been so shockingly neglected. Now, however, weeds pushed their way up through the gravel covering the drive leading from the gate to the house, where untrimmed shrubbery partially obscured the ground floor windows. What had once been a small ornamental lake appeared now to be no more than a stagnant pool choked with reeds, and the little temple at its center appeared, even at this distance, to be rather badly in need of paint. The clusters of larch trees that had lent their name to first the house and then the asylum seemed to huddle together in shared misery, their bare branches raised to the sky as if in supplication.

And then they were past the gate, and the property was shut off from view by a high brick wall.

"What a thoroughly unpleasant place," Julia said, wrinkling her nose in distaste. "If this young woman Mr. Poole spoke of really does live here, she must surely be a captive; I can't imagine anyone coming here by choice."

"And yet people do, according to Mr. Poole," Pickett pointed out. "I suppose it shows how great a hold opium has on them, and how badly they want to break it."

"Or others want to break it for them," she observed darkly.

"That, too," Pickett agreed, but it became clear that his mind was elsewhere when he pondered aloud, "I wonder if that wall goes all the way around the property." He rapped on the overhead panel and instructed the coachman to slow the horses to a walk, adding, "And if that break in the wall up ahead proves to be a track leading to the rear of the house, take it!"

This proved to be the case, and soon they were turning left into a narrow alley that paralleled the wall for some little distance past the house. There were no openings at all along this stretch, and so when the coachman called back to ask Pickett if he desired him to follow the bend in the wall where it ran along the back of the property, there being no room to turn the horses in so tight a space, what with the wall on one side of the track and woods on the other, Pickett agreed, at the same time adjuring him to keep his voice down.

Along the back wall Pickett discovered what he had been looking for: a second gate of much simpler design than the once-grand main entrance, and just wide enough to admit the tradesmen's wagons that must require access to supply the kitchen's stores, along with the other sundries necessary to the daily operations of so large a house, whether it served as an asylum or a private residence. At the moment, no such vehicle was drawn up to the door at the rear of the house, nor at any of the several outbuildings, one of which Pickett thought must be a stable. In fact, there were no signs of life anywhere.

Pickett might have thought he had come to an abandoned dwelling by mistake, had it not been for the wheel tracks indicating that this gate, unlike its more magnificent counterpart, saw traffic pass through on a more or less regular basis.

Having looked his fill, Pickett lowered the window and motioned to the coachman to continue, before the man could call to him for instructions, thus betraying their presence on what was very obviously *not* a public road. The carriage moved faster as the horses picked up their pace, and soon they reached the corner where both wall and track turned back toward the main road. There was no gate along this side of the wall, but there had been, once: a door-sized stretch of wall that did not quite match the rest indicated where an opening had been bricked up. Before the place was turned into an asylum, Pickett wondered, or after? It would be interesting to know, although it might not necessarily mean anything.

"You're thinking how best to get in," Julia observed, as they re-entered the main road for the return to Curzon Street.

"I am," confessed Pickett, somewhat taken aback. "How did you know?"

"My dear John, I can almost see the wheels turning," she assured him. "And what, pray, have you decided?"

He answered the question with one of his own. "Sweetheart, now that you've seen the place, would you be willing to come up here alone?" Seeing by her expression that she was far from delighted at the prospect, he added quickly, "Or ask Lady Dunnington to come with you, if you'd rather not do it alone."

"Do *what* alone?" she asked, all at sea.

"Have a look about the place. Get someone to show you around, if possible. Ask questions, the sort of questions one might ask if one were hoping to persuade a family member to become a patient."

"Of course, if you wish it, but wouldn't you prefer to ask the questions yourself?"

His gaze slid away from hers, and he suddenly became very interested in the passing scenery. "I—can't."

"Why not?" she asked in growing suspicion.

"Because," he said, "I'm the patient."

5

In Which Mr. and Mrs. John Pickett Disagree as to Method

She stared speechlessly at him.

"Think about it," he said quickly, taking advantage of the unexpected silence to make his case before she found her tongue. "I would have to either scale the wall or pick the lock on one of the two gates, then steal across a wide stretch of grass to reach the house, then, once inside, find a woman I've never seen before in my life, convince her that she ought to come with me—a complete stranger, as far as she's concerned—and then make my escape with the woman in tow, all without being caught. Or I can be admitted as a man with an opium habit, and have as much time as I need to learn my way about the place, make contact with the lady, win her confidence, and escape with her by whatever route I've determined would have the greatest chance of success."

"It was your breaking into the Bank of England that brought you to Mr. Poole's notice," Julia pointed out. "An asylum for opium-eaters can't possibly be more difficult to breach than that."

Pickett acknowledged the truth of this claim with a nod. "Perhaps. But that doesn't mean I'm obligated to break into the Larches. Mr. Poole left the method entirely up to me." Seeing she was not convinced, he added, "I'll admit the place hardly looks welcoming, at least from the outside, but what would you expect in November? It must have looked very different a month ago, when all the larches' needles were gold."

"Do what you're considering, and you might be able to see them next year for yourself!"

He smiled a little at that. "Sweetheart, it's an asylum for opium-eaters, not a prison."

"Lydia Bonner might beg to differ," retorted Julia.

"Perhaps. But most of the patients aren't going to be held there under duress—and between you and me and the lamppost, I'm not so sure Miss Bonner is, either. It's not unreasonable to assume she may have tried opium once or twice, say, in the form of the laudanum she'd taken for a toothache or some such thing, and liked it a bit too much for her peace of mind, given what happened to her brother. It's quite possible that she went there willingly before the stuff gained too strong a hold."

"If that's the case, then why isn't Mr. Poole allowed to see her?" challenged Julia.

"Maybe she doesn't *want* to see him. Maybe the attachment is stronger on his side than on hers. Or," he added, as a new scenario presented itself, "maybe she does care for him, and doesn't want him to see her at something less than her best."

Julia jabbed an accusing finger at him. "Now you're just creating situations out of whole cloth! You don't know that."

"No." Pickett readily conceded the point. "And I won't know until I ask the lady herself."

"You could always talk to the uncle, her guardian," Julia suggested. "He's unlikely to admit to a fiendish plot, even if one exists, but his reactions might tell you a great deal about how things stand between himself and his ward—or between his ward and Mr. Poole, for that matter."

Pickett sighed. "Yes, I'd thought of that. Unfortunately, Mr. Poole made me promise not to speak to her guardians until I'd got her safely away. That's why I'd hoped you would know the family well enough to pay a social call. But without that connection, the only mutual acquaintance is Mr. Poole, and I can't let them know he's taking a particular interest in Miss Bonner's welfare. Remember, the advertisement promised 'discreet' and 'private.' "

It was not to be expected that Julia would be satisfied with this answer; nor was she. The charms of the old Angel Inn, the historic St. John's Gate in Clerkenwell, the nearer attractions of Mayfair—all were ignored as they debated the issue throughout the drive back to Curzon Street, tabling the discussion only long enough to extend a civil greeting to Rogers and a rather warmer one to Kit before withdrawing to the privacy of their bedchamber, where they resumed the debate as they dressed for dinner.

"How long do you intend to keep flagellating yourself over things you were forced to do a child in order to survive?"

demanded Julia, who had never seen a boxing match, but could feel the rope at her back nonetheless.

"I'm not flagellating myself," Pickett insisted.

"Then you're putting yourself in harm's way for no purpose at all, which is worse!"

"All right, then," Pickett said, with an exaggerated patience in his tone that made Julia want to choke him, "what would you have me do?"

She didn't hesitate. "Tell Mr. Poole you've changed your mind."

"Don't you think it's a little late for that? He's already given me a draft on his bank for ten pounds!"

"You could always give it back, or tear it up. Please don't take this case, John. I have a—a bad feeling about it."

"A fine investigator I would be, if I folded my tents as soon as I was asked to do something that made me uncomfortable!" Seeing by her set expression that this argument failed to move her, he tried another approach. "This whole thing was your idea, yours and Mr. Colquhoun's, remember? I took your advice, I placed all those advertisements, I've waited a month for some answer to them, and now that someone finally wants to engage my services, I'm supposed to give it up and go meekly back to my position at the counting-house? Oh, wait! I no longer have a position at the counting-house, because *you* came and took me away from it, so I would be home in time to meet with Mr. Poole!"

"Yes, and if I'd had any idea what he was going to ask of you, I would have left you there!"

It was exactly the wrong thing to say. She knew it at

once—now that it was too late to take the words back. She'd only meant that, while he might be bored as a clerk at Ludlow & Ludlow, he would at least have been safe there. But she could not explain it, not while he regarded her with such a strange, unreadable expression on his usually open countenance.

"I'm going to take this case, Julia," he said, and although he spoke gently enough, there was a hint of steel in his voice. "I'd hoped to have your support, perhaps even your help, but I'll make do without them if I must."

Julia struggled for something to say, some argument to put forward that might change his mind. He had the sweetest nature of any man she knew, but he could be amazingly stubborn once his mind was made up. Perhaps fortunately, she was spared the necessity of a reply by a light tapping on the door. As she was nearer to the bedchamber door than he, she paused only long enough to ensure that he was decently dressed before opening it. Kit stood there, regarding her with a look of apprehension on his deceptively cherubic countenance.

"Yes, Kit?" she prompted. It seemed that, having succeeded in gaining their attention, he now seemed unsure of what to do with it. "What is it?"

"Rogers says dinner is ready." His wary gaze shifted from his sister-in-law to his half-brother. "I thought maybe you didn't hear."

Which means, thought Julia, filled with remorse, *that they can hear us quarreling from the floor below*. Aloud, she said warmly, "No, indeed we did not! Thank you for letting us know. Pray tell Rogers we shall be down in five minutes."

By tacit agreement, the subject was not raised at the dinner table, although Kit's anxious glances made it clear that he was fully aware of the tension between them. After dinner, when Pickett excused himself to the bedchamber to look over his notes, Kit trailed Julia into the drawing room, where he sat silently next to her on the sofa, for all the world like an unhappy little ghost.

"Is he going to go?" he asked at last.

"He hasn't decided just yet," she said reassuringly, tamping down the little voice inside her head that accused her of wishful thinking.

"If he goes away," Kit continued diffidently, "what'll happen to me?"

This simple question was sufficient to inform Julia that the boy had far greater fears than his half-brother's intention of having himself committed to an opium asylum. She felt a stab of guilt for having been, albeit unintentionally, the cause (well, one-half of the cause anyway) of his distress. "This is your home, Kit, for as long as you wish to live here. But as for John's going away, I fear you must have heard something and quite misunderstood. Your brother and I were having a—a bit of a disagreement on how he should proceed regarding Mr. Poole's request. People do disagree sometimes, you know, even when they love each other very much. It doesn't mean he intends to abandon us."

"Mum's old man left her, when he found out he wasn't my da after all," Kit said matter-of-factly. "Leastways, that's what Peggoty said."

"And who, pray, is Peggoty?" asked Julia, ready—even eager—to be distracted. "Is she a friend of your mother's?"

Kit nodded. "She's got a room in the house next door to Mum." Apparently feeling some further explanation was called for, he added, "She's a whore."

"Oh," said Julia in failing accents, taken aback as always by Kit's disconcerting combination of childish innocence and worldly wisdom.

It was perhaps fortunate that this exchange gave her something to recount to her husband later, after they had tucked Kit into bed and repaired to their own bedchamber; anything, she reasoned, would be better than resuming their interrupted quarrel. But although he smiled appreciatively at her description, it seemed to her that this reaction was somewhat mechanical; the disagreement that had prompted their argument was still there, hanging in the air like a tangible presence.

Nor did it dissipate after they had slid beneath the sheets and he snuffed the candle. Granted, the advanced state of her pregnancy made the more physical aspects of marriage awkward, to say the least. But now it was all too easy to imagine that the expanse of clean white cotton sheets that separated them had nothing at all to do with her pregnancy, and everything to do with their unresolved argument.

As her eyes adjusted to the darkness, she could make out the deeper shade of blackness that was his tailcoat, draped over the back of a chair. Had it really been only this morning that he'd put it on and set out on the long walk to Ludlow & Ludlow? *Utterly miserable*, she'd told his magistrate only twenty-four hours earlier. *And he would cut out his tongue before he admitted it . . .*

"John?" she whispered into the darkness.

"Mmm?" The response, though muffled, came so promptly that she wondered if he, too, was unable to sleep.

"John," she said again, "what do you want me to ask?"

"Come again?"

She repeated the question. "What do you want me to ask? At the Larches, I mean."

"Julia?" The mattress suddenly shifted, and his voice seemed to come from much nearer and rather higher, as if he had rolled over and was now propped up on his elbow, looking down at her. "Are you saying—?"

"About what I said earlier—I could never have left you at Ludlow & Ludlow, not when I knew you were so unhappy there, and I can't blame you for taking the opportunity, after you've waited so long for it. As you said, it was my idea, mine and Mr. Colquhoun's, so it seems to me that I have an obligation to help you make a success of the thing. Besides," she added on a lighter note, "the more information I can obtain for you, the easier your task will be, and the sooner you'll be able to come back to me, where you belong."

"Oh, Julia," he breathed, "I don't deserve you." His lips found hers in the darkness.

"So, the Larches," she reminded him somewhat breathlessly, when at last they drew apart. "What do you want me to ask there?"

"I'll make you a list," he promised, and did.

Eventually.

* * *

The following day, Pickett lingered in Curzon Street just long enough to see Julia off to Islington before setting out for the home where Dr. Thomas Gilroy lived and practiced his profession.

"Why, Mr. Pickett, this is a pleasant surprise," the physician greeted him, then added in some consternation, "Unless—is Mrs. Pickett perhaps—"

Pickett was quick to reassure him. "No—at least, not when I left the house."

"In that case, what may I do for you, Mr. Pickett?"

Pickett took a deep breath. "I want you to tell me everything you know about opium."

The doctor's eyebrows rose. "Thinking of taking up the habit, are you?"

"No!" Pickett said emphatically. "The stuff made me far too muddle-headed for my liking."

"Ah, but some of its practitioners claim that it broadens their minds and opens them to new sensations," Dr. Gilroy observed.

"Let's just say that it opened my mind to a great many new sensations I could jolly well have done without."

The doctor smiled knowingly. "Opium, you see, can be both a blessing and a curse. Nothing we have at present is even half so effective at easing pain—you with your broken head could no doubt attest to that—and yet there are some people who feel compelled to take it long after the medical need is past."

Pickett could not argue the point. Still, his craving for the black bottle had sprung from a very different source. After suffering a near-fatal cosh on the head, he could not wrap his brain around the idea that Julia, Lady Fieldhurst, should love him, even want to marry him. *Him*, John Pickett, Bow Street Runner and former juvenile thief. He'd been quite certain that anything so unlikely must be no more than an opium-induced fantasy. In fact, he'd been so sure of it that he was terrified of coming out from under the drug's influence, of waking up one morning with a clear head only to discover himself alone in his Drury Lane flat, with no one but his landlady coming up to his rooms occasionally to tend him. But once Julia had convinced him—had proven beyond all doubt, in fact—that it was no opium dream, he'd lost interest in the stuff; Julia's methods of persuasion far surpassed anything that might be found in a bottle, regardless of its contents.

He frowned. "And yet you keep supplying them?"

Dr. Gilroy fixed him with a scowl as fierce as any he'd endured from Mr. Colquhoun; Pickett wondered fleetingly if all Scots were born with the ability. "And why should you suppose I've been doing anything of the kind? For that matter, why should they come to me for it? Anyone who wants the stuff can buy it from any pub, grocer, even some street vendors sell it. Have you never heard of Godfrey's Cordial, or Darby's Carminative? Aye, I see you have."

Pickett had not only heard of them; he'd even bought a bottle of Darby's when it appeared Kit might be taking ill. As soon as he returned home, he resolved, he would take it down to the scullery and dump it into the basin.

"But tell me," the doctor continued, "what is the reason

for this sudden interest in opium?"

"It's—" Pickett hesitated. Would Mr. Colquhoun have told Dr. Gilroy, a personal friend as well as a professional one, about his departure from Bow Street? Unlikely, he decided. Surely the two would have more interesting matters to discuss. "It's a case I'm working."

"I see."

To Pickett's relief, Dr. Gilroy appeared to find nothing unusual in this claim. Having committed himself this far, he decided he might as well go straight to the point. "Are you familiar with a place called the Larches?"

The physician's eyes narrowed, and he regarded Pickett thoughtfully. "Now, why, I wonder, would you be asking about a place like that? Ah, well, I won't ask you to betray professional secrets. Aye, I can't say I know much about the place, but I have heard of it."

"And what, exactly, have you heard?"

"As I say, not much. I believe it's in Islington, an old country house turned into an asylum for opium-eaters looking to overcome the habit."

"That's all?" Pickett asked, disappointed that the doctor apparently knew no more about the establishment than he did himself.

"I only know of two people who went there for a cure," Dr. Gilroy explained apologetically. "Both of them are dead now."

"*What?*" demanded Pickett, leaning forward in his chair.

"I don't mean to suggest that the treatment they received there was in any way responsible for their deaths," the doctor added quickly. "I'm not familiar enough with the place to make any such claim, aside from the observation that some people do become so dependent on the drug that they find the prospect of life without it insupportable."

"But it can be done?" Pickett pressed on. "Overcoming such a craving, I mean?"

"I daresay it might, if one has sufficient desire to do so, and the strength of character to stay the course. I don't know what methods they employ at the Larches, but you may be assured that it would be a lengthy process."

"How would you go about accomplishing it, if someone were to come to you with such a request?"

"First of all, the 'accomplishment' would be his, not mine. Nothing can be done for the man who doesn't want to be cured, and want it very badly." Pickett nodded in understanding, and the doctor continued. "As to my method, first I would discover how much opium he was taking, how often, and in what form. I would ask the patient, of course, but if possible, I would seek confirmation from his wife, or someone else close to him, to make sure he was being truthful with me—not that I would expect him to lie, precisely, but it's amazing how one in the grip of a compulsion, whatever his particular weakness, can deceive himself as to the extent of his habit. Then I would supply him with the stuff, with the proviso that he was to purchase it from no other source. Assuming he agreed to my conditions, I would decrease the dosage a little at a time over weeks—months, if necessary—much as a mother might wean a nursing infant. Of course, there is no guarantee that the process will be successful, or that some future relapse will not occur."

"And these two people who died," Pickett said, "what can you tell me about them?"

"One was a military man," Dr. Gilroy recalled, casting his mind back. "Early thirties, distinguished career, pretty young wife. Then he was seriously injured at Maida, and I don't doubt he needed every grain of opium he could get, at least at first. But I believe many such men struggle to become acclimated to civilian life, even without the added complications of opium dependency. In any case, he entered the Larches several months later. Within six weeks, he was dead."

"What was the cause of death?" Pickett asked. "Surely there must have been an inquest."

"The coroner's jury brought in the merciful ruling of 'suicide while of an unsound mind.' " The doctor's voice was carefully neutral. "The pretty young wife did not mourn for long, but married one of his fellow officers only a few months later. Granted, hasty remarriages are not unusual in military circles, although they are usually between the enlisted men and widows who have been following the drum, women who would otherwise find themselves left alone and unprotected in a strange land. Still, I can't help wondering if there was already something afoot between the young wife and her husband's brother officer, and the poor fellow found out." A delicate cough, and then the doctor added, "His injuries, you understand, were not of the sort that are conducive to a happy marriage."

"I see," Pickett said. "And the other one? The other man

who died after seeking treatment at the Larches, I mean," he added hastily, since the physician's recollections had taken them quite some distance from the original query.

Dr. Gilroy frowned thoughtfully. "I confess, that one puzzles me. Scarcely more than a boy, he was, and anyone less likely to take up the opium habit would be hard to imagine."

"His name wouldn't be Philip Bonner by any chance, would it?"

"You know him?" the physician asked sharply.

Pickett shook his head. "I've never met the fellow. But it might interest you to know that his sister is one of the Larches' current residents."

"*Lydia Bonner?*" The doctor was frankly thunderstruck. "What in God's name is *she* doing there?"

"That," said Pickett, "is exactly what I intend to find out."

6

In Which Julia Carries Out a Reconnaissance Mission

While her husband was closeted with the doctor, Julia returned to Islington, where she now sat in what at first glance appeared to be an elegant albeit somewhat outdated drawing room, but which actually served the Larches as a business office, as evidenced by the large cabinet (better suited to a gentleman's study than a lady's drawing room) situated behind a wide oak desk upon which stood a small brass plate with "C. H. Danvers" engraved upon its gleaming surface. Tall windows flanked the cabinet, their sadly faded curtains of satin brocade drawn back to offer a view of the front lawn, readily identifiable by the reed-choked pool crowned with its seedy temple.

"And this is your husband, you say?" asked the woman who regarded her thoughtfully from the opposite side of the desk, which had been set for tea just as if this were a social call. She was, Julia noted, a handsome female of about fifty, whose dark hair was threaded with silver and tightly pinned back from her face in a severe style that should have been frumpy, but which somehow enhanced the fine bone structure—and would still do so when she was eighty, long after the silver locks had completely overwhelmed the darker tresses. "How long has he taken opium, and in what form?"

"Laudanum," Julia replied, recalling the tall black bottle from which she had dosed Pickett in the aftermath of the Drury Lane Theatre fire of the past February. They had agreed that she should tell the truth as much as she was able; it was, after all, a well-known axiom that once one told a lie, one was inevitably obliged to tell more lies to cover the first, which in their turn necessitated still more lies, until the whole tangled web eventually collapsed of its own weight. With commitment to truth in mind, she added, "He was injured, you see, on the night of the Drury Lane fire, when he was struck in the head by a—a fallen beam." She was rather pleased with her use of the word "fall*en*" rather than "fall*ing*"; it had certainly been lying on the ground prior to being picked up and used as a weapon, and yet the two words sounded so similar that no one hearing the former would hesitate to interpret it as the latter. Thus were the conflicting objectives of honesty and expedience equally satisfied.

Mrs. Danvers nodded in sympathetic understanding. "It happens so often," she said in a voice that suggested long familiarity with just such a scenario. "First, one needs the laudanum to ease the pain; then one needs it to sleep; then one simply—needs it, never mind the reason why. Never fear, Mrs. Pickett, I believe we here at the Larches can do something for you."

Julia frowned slightly. "I would rather you do something for my husband."

"Of course, that goes without saying," Mrs. Danvers was quick to reassure her. "I promise you, Mr. Pickett will be taken care of."

"Mrs. Danvers," Julia began hesitantly, unsure exactly how to couch the question she knew she must ask, "what is it, exactly, that you do here?"

"Come now, Mrs. Pickett, you cannot really expect me to give away *all* of my trade secrets!" the older woman chided her with a somewhat brittle smile.

"No, of course not, but—well—he *is* my husband—"

Mrs. Danvers nodded sagely. "Believe me, Mrs. Pickett, I quite understand. And yet, when one finds that her husband is no longer the man she married, what else is she to do? Marriage is, after all, 'until death do us part.' " Seeing from Julia's expression that this was not at all the answer that lady had hoped for, she added, "As to the exact method that will be employed, that depends on the individual. I regret that I cannot give you a more specific answer at present. We shall have a better idea of how to proceed once we have had Mr. Pickett in our custody long enough to evaluate him."

Julia's brow puckered. "Your custody? You mean your care, surely?"

"If you prefer. It amounts to very much the same thing, do you not agree?"

In fact, Julia was not at all certain she did, but before she could voice an objection to what she told herself must surely be merely a matter of semantics, Mrs. Danvers had risen from her desk, saying briskly, "But perhaps you will feel more confident once I have shown you about the place."

"I should like that," Julia confessed. "My husband and I did take a drive about the perimeter, but the wall impedes much of the view." There was no particular reason why she should not disclose that earlier visit, as anyone in the house who had chanced to look out a window might have noticed the carriage creeping past.

"In that case, you no doubt saw enough to recognize that the grounds are sadly neglected. This was my childhood home, and I confess it pains me to see it in such a condition, but we have only the one gardener, and he can't keep up so large a property all by himself—certainly not in addition to his other duties."

Julia had no time to wonder what "other duties" a gardener might be expected to perform, for her hostess ushered her out of the office and up the stairs. They had not gone far down the corridor when she stopped before an open door and gestured for Julia to precede her into the room. It proved to be a small chamber containing a narrow bed, a writing desk with a ladder-backed chair pushed into its kneehole, and a second, upholstered wing-backed chair of the sort in which one might settle with a book before a roaring fire; in fact, three volumes, bound in red cloth and held upright by bookends, stood upon the mantelpiece as if holding themselves in readiness for just such a purpose. The furnishings were undoubtedly worn—Julia had only to look at the threadbare rug beneath her feet for proof—but everything was scrupulously clean, and the faint, honeyed scent of beeswax testified to the furniture's having been recently polished. Curtains of slightly faded brocade had been drawn back from the single window, revealing the front lawn with the same depressing prospect she'd noticed from the office windows.

Noting the direction of her gaze, Mrs. Danvers returned to what was clearly a sore subject. "The grounds may be sadly neglected, and comprise only a fraction of what they were in my younger days, but they are extensive enough to allow for some very pleasant exercise on fine days. Then, too, there is a library on the ground floor, from which guests are welcome to select books to take to their rooms. There is also a room where they may play billiards or cards, either alone or with their visiting family members or fellow guests—although these cooperative amusements must be closely monitored, lest one lead another astray. I fear that in spite of our best efforts some contraband opium occasionally finds its way in, no doubt smuggled in by some well-meaning visitor."

She led Julia back down the stairs to inspect the common rooms: the billiard room she had mentioned earlier, as well as a dining room ("although guests may take their meals privately in their own rooms, if they prefer," Mrs. Danvers said, adding rather cryptically, "Sometimes it's easier that way"), until finally they reached the library, where a somewhat stout man in an old-fashioned bag wig balanced rather precariously on the third rung of a library ladder as he restored a volume to its place on the shelf.

"Just returning *Tristram Shandy* from Mr. Lester's room," he said without turning around. "Not as if he'll be needing it again, what?"

"*Ahem!*" Mrs. Danvers very pointedly cleared her throat, and the man wheeled about, regarding the ladies with an expression of almost comic dismay in his protuberant light blue eyes.

"Beg pardon, m'dear!" he said somewhat breathlessly, scrambling down the ladder with a speed that made its side rails lurch drunkenly from side to side. "Didn't know we had a visitor—er, a new guest, perhaps?"

Mrs. Danvers could not have failed to hear this speech, although she did not acknowledge it in any way, addressing herself instead to her visitor. "Mrs. Pickett, may I present my husband? Mr. Danvers, make your bow to Mrs. Pickett. She is thinking of leaving her husband with us for a time. Laudanum," she added darkly.

"Is that a fact?" Having reached the floor without incident, he made Julia a courtly little bow. "Dear me, what a pity, ma'am and you such a pretty young thing. Ah well, never you mind. My wife and I will take care of him, just see if we don't!"

"I'm pleased to make your acquaintance, Mr.—" Julia began, only to be interrupted by her hostess.

"Now that you have seen the house, let us take a look at the grounds."

Obeying a gesture indicating that she should precede her guide from the room, Julia said all that was proper to Mr. Danvers, then stepped through the library door—and almost collided with a man on the other side.

"*Oh!*" she cried, startled into involuntary exclamation. "Oh, I do beg your pardon, sir. I didn't realize you were there," she said, with a shaky little laugh at her own folly.

The gaunt man was clearly one of the residents—no, "guests"—for surely no one else would still be wearing his nightshirt at this hour, and this, along with the untidy white hair sticking up from his head at all angles, made it obvious to the meanest intelligence that he had only just arisen from his bed. The man was more deserving of her pity than her fear, she reminded herself. There was no reason, save for her coming upon him so unexpectedly, for her heart to pound against her ribs like a blacksmith's hammer upon an anvil.

"Do you have it?" he asked urgently, clutching at her sleeve with one clawlike hand. "Have you brought it?"

"I—I believe Mr. Danvers has it," she began, just as her hostess turned to call to her husband.

"Come down from that ladder, Mr. Danvers, and give Mr. Tomkins his medication while I show Mrs. Pickett about the grounds. You may go into the library, Mr. Tomkins, and Mr. Danvers will see to you directly."

"Was that not Mr. Lester, then?" Julia asked in some confusion as they exited the house through the wide double doors that were the focal point of the façade facing the street. "I assumed it was he, coming in search of his *Tristram Shandy*."

"No, that was Mr. George Tomkins, another of our guests. Mr. Lester is no longer with us."

Julia waited for some further explanation, but when none came, she asked, "How many, er, guests do you have at present?"

"Three. Your husband, should you choose to entrust him

to us, would be the fourth. We don't like to have more than half a dozen in residence at any given time. The larger our numbers, the more difficult it is to give each guest the individual attention his case requires."

" '*His* case,' " Julia echoed, fixing upon the masculine pronoun. "Are all of your guests gentlemen, then?"

In fact, she knew quite well that one, at least, was not, and Mrs. Danvers confirmed this.

"That is usually the case, but not always," the older woman acknowledged. "I don't know if gentlemen are more susceptible to the habit, or simply more likely to indulge to such an extent that some action becomes necessary. But as it happens, we have a lady staying with us at present. Her bedchamber is on the floor above that of the men. My husband and I occupy a suite of rooms on the same floor, so the demands of propriety are met."

Dead grass and fallen leaves crunched beneath their feet as they set out across the lawn in the direction of the lake. Mrs. Danvers did not lead her all the way to the water—an omission which was hardly surprising, given its present state—but veered to the right about halfway down the slope, as if to make a wide circuit about the house.

As the most prominent of its outbuildings came into view, she pointed out the stable—alas, home now only to one carriage and a pair of job horses—as well as the ice house, the smokehouse, and the root cellar. There, too, were the now-unused remnants of more prosperous days: the abandoned dairy, the tumbledown henhouse, and the roofless dovecote, where the descendants of its long-ago occupants occasionally returned to make their nests.

Julia had little attention for these relics, however, for she had glanced back toward the house, and seen a pale face watching them from one of the second-floor windows. Even as she recognized the thin, lined face of Mr. Tomkins, he put a hand up as if to signal her. She gave an infinitesimal nod that was half acknowledgement and half apology for her earlier *faux pas*, and turned her attention back to Mrs. Danvers.

"The groom, who also serves as coachman when the need arises, lives above the stable, as does the gardener," that lady was explaining, seemingly oblivious to this silent exchange. "The butler and the cook are brother and sister, and come in daily from Clerkenwell, as does the girl who cleans the house. Those are all who remain of what was once a staff of more than fifty."

Given the spotless condition of the small bedroom, Julia wondered at the daily girl's ever being able to leave the house at all, if she alone was responsible for cleaning the entire house. Aloud, she merely observed, "It must be a lonely life, your being the only female amongst so many men."

"It can be lonely at times, Mrs. Pickett. And yet it seems a small price to pay to be able to keep my family's home beyond reach of the auctioneer's gavel."

They drew abreast of a short expanse of wall where the bricks did not quite match, which Julia instantly recognized from their preliminary survey the day before.

"That was once a gate with a deer park on the other side," said Mrs. Danvers, pointing toward the bricked-up section.

"Ah well, if it hadn't been bricked up decades ago, it most certainly would be now, as a precautionary measure. As for the ornamental gates at the front of the house, it has been so long since they were opened that I should be hard-pressed to lay my hand on the key."

"And yet the back gate is ajar," Julia noted, recalling that it had been closed when she had seen it the day before.

"Yes, for we are expecting a delivery from the greengrocer. It is locked when not in use, of course, and Ned—the gardener, that is—checks it every night. At one time, it led to the farms that provided my family's income, but these were sold many years ago—in fact, a row of quite hideous terrace houses now occupies the plot where my father's tenants once raised barley—but at least the house remains, albeit a shadow of its former self."

"I'm sure it must have been lovely a month or so ago," Julia said encouragingly, recalling her husband's words.

"A month or so?" Mrs. Danvers's voice had an edge that had not been there before. "Why a month or so?"

"After the trees had all turned color," Julia reminded her, "but before their leaves fell."

"Oh, yes. Of course." Mrs. Danvers gazed out over the bare branches, but Julia had the impression she was not really seeing them. What had happened a month ago, she wondered, to provoke such a reaction? The death of Miss Bonner's brother six weeks ago might be described in such terms as "a month or so"; Coincidence? She could hardly ask such a question outright, but the conversation had provided an opening for another that she could—indeed, must—ask.

“It must be frightfully expensive to maintain such a place,” she remarked sympathetically.

“It is, even when one practices the most stringent economy, which of course we do, as much as we are able.”

“How much, then, should I expect to pay for the—the full course of treatment for my husband?”

The cost of the “full course of treatment,” as it transpired, proved to be staggering. Julia wondered how much of her guide’s mournful account of fallen fortunes and lost status were intended to evoke sympathy in her audience before she presented her bill of sale. She reminded herself that it would ultimately be Mr. Poole who would bear the expense, and assured her hostess that Mr. Pickett’s successful treatment must be worth any price.

“I realize this is not a step one takes lightly, Mrs. Pickett,” Mrs. Danvers said, after the tour was concluded and they had returned to the house. “But you need have no fear. It will all be over very soon.”

As she took her leave, Julia couldn’t help wondering why these reassuring words had sounded so very ominous.

7

In Which Julia Makes Her Report

"And then," concluded Julia, having recounted the results of the interview to her husband over tea, "she said, 'Come now, Mrs. Pickett, you cannot really expect me to give away *all* of my trade secrets' in the most *odious* fashion! Yes, you may laugh, but you must own that it doesn't help us much."

"Never mind," Pickett said consolingly, suppressing his grin with an effort. "I'm sure I'll find out soon enough."

"That is exactly what I'm afraid of," retorted Julia, unappeased.

"But you said she showed you about the place. Did you learn anything useful?"

"I think so, but you would be the best judge of that. First of all, the gate at the back of the property is certainly your best escape route, as it is the only one used regularly and left unlocked at least during daylight hours, when some delivery is expected. The bricked-up entrance was closed off many years ago, when the land on that side of the house, formerly a deer park, was sold. As for the main gate that opens onto the road, it has been locked up for so long that Mrs. Danvers has lost the key."

"Or so she says," Pickett put in.

"So she says," agreed Julia. "Still, I should think the hinges of any gate as long disused as Mrs. Danvers claims this one is would very likely resist any attempt to push it open with shrieks loud enough to sound the alarm, even if you should succeed in finding the key—or picking the lock, which I must say sounds much more in your usual style. So if you have any thoughts of throwing the gates open wide and strolling through in triumph with Miss Bonner on your arm, I fear you had best abandon them."

"John don't need no key," a slightly indignant voice came from an apparently offended drawing room curtain.

"Kit, you abominable child!" Julia cried, noting the bulge in the draperies that had certainly *not* been there that morning. "Come out from there at once! How long have you been hiding?"

"I wasn't hiding," insisted her young brother-in-law, emerging somewhat reluctantly from the folds of straw-colored satin brocade. "I was just listening."

"And do you always feel the need to conceal yourself behind the curtains when you 'listen'?"

"Only when I think I might hear something interesting," Kit said with a shrug.

"Exactly what did you hear?" Pickett asked. "Was it interesting enough for you?"

"You're going someplace, only Julia don't want you to go."

"Julia doesn't want you to go," she corrected him gently.

"*I'm* not going," Kit insisted. "*John* is. Mind you, I would go, if he'd let me, only I'll bet he won't."

"You're quite right," Pickett said. "What else have you heard?"

Kit screwed up his face in concentration. "You're going someplace, and while you're there, you're supposed to rescue some lady." He considered this for a moment. "When you've got her, will you be bringing her here to live, too?"

"Not if he knows what's good for him," Julia said sweetly, regarding her beloved with a baleful eye.

"I expect I'll hand her over to Mr. Poole," Pickett told him. "Now, why don't you go upstairs and play—"

"But I'm not done yet!" protested Kit. "I'd only just got to the part where you have to find a key to get in. Or maybe to get out. Anyway, you don't need a key, because you know how to open locks without one."

"*You* know that, and *I* know that, but maybe it's best if we keep it to ourselves," suggested Pickett. "The neighbors wouldn't much like it, you know."

"Are you hungry?" Julia asked. "Come tell me what you would like, and I'll make up a plate for you to take to the schoolroom."

The suggestion of food never failed to please, and so neither Julia nor Pickett was surprised when Kit abandoned his hiding place in favor of the tea tray with its tower of cakes.

"I believe these are the apple biscuits you like so," Julia

said, putting two of them on a plate.

"Cook used to make all *my* favorites," Pickett grumbled with mock resentment. "My nose has been put out of joint by my own brother."

Once Kit had been dispatched to the schoolroom with, as Julia observed, enough food to maintain any number of ten-year-old boys for at least a week, she turned to Pickett. "He does need to be in school, you know," she said, refilling his cup and moving the sugar bowl within reach. "It's not that I mind having him here—how could I, when he's such a darling?—but he needs to be with other children, to say nothing of his education, which as far as I can tell has been shockingly neglected! I have winnowed the field down to two possibilities: the Fountainhead Academy and the Chesterfield School. Perhaps after you've finished with this case for Mr. Poole, a visit to both campuses might be in order. Would bringing Kit along to meet with the headmaster be a help or a hindrance, do you suppose?"

"Not only a hindrance, but a completely unnecessary one," Pickett answered without hesitation. "I suspect he'll become very well-acquainted with the headmaster within a very short time of enrolling. But I agree that we should have a look about the two schools, if for no other reason than putting their headmasters off the scent by introducing them to Kit's gently bred sister-in-law."

"Which means," said Julia, steering the conversation back to the matter at hand, "that if we intend to make the trip before my confinement, you had best make short work of this business at the Larches."

"All right, then," Pickett said, "what else have you got for me?"

Julia took a deep breath, and picked up where she had left off. "The number of servants actually living on the premises appears to be quite small. The groom and the gardener live above the stables, but the house servants—the butler, the cook, and a girl who cleans—are apparently dailies who come in every morning from Clerkenwell. At least you need not fear stumbling upon them in the dark, should you be obliged to spirit Miss Bonner out of the house under cover of darkness."

"One minute," Pickett said, fumbling in the inside pocket of his coat for his notebook and pencil. He scrawled frantically for a few seconds, then looked up. "Sweetheart, you are a marvel. Thank you! This is—"

"Oh, but I'm not finished yet! There are three patients currently in residence, two men—one is named Mr. Tomkins, but I don't believe the other was ever mentioned by name—and Miss Bonner, the only female. Her room is on the floor above that of the gentlemen, and Mr. and Mrs. Danvers occupy a suite on the same floor, which might complicate things a bit. As for the men, Mr. Tomkins's room appears to overlook the back of the house—at least, I saw him watching from one of those windows while Mrs. Danvers was showing me about the grounds. I don't know about the other man, except that he is housed on the same floor as Mr. Tomkins. The rooms themselves were a pleasant surprise: scrupulously clean, and comfortably, though not luxuriously, furnished. The property is what's left of Mrs. Danvers's family's estate.

There is a Mr. Danvers—have I mentioned him?—but unless I miss my guess, it is she who rules the roast. He certainly seemed eager to placate her after we came upon him in the library. He had his back to us, you see, and he spoke to her thinking they were alone."

"Placate her? Why? What did he say to offend her?"

Julia shrugged. "Nothing out of the ordinary, as far as I could tell. He was up on the library ladder shelving books, saying Mr. Lester no longer needed them."

"Mr. Lester," echoed Pickett, making note of the name. "The other male patient, perhaps?"

"No, although I thought the same thing when Mr. Tomkins came in. I assumed he must be Mr. Lester coming to retrieve his book, thinking perhaps he wasn't finished with it after all, but Mrs. Danvers said Mr. Lester is no longer with them."

"That's rather ambiguous," Pickett said, looking up from his notebook with a puzzled expression. "No longer with them as in completed his cure, or no longer with them as in dead?"

"I never thought to ask," she confessed, conscience-stricken. "I noticed at the time that it seemed an odd turn of phrase, but I was too mortified over my *faux pas* with Mr. Tomkins to press Mrs. Danvers for details. I'm so sorry!"

"Never mind," he said reassuringly, shutting the notebook with a snap. "It's a comfort to know that you can make them, too."

He returned the notebook and pencil to the inside pocket of his coat, then picked up his cup and tossed back the last of his tea.

"I have to go now," he said, returning the teacup to its saucer as he rose to his feet. "I don't think I should be gone too long, but in the meantime, I would be obliged to you if you would oversee the packing of my bag for an indefinite stay at the Larches. Oh, and would you mind if I took a couple of your hairpins? I would hate for Kit's faith in me to be utterly destroyed."

Julia agreed, her dread of his departure leavened by the realization that she had not seen him so happy in weeks. She felt a pang of guilt at the recollection that she would have considered, even for a moment, denying him the opportunity to do what he did best—well, second-best, in any case.

"Some men," she said with a sentimental sigh as she accompanied him to the door, "ask for a ribbon from their ladyloves' hair as a token before going into battle. Mine asks for a pin, so he can go skulking about in places he shouldn't."

"And you love him for it," he said, taking her in his arms.

"I do," she agreed, and lifted her face to be kissed. At the conclusion of this protracted and mutually satisfying exercise, she asked, "In all seriousness, John, what do you intend to do next?"

"Come now, Mrs. Pickett," he chided, "you can't really expect me to give away *all* of my trade secrets."

And with this Parthian shot, he dropped a kiss on her indignantly parted lips and set off up the street with a spring in his step that had not been there in quite some time.

8

In Which John Pickett Returns to Bow Street

By the time he drew abreast of the looming edifice that was Covent Garden Theatre, Pickett's steps were no longer quite so jaunty. He had not come back to the Bow Street Public Office since tendering his resignation, although not a day had gone by that he had not thought of it, often with a stab of longing so powerful that it was almost a physical pain. The last time he had seen any of his former colleagues, they had been witnesses to his arrest for robbing the Bank of England, and one of them—he wasn't sure who, which was probably just as well—had been the man to put him in irons. He had no idea how they would receive him now—if, in fact, any of them chose to acknowledge his presence at all, which was by no means certain.

All too soon, he found himself stepping up onto the front stoop, with nothing to do but open the door and go in. He set his shoulders, took a deep breath, and opened the door.

"Well, stap me if it isn't our Mr. Pickett!" Dixon

exclaimed as Pickett strode across the familiar threshold. "Where've you been keeping yourself?"

A hard knot in the pit of his stomach began, ever so slowly, to uncoil. "Mr. Dixon," Pickett said, accepting the older man's proffered handshake and returning (albeit somewhat warily) the always-taciturn Maxwell's nod. The last time he'd seen Maxwell…

Before his brain could form the thought, his attention was caught by a remarkably good-looking young man a few years older than himself, a fellow rejoicing in a head of windswept golden hair and a garish toilette comprising a tailcoat of mustard-colored wool worn over an olive-green waistcoat. Pickett was startled into unwise speech.

"Out of uniform, Mr. Carson?"

"As you see," boasted Harry Carson. "I've hung up the red waistcoat for good."

"You've quit the Horse Patrol?"

"I should think not!" protested Harry, grinning broadly. "I've taken over *your* job!"

"Oh," Pickett said, feeling rather as if the ground were giving way beneath his feet. "Well, that's—that's—"

The door to the magistrate's office flew open. "I know that voice!" Mr. Colquhoun came forward with every appearance of pleasure. "Welcome back, Mr. Pickett. What brings you, er, that is—" The keen blue eyes shifted from Pickett to Carson, and back again.

"I haven't come to ask for my position back," Pickett assured him hastily. He turned to Carson and tried to look pleased. "And it sounds as if I would be a bit late to the fair if

I had. Harry tells me he's taken it."

"And I don't intend to give it back," Carson put in impudently. "Still, it might interest you to know that it takes two men to replace you."

"Oh?" Pickett, bewildered, looked to Mr. Colquhoun for enlightenment.

"Mr. Carson will be working with an assistant from the Foot Patrol," offered the magistrate by way of explanation, then raised his voice to address someone on the other side of the room. "Mr. Yates!"

"Yes, sir?"

Pickett had been vaguely aware of a slim figure on the opposite side of the room, but if he had thought about this person at all, he would have supposed it to be one of the many young thieves arrested and hauled before the magistrate on any given day—as he had cause to know, having formerly been one of their number. As the youth approached, however, Pickett recognized the distinctive blue coat and red waistcoat of the Bow Street Foot and Horse Patrols. He had worn just such a uniform himself from the age of nineteen to three-and-twenty, at which time he, like Harry Carson, had put it aside upon his promotion to principal officer.

Pickett had endured too many remarks about his own age (or, rather, lack thereof) to subject another to the same insult. Still, his nineteen-year-old self must seem a regular Methuselah compared to a stripling who could surely have no more than sixteen years in his dish. He glanced at his former magistrate, wondering what Mr. Colquhoun was about, but found his mentor wholly absorbed in making introductions.

"Mr. Pickett, this is Mr. Yates, the newest member of the Foot Patrol. He will be assisting Mr. Carson. Mr. Yates, make your bow to Mr. Pickett, a principal officer until quite recently, when he abandoned us to take on private commissions."

"H-how do you do?" The youth stammered slightly, and a flush spread over cheeks that had certainly never known a razor. "I'm pleased to meet you, Mr. Pickett. I've heard a great deal about you, for Mr. Carson thinks very highly of you."

"I do not!" objected Harry, stung.

"It's very kind of you to say so, Mr. Yates," Pickett said with a smile, "but if Mr. Carson is your only source of information, I can only wonder at your being willing to speak to me at all."

"Oh, but he said—*ow!*" Mr. Yates broke off with a yelp as Carson trod squarely on his booted foot.

"Don't you have something to do, Mr. Yates?" Carson asked, in a voice that warned his hapless assistant to answer in the negative at his peril.

"Tell me, Mr. Pickett, what brings you back to Bow Street?" asked Mr. Colquhoun, steering the conversation into more appropriate channels and at the same time deflecting attention from a *faux pas* that had deepened young Mr. Yates's flushed countenance to crimson.

Pickett, feeling a certain sympathy for the youth where Harry Carson was concerned, answered readily. "I'm working on an investigation, and a question has come up that I thought perhaps you might be able to answer."

"Oh-o, so you've an investigation going, have you?"

Pickett might have wished Mr. Colquhoun had sounded less surprised, but there was no denying the pleasure with which the magistrate greeted the news. "Come into my office and tell me about it."

He accepted the invitation with alacrity, feeling only the smallest pang of regret at being denied the opportunity to watch young Mr. Yates giving Carson grief in just the same way that Carson had once done to him. Pickett was just about to follow Mr. Colquhoun to his office when he remembered his manners, and turned back to excuse himself to Mssrs. Carson and Yates. Harry was addressing his assistant in hushed tones, but Pickett didn't need to hear the words to recognize that he was giving the lad a rare trimming. Yates, for his part, was no longer timid and blushing, but regarded his superior with his smooth jaw set, and his pointed little chin thrust defiantly forward. *On second thought*, Pickett amended mentally, regarding the pair with a thoughtful frown, *perhaps not in* quite *the same way after all...*

"About this assistant of Carson's—" he began as the magistrate closed the office door, allowing them to speak privately.

But Mr. Colquhoun's mind was on other matters. "So, you finally got a response to your advertisement, did you? Who was it?"

"His name is Poole. Edward Poole," Pickett answered impatiently. "But sir, about Harry's assistant—"

"Mr. Yates need not trouble you," the magistrate said dismissively. "Poole, you say? I don't believe I know anyone of that name. What is he asking you to do? Of course, if you're sworn to secrecy, I wouldn't ask you to betray a confidence," he added quickly.

"I have no qualms about confiding in you, sir, but I think you should know that this Mr. Yates you've taken on—"

"I know all about Mr. Yates." The absolute certainty in his voice, made it impossible to argue. And yet…

"You do?" The words themselves might have suggested agreement, but the tone in which they were uttered indicated only stunned disbelief. "Then you know Mr. Yates is—"

"I assure you, John, you can tell me nothing about Mr. Yates that I don't already know."

"Yes, sir," said Pickett, reluctantly conceding the point. "I suppose you know your own business best."

"I should certainly hope so."

Pickett considered the implications of this claim for a long moment, then asked, "What about Harry? Does he know?"

"Mr. Carson has not mentioned the matter to me." Mr. Colquhoun's voice was carefully neutral, but Pickett was not deceived.

"Which would seem to suggest that he doesn't." Pickett's face split in a wide grin. "What I wouldn't give to be here to watch what happens when he figures it out!"

"That's quite enough about Mr. Carson," the magistrate said, seating himself behind his desk and regarding his protégé somewhat sternly through keen blue eyes, quite like old times. "Tell me about this Edward Poole of yours."

Pickett leaned against his mentor's desk, resting one hip and thigh on its surface in a half-sitting posture that would have been a shocking breach of protocol only six weeks earlier. He regaled the magistrate with a vivid account of Julia's invasion of the hallowed portals of Ludlow & Ludlow, culminating in his own departure from the premises.

"So you see why I have to make this work," he concluded, suddenly serious. "As far as Ludlow & Ludlow is concerned, I'm afraid I've thoroughly burned my boats."

"Harrmmph." Mr. Colquhoun made a very Scottish growl in the back of his throat. "I can't say I'm entirely sorry, for if ever there was a waste of—but I believe you know my views on that particular subject, so I won't repeat them. What does this Mr. Poole want from you?"

Pickett gave a sheepish little laugh. "I know it sounds like something out of a gothic novel, sir, but—well, he wants me to rescue a damsel in distress." He recounted the story of Miss Bonner, an heiress committed to an asylum by the guardian who, according to Mr. Poole, hoped to maintain control over her considerable fortune. "I'm not sure how much of it is true, and how much is nothing more than the baseless fear of a man whose matrimonial ambitions are not progressing as he'd hoped," Pickett confessed at the end of this narrative. "Still, I should think it must be significant that her brother was known to take opium, and that he died while seeking treatment in the very same establishment."

"Oh, certainly significant," Mr. Colquhoun agreed readily. "And how, pray, do you intend to accomplish the thing?"

"I drove out to Islington yesterday to have a look about the place, or at least as much of it as can be seen from the road.

Then this morning Julia spoke to the proprietress about having me committed." Seeing the magistrate's bushy white eyebrows lowering ominously, Pickett hastily added, "You must admit, effecting a rescue will be much easier from the inside, and after I've had plenty of time to explore the lay of the land, so to speak, before making the attempt."

"Aye, but surely there are less drastic methods than being confined there yourself," countered the magistrate.

"With all due respect, sir, I don't think there are. I can't afford to arouse suspicions by asking a lot of questions—or having Julia ask them on my behalf, for that matter."

"No, but the residents are surely allowed visitors, are they not? What is to keep you from putting your questions to Miss Bonner herself?"

Pickett shook his head. "Mr. Poole has tried to visit her several times without success. If she refuses to see an old friend of her brother—or if Mrs. Danvers won't allow her to see him, which just might be the case—then it's unlikely that I'll succeed where he failed, and in the meantime, I'll have roused all Mrs. Danvers's suspicions." After a delicate pause, he added, "Then, too, there is the fact that I know something of what it's like to hear that black bottle calling in the middle of the night."

"What's this?" If it were possible, Mr. Colquhoun's scowl grew even fiercer. "You don't mean to equate taking laudanum to ease the pain of a head injury with using opium as the doorway to a fantasy world simply because one hasn't the gumption to face real life!"

"Actually, the line between the two isn't as clear as you

might think," Pickett confessed somewhat reluctantly.

He immediately wished he'd held his tongue, for the magistrate looked as if his protégé had just struck him. "You don't mean to say that *you*—"

"No, sir, not as bad as all that," Pickett assured him hastily. "It's just that—well, I was a bit muddled in the head at the time—"

"Only a bit?" put in Mr. Colquhoun, quite in his old manner.

"And sometimes I would wake up and I would see Julia there. That didn't seem likely—in fact, the very idea was ridiculous—so I thought it must be the laudanum. And I didn't want to give it up, because it would mean giving *her* up. Or so I thought."

"It doesn't appear to have taken her long to enlighten you," Mr. Colquhoun remarked dryly.

"Er, no, sir," Pickett said, with a reminiscent gleam in his eye at the memories this simple observation evoked. "But the point is, I'm familiar enough with its effects to make a good show of it—good enough, at least, that no one will question my need for a 'cure' while I try to make contact with Miss Bonner."

"And just how long do you expect that to take?"

Pickett pondered the question before answering. "I shouldn't think it would take more than a couple of days, provided I can persuade Miss Bonner to trust me. I'll do my best to speed the process along, but I mustn't appear to be importuning her in any way; I can't imagine a gently bred young woman readily agreeing to entrust her safety to a man she's never seen before in her life, especially not after being betrayed by those closest to her."

"If she's truly being held there against her will, I should think she'd be ready to fall on the neck of any rescuer, be he stranger or no. Then, too, there is the fact that your countenance is hardly the sort to strike terror into the heart of any gently nurtured female."

"I'm trying to decide," Pickett said thoughtfully, "whether to feel flattered or insulted."

"You'll have to put that one to your wife. Speaking of Mrs. Pickett, what does she think of this plan of yours?"

Pickett sighed. "She is—not enthusiastic, sir."

The magistrate nodded. "It's a wise woman you've married," he said. "But you said there was a question you wanted to ask."

"Yes, sir," Pickett said eagerly, relieved to discover that, however much Mr. Colquhoun might disapprove of his course of action, his mentor at least had no intention of trying to persuade him to abandon it. "When my wife interviewed the mistress of the Larches, the woman made mention of a Mr. Lester, who had recently been a resident there, but who is now, according to Mrs. Danvers, 'no longer with us.' It occurred to me to wonder whether she meant he was finished with his course of treatment, or he was dead. Do you know of any man named Lester, first name unknown, who has died under suspicious circumstances in the last, say, six months?"

"Lester, Lester," the magistrate muttered to himself. "I seem to remember seeing something in the *Morning Chronicle* only a week or so ago, mentioning a Mr. Horace

Lester of Islington—no, it said 'late of Islington,' or something to that effect; I recall thinking it was oddly worded, as if that wasn't the fellow's usual residence."

"And this man had died?" Pickett asked eagerly. "Did it mention the cause of death?"

"As I recall, it was ruled death by misadventure. It was the kinder verdict, the only alternative being suicide. He was killed when he fell from the roof," he added by way of explanation.

" 'Fell'?" echoed Pickett cynically. "Was pushed, more like."

"Quite possibly, but you have absolutely no evidence to prove such a thing. You don't even know if this man had ever set foot in the Larches at all. It's not an uncommon name"

"Still, you must admit it looks suspicious. Two men living in the same section of Town, possibly in the same house, both of them dying within a short space of time—what?" Considerably deflated, Pickett broke off upon seeing Mr. Colquhoun shaking his head with the air of one regretfully dashing a last, best hope.

"If we were speaking of the general population, perhaps, although even that would be a stretch. Do you have any idea how many people currently reside in Islington? But we're not speaking of the general population; we're talking about the residents of a house offering a cure to people who have already demonstrated, I wouldn't call it a weakness of character, but let us say a certain difficulty in coping with the demands of daily life without narcotic aid. Even supposing that this man Lester is the same man who once sought treatment at the Larches, it's not inconceivable that more than one opium-eater has come there for a cure, only to find the prospect of life insupportable without that substance. Nor that one such man, having put an end to so bleak an existence, might not inspire another to follow suit."

"Yes, sir," Pickett conceded with a sigh.

"You will, of course, do as you think best—I've no power to stop you—but before you seal yourself off from the outside world, I should advise you to see what you can discover from the coroner's reports on both the Lester and the Bonner deaths." The magistrate gave a discreet cough. "Of course, you need not volunteer the information that you are no longer with Bow Street."

"Thank you, sir," said Pickett, much gratified.

"And John—"

"Yes, sir?"

"Get off my desk."

9

In Which John Pickett Renews an Old Acquaintance and Resumes Old Habits

Upon leaving the magistrate's office, Pickett exchanged a hearty handshake with Dixon, acknowledged Harry Carson with a careless wave, touched his hat to young Mr. Yates, and stepped outside, where he found Maxwell on the portico, leaning against one of the pillars and smoking a *cigarillo*, as was his usual habit. If Carson were to be believed (which Pickett thought doubtful), Maxwell had adopted the practice less from a craving for tobacco than from unrequited love: specifically, a desire to see the celebrated actress Mrs. Cummings arrive at Covent Garden Theatre for rehearsals. Still, there was the fact that here Maxwell stood, his back to the Bow Street Public Office and his face toward the theatre adjacent.

Even as the thought formed in Pickett's brain, Maxwell turned to look over his shoulder, alerted, no doubt, by the sound of the door opening behind him. "Mr. Pickett," he said, giving his erstwhile colleague a terse nod.

Pickett returned the gesture, somewhat surprised that it had been made at all. He was never quite sure how much of Maxwell's cool demeanor toward him was due to the man's natural reticence, and how much was acute dislike, born of the fact that Pickett had deliberately undercut Maxwell's investigation and pursuit of a criminal gang—a gang that had included Pickett's own brother. Still, Kit was safe and happy, and that was what mattered; the loss of his own reputation, along with a position he had loved, was perhaps a steep price to pay but, as he frequently reminded himself, the reward was ultimately worth the cost.

"Mr. Maxwell." Pickett's gaze shifted from the man to the theatre beyond him. "Have you drawn theatre duty, then?"

Maxwell's countenance grew even more wooden than usual. "I don't know what you're talking about."

By Jove, Harry was right, Pickett thought. *The poor fellow thinks I'm mocking him for his interest in Mrs. Cummings*. In fact, Pickett was the last man on earth to taunt anyone else for nursing a hopeless passion, having himself fallen in love with a viscountess in spite of his magistrate's warnings and his own best efforts to resist an attraction that could only lead (or so he had thought) to heartbreak. "Theatre duty," he said again, jerking his thumb in the direction of the edifice under discussion. "You know, don't you, that the theatres always hire a principal officer to be on hand during performances?

He had the satisfaction of seeing Maxwell's face register something resembling human emotion. "No, I wasn't aware of any such arrangement."

"Dixon usually covers Covent Garden, but he might be willing to swap places with you from time to time. If you've any particular interest in the stage, that is," he added, with a look of bland innocence that would have done Maxwell himself proud.

Maxwell nodded. "I'll do that," he said, regarding Pickett with more warmth than he had ever shown before. "Thank you, Mr. Pickett. I'm obliged to you."

"Not at all," Pickett said modestly, and stepped off the portico.

"Before you go, Mr. Pickett—" Maxwell said abruptly, delaying his departure.

"Yes?"

"Mr. Colquhoun explained to me why you did what you did. Can't say I blame you. I once had a lad of my own very near the same age. How is the boy?"

"He's—doing very well, thank you," Pickett said, taken aback by this sudden burst of loquaciousness. *Had* a lad Kit's age? What had happened to him? Even as Pickett cast about in his mind for some tactful way of framing the question, Maxwell spoke again, and the moment was lost.

"No hard feelings, then?"

"None at all," Pickett assured him.

Maxwell nodded again, as if satisfied, and turned back toward the theatre. Clearly, the conversation was over. Still, Pickett thought as he strode up Bow Street, it was remarkable that it had taken place at all. Upon reaching the Strand, he hailed a hackney and instructed the driver to set him down at the Coroner's Office for Islington, just off Clerkenwell Green.

As the carriage jolted its way northward, Pickett mentally rehearsed how best to frame his request to the coroner. *You don't have to tell him you're no longer with Bow Street*, Mr. Colquhoun had said, but Pickett wasn't certain it would matter in the end. Most of the inquests in which he'd been obliged to participate had been conducted under the auspices of the coroner of London or, more recently, Westminster; he'd never had dealings with the coroner for Islington before, therefore the man who held that office would have no knowledge of John Pickett at all, either as a principal officer at Bow Street or as a private citizen.

Or so he thought, until he entered the coroner's office and discovered a tall, cadaverous man of late middle age—a man, moreover, who he had hoped might never cross his path again.

"*Mr. Bagley?*" Sheer incredulity banished every word of his carefully rehearsed speech from his brain. "Bartholomew Bagley?"

The man looked down his long nose at Pickett with the same distaste he might bestow upon a fly in his soup. "And who, pray, might you be?"

"John Pickett, of—" No, *not* of Bow Street. Not any longer, and not ever again. He tried a different approach. "I believe you were with the Westminster office, were you not?"

"I served there for a time as interim, and turned my experience to good account, as it led to my securing a permanent post at Clerkenwell. Why do you—" He broke off and regarded Pickett through narrowed eyes. "I remember you! You're that damned impudent young upstart who kept poking his nose into that Washbourn affair!"

"The very same," Pickett declared, perversely pleased with this unflattering description of himself. "And if you'll recall, I was—" He stopped himself just in time. *I was quite right; it* was *murder*, he'd almost said. But Mr. Bagley would recall no such thing, for the results of that investigation had been hushed up (and at his own instigation) in order to protect the reputation of His Majesty's envoy to the Turks at Constantinople. "I was accompanied by Mr. Colquhoun of the Bow Street Public Office on that occasion. In fact, it was he who suggested I apply to you—well, not to you personally, of course, but to the coroner for Clerkenwell for help."

"All right, then, what does he want me to do for you?" Mr. Bagley's concession sounded more than a little grudging, and Pickett remembered that the coroner had a certain reason to resent Mr. Colquhoun; the magistrate had, after all, very neatly coerced him into making Pickett's evidence, along with his suspicions, a matter of public record.

"I should like to have a look at the records of two recent inquests, if I may," Pickett said.

"And which inquests might those be?" asked Mr. Bagley, clearly unwilling to commit himself.

"The inquests into the deaths of Mr. Philip Bonner and Mr. Horace Lester," Pickett replied. "Both residents of a house called the Larches, an asylum for those seeking a cure for an opium habit."

"I remember them well," the coroner said, frowning. "Sad business, both of them."

"Then you should have no objection to my reading about

the inquests," Pickett observed blandly.

Mr. Bagley opened his mouth to correct this false assumption, but before he could voice whatever objections he harbored, the door burst open to admit a breathless lad still in his teens, who had clearly arrived there with all possible speed.

"Begging your pardon, sir—sirs," the boy said, glancing from Pickett to Bagley and back again, as if unsure precisely which man he had been dispatched to fetch. "There's a body been found behind the workhouse at St. Sepulcher. Knifed in the back, he were." This last detail was clearly addressed to Pickett, whom he had apparently judged to be, if not the coroner himself, certainly the more sympathetic of his hearers.

"Yes, I'll come at once," said Mr. Bagley, and although he was speaking to the boy, he glared at Pickett in a manner that suggested he fully expected the Bow Street magistrate's protégé to horn in here, too, just as he had at that earlier inquest. To forestall any such intrusion, he added to Pickett, "Look here, Mr. Plunkett—"

"Pickett," the possessor of that name corrected him gently, and was ignored.

"—I've no more time for you. I must go."

Pickett nodded. "I understand, sir," he said with a meekness that would have instantly raised the coroner's hackles, had he been better acquainted with his adversary. "I'll go at once."

And so he did.

But he'd made no promises as to exactly *where* he would

go, or how long he might remain there. He retraced his steps to Clerkenwell Green, where he spent the next ten minutes strolling along its perimeter. He had no very clear idea of the exact location of the St. Sepulcher workhouse, or how long it might take Mr. Bagley to reach his destination; nor did he have any idea of how long it might take him to discover what he sought. At last satisfied that Mr. Bagley would not turn back to collect some forgotten implement of his profession, Pickett judged it safe to return to the coroner's office. He tried the door and was not surprised to find it locked; still, it was the work of a moment to let himself in with one of his wife's hairpins which he had confiscated for just such a contingency. Once inside, he closed the door behind him, then turned his attention to the rows of drawers banked up against the opposite wall. Unless he missed his guess, this was where the coroner's records would be kept; he had only to find which one, or ones, contained the accounts he sought.

This, it soon became apparent, was a good deal easier said than done. Mr. Bagley's predecessor appeared to have shoved papers willy-nilly into whichever drawer was nearest to hand, resulting in Bills of Mortality from 1804 stuffed cheek-by-jowl between inquest records from 1808 and witnesses' statements from 1799. Resigning himself to a long and tedious search, Pickett only hoped that, whatever the situation awaiting Mr. Bagley behind the workhouse, it would keep the coroner busy for a very long time. He pulled out the topmost drawer on the left side and sat down in Mr. Bagley's chair with the drawer on his knees.

He was obliged to work more quickly than he would have

liked, all too keenly aware that he was acting without the coroner's knowledge or permission, and that Mr. Bagley might return at any moment to inform him of the fact, perhaps even to take whatever legal action he could—trespassing came to mind, to say nothing of breaking and entering—to ensure that his erstwhile nemesis was unable to repeat the offense. Never had Pickett been so conscious of the fact that he could no longer claim the protective authority of Bow Street.

The first drawer yielded nothing pertinent to his needs, so Pickett returned it to its slot and pulled out the drawer directly beneath it. Unlike its fellow, this one made a curious rattling noise, and the reason soon became evident: tucked into the rear right-hand corner of the drawer was a chipped porcelain cup containing a handful of coins; clearly, this was where the coroner kept his petty cash.

"For shame, Mr. Bagley," scolded Pickett, turning his attention to the papers at the front of the drawer after having solved this minor mystery. "You shouldn't leave your money lying about where anyone with a hairpin could steal it—hallo, what's this?"

It was the report of an inquest into the death of one Horace Lester, dated 2 November 1809: in fact, Pickett noted, less than a fortnight earlier. A closer reading revealed that at approximately ten minutes before eleven o'clock on the previous morning, the deceased had, according to the testimony of three witnesses, leapt from the roof of the asylum known as the Larches, apparently laboring under the illusion (clearly an effect of the substance for which he had sought treatment) that he could fly.

The coroner's jury had rendered a verdict of death by misadventure, having ruled out suicide based on the lack of any evidence that Mr. Lester had contemplated the intentional taking of his own life. One of the three witnesses, Pickett noted, was none other than Mr. Joseph Danvers; another, a man by the name of Ned Stubbing, had given his occupation as gardener and general factotum at the Larches. The third witness was one George Daniel Tomkins—clearly the same Mr. Tomkins who had so disconcerted Julia, as evidenced by the testimony of the attending physician, who suggested that the habits of this particular witness might cast some doubts as to the veracity of his claims.

Pickett had hoped to copy down any pertinent information in the small notebook he carried in the inside pocket of his coat—a habit derived from the occurrence book of his Bow Street days—but given that his time must surely be growing short and his task only half-completed, he instead rolled up the entire document and stuffed it into his pocket. Then, because he reckoned he owed the fellow something for having confiscated official records without permission, he fished in the pocket of his coat for a sixpence and added it to the cup with a *clink* of silver upon porcelain that sounded unnaturally loud in the quiet office.

He had not long to seek for the inquiry into the death of one Philip Bonner, also resident at the Larches, whose body had been discovered in one of the outbuildings belonging to the property at seven o'clock on the morning of 14 September 1809, some six weeks before Mr. Lester had met his own tragic fate. However, Pickett sought in vain for any mention of the jury's verdict. Unlike the coroner's report on Mr. Lester, which ran to several pages, the account of young Mr. Bonner's death scarcely filled a single sheet of paper. There must surely be more than this. Who had discovered the body, for instance, and in what condition had it been found? These questions must have been raised at the inquest, and their answers recorded. So where were they? Had this particular page been separated from the rest, and the bulk of the report left to languish, forgotten, in some other drawer? Given the lackadaisical filing system—if one could call it that—prevailing in the few drawers he'd searched thus far, it wouldn't be at all surprising.

And yet, given Mr. Poole's concerns, the incompleteness of that particular report seemed a bit too coincidental for Pickett's liking. It appeared that someone—or several some-ones—did not want to leave any record of how young Bonner had died. Mentally adding this to his list of questions to put to Miss Bonner, he shoved the coroner's report, incomplete as it was, into his coat pocket along with its fellow, and within seconds was out the door and standing on the edge of the green, trying to hail a hackney.

The vehicle drew up just as Bartholomew Bagley, puffing from exertion, rounded the corner of Turnmill Street. Upon recognizing the young man climbing into the carriage, the coroner's eyes narrowed in sudden suspicion, and he picked up his pace accordingly. Pickett, returning his gaze with one of detached interest, touched the brim of his hat in farewell, then ducked inside the conveyance and closed the door. By the time Mr. Bagley reached the spot where Pickett had stood, the horses had found their rhythm and were bearing the hackney southward at a brisk trot.

The coroner could never afterwards be quite certain of what Pickett had been doing during the time that he himself was occupied at St. Sepulcher. Still, he always wondered where that extra sixpence had come from.

10

In Which John Pickett Commences Putting His Plan into Action

"To look at the pair of you," Pickett said, his gaze shifting from his wife, seated to his right at the breakfast table, to his half-brother, seated to his left, "anyone would think I was going to the Antipodes, rather than to a private house in Islington."

"It's not the 'where' that troubles me, but the 'how long.' " Julia said.

"Where's that?" asked Kit, frowning.

"Just north of Holborn," Pickett said reassuringly. "Not really that far at all."

"Not *that!*" Kit retorted, with all the scorn of which a slighted ten-year-old is capable. "I mean the An—An—"

"The Antipodes," said Pickett, as light dawned. "I suppose you could say it's another name for Botany Bay."

Kit nodded sagely. "Where Da is."

"That's right." Pickett kept his voice carefully neutral, as he always did when discussing their father or Kit's mother in front of the boy.

"I'm going to go there someday," announced Kit. "I'm going to go to the An—whatever you said. I'm going to find Da and tell him I'm his son. And he'll have to believe me, 'cause everybody says *I* look just like *you*, and *you* look just like *him*."

"How exciting that sounds!" Julia exclaimed, playing along. "But I hope you won't go until John returns, for I should hate to be left here all alone while the pair of you are off having adventures."

"I shouldn't think I'll be gone that long," Pickett assured her. "Only long enough to find my way about and determine the best way to escape, and then to establish a rapport with the lady and get her out. No more than a couple of days, maybe three at the most. Mr. Colquhoun predicts that if she's really being held against her will as Mr. Poole claims, she'll very likely fall on my neck."

"Is that supposed to make me feel better?" Julia challenged. "You, locked up in close quarters with a beautiful woman—"

"What makes you think she's beautiful?" asked Pickett, bewildered by this leap in logic.

"My dear John, do you honestly think Mr. Poole would be so desperate to rescue a lady who was not?"

He shrugged. "There's always her money."

"Very well, I concede the point," Julia said impatiently, and moved on to her next objection. "But must you go today? I should have thought there would be preparations you would wish to make first: studying those reports, for instance, and—what?" She broke off, seeing him shaking his head.

"I've already done it, and made notes besides." He put his hand inside his coat as if to withdraw the small notebook he kept there. "I did it while you were still asleep. Would you like to see?"

Julia declined this offer, but was by no means resigned to his imminent departure. "I was thinking just yesterday that your hair is in need of a trim. Perhaps you should see to it before you go."

"All the better for posing as someone who spends most of his time in an opium haze, wouldn't you think?" Seeing she was not convinced, he took her hand and cradled it in both of his own. "Sweetheart, what is it that's troubling you? What do you think is going to happen to me?"

Julia shook her head. "I suppose you think I'm being very foolish. But that house—" She gave a shudder. "There was nothing wrong with it, at least nothing beyond a general air of neglect. And yet it felt—I don't know—unpleasant."

"Well, that settles it." Releasing her hand abruptly, Pickett leaned back in his chair and crossed his arms. "I've never been anywhere unpleasant before, and I don't intend to start now."

Julia choked back a reluctant little laugh, which was precisely the reaction he had hoped to provoke. "All right, you've made your point."

"But seriously, sweetheart, I should think the very nature of the place and what they're trying to accomplish there would be enough to give it an atmosphere of unpleasantness, wouldn't you? After all, people go there—or are sent there—in the hope of freeing themselves from a habit they've become very, *very* attached to. Add to that the fact that two of its residents have died within a short space of time, plus the possibility that at least one of the current occupants is not there by choice, and—well, what would you expect?"

With a sigh of resignation, Julia removed the crumpled linen serviette from her lap and placed it on the table. "I can see you are going to have an answer to every argument I put forth, so I might as well save my breath."

"Look at it this way," Pickett added, seeing she was still far from convinced, "The sooner I go, the sooner I can come home. I'll have to make short work of it, if I'm going to be back in time to meet little Master or Miss Pickett."

"Can I come with you?"

Kit bounced up from the table with such eagerness that he set the cups rattling in their saucers. Pickett, taken by surprise with his coffee cup halfway to his lips, gave an instinctive jerk, splashing the contents of his cup over the left lapel of his fawn-colored tailcoat.

"I'm sorry!" cried Kit, turning stricken eyes on his brother, who was wiping at the spilled coffee with his serviette, a process that only served to spread it further. "I didn't mean to—it was an accident!"

"Of course it was an accident." Pickett, realizing that wiping at the mess was not having the desired effect, abandoned this process and began dabbing at it instead. "Kit, you wretched brat! You needn't look at me as if I was going to beat you!"

Kit's gaze shifted uncertainly to his sister-in-law, and Pickett realized a beating was the least of Kit's worries; even after a month beneath their roof, his young half-brother was not entirely convinced they weren't going to return him to his gin-soaked mother in the rookery of St. Giles. He put his arm about the boy and drew him close.

"Accidents can happen to anyone. Besides," he added bracingly, "you heard what I told Julia about my hair, didn't you? Well, the same thing holds true for my clothes. You might even say you helped me with my disguise."

Kit looked as if he rather doubted this, but at least he appeared to have lost his fear of being put out on the streets. "Really?"

"Really," echoed Pickett.

Apparently satisfied on this point, Kit returned to the matter at hand. "So, can I come, too?"

"I'm afraid not."

"I know I couldn't stay there with you—I know better than *that!*—but couldn't I just ride up to Islington with you? I wouldn't even get out of the carriage; I'd just look at it from the outside, just so's I'd know where you'll be."

Pickett shook his head, albeit not without sympathy. "I'm sorry, Kit, but I'm afraid not."

"It's because I'm just a kid, ain't it?" Kit said bitterly, his tone challenging his brother to deny it if he dared.

"Your age has nothing to do with it," Pickett said. "It's just that—that—" He broke off, realizing that he was poised on the horns of a dilemma. To enumerate for Kit all the reasons why he should not accompany them would be to admit to Julia that she had cause to fear for his own safety. "It's just that someone needs to stay here in case Mr. Poole should call to inquire as to my progress."

Kit considered this explanation for a long moment, as if trying to decide whether or not he found it acceptable. It soon became clear that he was not convinced, for he gave it as his opinion that "Rogers could tell him."

"No, that wouldn't do at all," Pickett replied without hesitation. "He would be asking for Mr. Pickett, and the only Mr. Pickett besides me is you."

With this reasoning Kit was forced to be content, and so it was that within the quarter-hour Pickett was in the carriage en route to the Larches, with Julia beside him and his valise at his feet.

"Have I told you lately that you're going to make a wonderful father, Mr. Pickett?" Julia asked, tucking her hand into the curve of his arm.

"Hmm," was Pickett's noncommittal reply. "I wonder if Kit would agree."

"He will," she predicted confidently. "Not today, perhaps, but eventually."

Pickett regarded her with skepticism writ large upon his expressive countenance. "When?"

"Possibly not until you come home." Giving his arm a little squeeze, she leaned toward him until her cheek pressed against his shoulder. "But he'll have to wait his turn, because I'm going to want you all to myself for the first se'nnight, at least."

"What, only a se'nnight?"

"Make it a fortnight, then." In a more serious she added, "In fact, that's why I didn't encourage you to allow Kit to accompany us. I wanted to spend a little time alone with you before leaving you there in that dreadful place."

"To tell you the truth," Pickett confessed, "I'd hoped to discuss something with you that I didn't want Kit to hear."

Julia sat up straight. "Oh?"

"I've been thinking about the best way to approach this, and I believe it would be best if I were to act as if I'm taking the cure under duress. Not held captive, as Mr. Poole suspects Miss Bonner is, but unwilling nonetheless. Perhaps our income derives not from your first husband, but from your father. That wouldn't be inconceivable, would it? After all, anyone with eyes in his head can see that you married beneath yourself."

"You do yourself less than justice, but go on."

"All right, then, your father couldn't stop the marriage—did we elope, perhaps? Yes, let's say we eloped—but he didn't want you to suffer for your lapse in judgment any more than you had to, so he makes me an allowance so that I can support you in the manner to which you are accustomed. Unfortunately for you, your parents were right about me all along, and now, having married a wealthy woman, I spend all my days sitting on my—er, sitting on the sofa and indulging my opium habit."

And that, my poor love, is exactly how you think others regard you, Julia thought with a sudden flash of insight. *Not the opium, perhaps, but the rest of it...*

She wished she'd made that connection months earlier,

when her money, and his reaction to it, had created a conflict that had very nearly wrecked their marriage, then in its third month. She would have been gentler with him, would have tried harder to understand his reservations.

It was too late to undo what they'd said and done then, but she would remember it in the future, just in case the successful resolution of Mr. Poole's dilemma was not followed by a cavalcade of other clients in need of similar services.

"Well?" Pickett prompted, when no opinion was forthcoming. "What do you think?"

"I think anyone who knows you at all would scoff at the very idea," she informed him bluntly. "Granted, Mr. and Mrs. Danvers don't seem to be among that number, so I daresay you might convince them, but—John, why?"

"Because if I should happen to be discovered in the middle of the night someplace I ought not to be, it might be useful to have an excuse ready to hand."

"Oh. Yes, I can see how it might."

"But if we expect them to believe it then, we'll have to convince them of it now."

She knew he was leading up to something, although what it was, she couldn't tell. "What are you saying?"

"Sweetheart, depending on how the conversation goes, I may have to say things that will hurt you. Worse, I may not have a chance to make it up to you afterward. God only knows if we'll have a moment alone, even to say our goodbyes, without someone listening at the keyhole."

"In that case," Julia said with a bravado she was far from

feeling, "I suppose you had better start making it up to me now."

Pickett, nothing loth, did exactly that.

11

In Which John Pickett Takes Up Residence in a New Abode

"Why, it's no better than a prison cell!" Pickett, who over the course of his six-year career at Bow Street had certainly seen enough prison cells to know better, regarded with disfavor the small, spartan chamber that was to be his home for the foreseeable future.

Mr. Danvers, engaged in unpacking the new arrival's valise and stowing its contents in an ancient chest of drawers, looked up from his task long enough to utter a mild reproof. "There, there, Mr. Pickett, no need to take on so. I'll wager this 'cell,' as you call it, will be vacant again in no time at all."

Mrs. Danvers bent upon her husband just such a look as a nursery governess might bestow upon one of her young charges who had spoken out of turn, then addressed the newest of the Larches' residents. "What my husband means to say, Mr. Pickett, is that the success of your stay here depends very much on the attitude you take. A recalcitrant guest who resists treatment will undoubtedly find his stay here much more irksome, and much longer, than will his more cooperative fellows. You might do well to ask yourself which sort of guest you intend to be."

"I might do even better to ask you how long you intend to keep me here," he retorted, and although the question was addressed to his hostess, the glare that accompanied it was divided more or less evenly between her stern visage and Julia's strained, white face.

"John, darling, we talked about this before," she said in a voice just loud enough to be overheard while still sounding as if she were trying to speak to him privately.

Pickett, noting the tension in her voice, wasn't quite sure whether his love was displaying a hitherto unsuspected talent for acting, or reminding him of her own dislike of the scheme. Either way, he could offer her no reassurances; having come this far, they were committed to the ruse, and he knew what he had to do.

" 'We'?" he echoed indignantly. "This whole thing was your father's doing, with your full cooperation. *I* don't remember being consulted in the matter at all!"

"John, please," she chided in an undervoice, casting a loaded glance in Mrs. Danvers's direction.

"What, you don't want my hostess to know that I'm here under duress?" Turning away from Julia, he addressed himself to Mrs. Danvers. "I'm afraid you've been misled, ma'am. I have no need of a cure. This whole charade was concocted by my loving wife"—he cast a resentful look at Julia—"and her father. It seems they don't approve of my spending a very small part of her money on a harmless bit of pleasure.

Although what else a man is supposed to do, when he's not even master of his own house, but beholden to his wife for every farthing…"

It was frightening how easily the old resentments rose to his lips, almost as if they had never truly gone away, but lurked just beyond the realm of his consciousness, waiting to be roused at the slightest remembrance. Partly to convince Mrs. Danvers, and partly to distance himself from a claim that struck a bit too close to the truth, he rambled on in this vein, muttering vague imprecations against his father-in-law that, while never containing outright falsehoods, contrived to paint Sir Thaddeus Runyon, not as the bluff country squire he was, but as a vaguely sinister figure with a will of iron who controlled his daughter and, by extension, her husband through unspecified but terrible means.

"John!" Julia exclaimed, with a tremor in her voice that anyone less well-acquainted with her would have taken for incipient tears. Pickett knew that it indicated quite the opposite—in fact, she was dangerously close to demolishing his carefully crafted story by dissolving into laughter—and so the pain of parting was considerably allayed by the knowledge that he was at least sending her away with a smile on her face, albeit one concealed behind the lace-edged handkerchief with which she blotted her suspiciously dry eyes. If they were denied the opportunity for more private farewells, this, at least, would suffice.

"Come, Mrs. Pickett," Mrs. Danvers said, taking Julia's arm and steering her toward the door. "I think we had best leave your husband to settle in while we review a few last details. If you will come with me…"

Her voice faded as the two ladies proceeded down the corridor. Mr. Danvers, having finished unpacking Pickett's valise, nodded in farewell and made as if to follow.

"My bag," Pickett protested, only to be cut off.

"You'll not be needing it for a time yet, and there's no room for it here. I'll just put it in the box room up in t'attic, and it'll be waiting there safe and sound until you're ready to leave us."

He then undid the calming effect these soothing words were intended to produce by scurrying from the room as if fearful Pickett would attempt to wrest the bag from him by main force, foiling pursuit—or at least delaying it—by closing the door on his way out.

What an odd little man, thought Pickett, watching him go. Julia had said it was Mrs. Danvers, rather than her husband, who ruled the roast, and it appeared she'd got it right. But there was more to it than that. Mrs. Danvers was clearly a gentlewoman, or had been, until reversals in her family's fortunes had compelled her to put her family home to commercial purposes; her husband, on the other hand, appeared to have come of humbler stock.

You should talk, Pickett chided himself, even as his brain insisted that the two cases were not at all the same. Mr. Danvers's humbler origins were betrayed not only by the man's speech, but also—and perhaps more significantly—by his subservience to his wife. It appeared that, at least in this case, he—or she—who paid the piper did indeed call the tune. But Julia had never expected her own low-born husband to show her the same deference—and he suspected she would not at all like it if he did.

Still, the fact that he and his host appeared to have this circumstance in common might prove useful, if he should need an ally. In the meantime, he would take advantage of this possibly brief time alone to make his preparations. He first counted slowly and silently to ten, allowing Danvers sufficient time to reach the stairs and be well on his way to the attic. Satisfied on this point, he opened the door just wide enough to ensure that the corridor was indeed empty before closing it again, turning the key in the lock for good measure.

He then withdrew the little notebook and its pencil from the inside pocket of his coat and tucked them away in the top drawer of the wardrobe, concealed beneath his supply of clean and starched cravats. The notebook was followed by his coin purse, which he had emptied of its contents save for just enough to procure some form of transportation for himself and Miss Bonner once they had won free of their prison.

Finally, he extracted from his pocket that feminine accoutrement so useful for burglary, a hairpin filched from his wife's abundant supply. He frowned at the thought of placing it into the drawer with the rest of his belongings, where it might roll about or fall through a crack. Attempting to retrieve it in the middle of the night, and by candlelight, would be almost literally searching for a needle in a haystack. Placing it carefully on top of the wardrobe, he retrieved the notebook, tore out a page, and folded up the hairpin inside, then returned the whole to its hiding place amongst the cravats.

No sooner had he closed the drawer and turned away

from the wardrobe than he changed his mind. He retrieved the whole kit and boodle from the top drawer and moved the lot to the bottom, this time tucked within the folds of the gorgeous crimson-and-gold banyan which his valet, Thomas, had apparently deemed necessary for his comfort.

A moment's reflection was sufficient to convince him that this, too, was unsatisfactory. Stooping to reach the bottom drawer was certainly less convenient than opening the top one, but anyone intent on searching his belongings would not be put off by the necessity of kneeling.

Once again, he removed the tools of his trade from their rather exotic nest, then lifted a corner of the mattress and placed them directly beneath the spot where his head would lie. The mattress upon which he was expected to sleep during his stay at the Larches was so thin and lumpy that he had to wonder at his wife's idea of "comfortable, though not luxurious"; it appeared the bedchamber that was shown to prospective clients was a far cry from those actually assigned to the establishment's "guests." Still, his bed's inadequacies might prove to be an advantage; it was unlikely that anyone could steal a hand beneath the mattress to pilfer his possessions while he slept without his being instantly aware of it.

Having stowed his belongings to his satisfaction, he crossed the small room to the window and twitched the curtain aside. He had been given a room at the front of the house, and the view afforded by its single window must once have been excellent, overlooking as it did the spacious grounds with their gentle slope down to the ornamental water, as well as the wide gravel drive down which carriages would have approached the house from the scrolled iron gate to deposit visitors at the foot of the portico.

From this angle, however, the full extent of the neglect was laid bare: the lawn badly in need of scything, the water green with scum, the drive choked with weeds and, perhaps worse, abandoned in favor of a rough utilitarian track that had been cut around one end of the house to join not the London Road, but the narrow lane at the rear. He supposed the Danverses could hardly be blamed for the bare limbs of the larch trees that gave the property its name, but these certainly added their share of gloom to an already uninviting landscape.

Turning his mind to more practical matters, he noted that his room was too far from the ground to climb down, even had there been a conveniently placed tree or downspout to employ in such a cause. He glanced from the fold of curtain still in his hand to the sheets on the bed, the latter slightly disarranged from his operations there. A rope of these tied end-to-end might suffice—it had certainly served the purpose well enough to enable an escape from the burning Drury Lane Theatre—but the drop would still be precipitous, and that was assuming he could persuade Miss Bonner to undertake such a descent on the word of a stranger.

Then, too, there was the window itself, which bore the appearance of not having been opened in a very long time. Pushing open the sash, assuming it could be done at all, would very likely result in enough noise to rouse the house. Nor would breaking the glass be of any use; quite aside from the noise this would produce, the window was made up of a dozen panes, each one far too small for even the daintiest lady to pass through, to say nothing of his own six-foot-three-inch frame. The idea that his pencil might serve as a tool with which he might unscrew the bolts and remove the entire window frame from the wall was likewise rejected; if this could be accomplished at all—an outcome which was far from certain—it would very likely be a lengthy (and far from silent) process, and would undoubtedly destroy his pencil into the bargain, leaving him with no implement for making notes.

Having eliminated the window as a means of clandestine egress, he would have dropped the curtain back into place and turned away when a movement below caught his eye. A carriage approached, not down the weed-choked drive leading from the street, but from the northern corner of the house, along the rude track that circled back to the stables, or whatever was left of them. The vehicle drew to a stop before the portico, and although the double doors at the front of the house were blocked from his view by the pediment crowning the portico, he had no difficulty at all in identifying the foreshortened figure in bonnet and pelisse being ushered out of the house and handed into the carriage.

Suddenly it was of the utmost importance that he should get her attention, that their eyes should be able to make to one another the promises their lips were denied. Should he rap on the glass? *Could* he, without breaking character? Yes, he decided; beating on the glass was just the sort of thing a man would do, if he were being left in this dismal place against his will and without his beloved opium to sustain him.

"Look up," he muttered, rapping his knuckles against the

glass with as much force as he dared. "Julia, sweetheart—*look—up!*"

He had known they might not have an opportunity to exchange private farewells; he had warned her of that very possibility. And yet he was unprepared for the sense of abandonment that overwhelmed him as the door of the carriage was closed behind her and the vehicle lurched forward. He leaned closer for a better view from which to watch it go—watch *her* go—until the carriage disappeared around the southern end of the house, leaving him alone before the window, his face pressed to the glass.

Alone. For the first time, he considered Miss Bonner's situation, not from the perspective of Edward Poole, a concerned outsider, but from that of the lady herself: trapped and alone, unaware that there were those even now who knew of her dilemma and were working to effect her rescue.

He turned away from the window and let the curtain fall back into place. There would be time later (very likely tonight, as he lay on the thin mattress trying to sleep) when he could be as maudlin over Julia's absence as he pleased. For now, the sooner he made contact with Miss Bonner and plotted their best course of action, the sooner they could escape.

Both of them.

* * *

While Pickett judged how best to conceal his belongings from prying eyes, Julia accompanied Mrs. Danvers down the wide, sweeping staircase to the office on the first floor.

"A good-looking young man, your husband," Mrs. Danvers observed, gesturing for her guest to precede her through the door. "I can certainly see why you succumbed to his charms—and why you now feel compelled to give him over into our care," she added darkly.

"He is not usually so belligerent," Julia said apologetically, and with perfect truth. "How long do you think it will take? That is, how long must he remain in residence here?"

The time could not be short enough to suit her, and yet she knew it would place him in a very awkward position if Mrs. Danvers should pronounce him "cured" before he'd had time to complete his mission.

Mrs. Danvers cast a loaded glance in the direction of Julia's swollen middle. "I daresay you will want your husband's case settled with all due haste."

"Well, yes," Julia said, judging this to be a safe answer as well as a perfectly honest one; surely any woman facing childbirth would want her husband near at hand. "Of course, I understand that these things take time—"

Mrs. Danvers cut her off. "Depend upon it, by the time of your confinement, all of this will be nothing but a distant memory." After a delicate pause, she added, "Of course, such immediate results require a great deal of effort, and although one hates to be so vulgar as to speak of money..."

The words trailed off on a note of expectation, and Julia could not fail to take her meaning. "Of course," she said hastily, tugging open the drawstrings of her reticule.

She removed a roll of bank notes and counted out enough to cover the price Mrs. Danvers had quoted on her earlier visit, then handed it over, albeit not without a pang of uneasiness at parting with such a sum. Mr. Poole would reimburse any expenses incurred on his behalf, of course, but until Miss Bonner's fate was settled, his name must not appear in the matter at all. In the meantime, it was the Pickett household that would bear the expense.

"Thank you, Mrs. Pickett," Mrs. Danvers said briskly, stowing the bank notes in the top drawer of the desk and turning a small brass key in the lock. "And now, if you will sign these documents—there are two, you see—all will be settled. You have my word that we shall resolve the matter as quickly as is safely possible."

Julia assured the woman that she quite understood the need for caution, but it appeared that Mrs. Danvers, her gaze shifting to focus on some point over Julia's shoulder, was no longer attending.

"Ah! Here is my husband to show you to your carriage."

Julia turned, and was dismayed to discover Mr. Danvers hovering just inside the doorway, clearly ready to usher her gently but firmly from the premises. "Oh, but must I leave at once? May I not say goodbye to Mr. Pickett first?"

Mr. Danvers shook his head sadly, but it was his wife who spoke. "I'm afraid not, Mrs. Pickett. In such cases as this, an abrupt change is more effective. Suddenly bereft of all that is familiar, the patient is more open to practices that are *un*familiar." Julia's face must have expressed her doubts, for Mrs. Danvers continued in a rallying tone. "Come, Mrs. Pickett! Having got this far, surely you would do nothing to delay the very results you seek."

"No," she said with a sigh. "No, of course not."

Conceding defeat, she allowed Mr. Danvers to lead her to the wide double doors at the front of the house. He flung these wide, and she was surprised to see the carriage already drawn up before the portico. Clearly, the Danverses were ready to be rid of her, presumably so that they might begin the course of treatment, whatever it was, without delay. “In such cases as this,” Mrs. Danvers had said. Had she meant cases where prompt results were desired, or cases in which the patient was supposedly submitting to treatment under duress?

Obeying a sudden impulse, she snatched her elbow from Mr. Danvers’s grasp and turned back toward the house just in time to see the door close. Was it her imagination, or did she really hear the faint rasp of metal on metal, as if the bolt had been shot home?

“Never you mind, Mrs. Pickett,” Mr. Danvers said soothingly, taking her arm once more and steering her toward the carriage. “It’ll all be over before you know it.”

“I’m sure you’re right,” Julia said with more warmth than she felt, gathering her skirts as he handed her up into the vehicle. “Only—you will take care of him, won’t you?”

“Aye, we’ll take care of him,” he assured her, and closed the carriage door.

It was exactly what she had wanted to hear, and yet she could not be easy in her mind. At that moment she would have given anything to have her husband seated beside her, teasing her out of her fears as he had (at least temporarily) at breakfast that morning. But the carriage started forward with a lurch, and there was nothing for it but to put on a brave face for Kit’s sake.

She collapsed against the squabs and pressed her hands to her face. Such was the life of any woman in love with a man who felt it his duty to right all the world's wrongs.

12

In Which John Pickett Is Discovered in a Compromising Situation

Impatient as he was to make contact with his quarry, Pickett was obliged to cool his heels for the better part of the day; any man installed here against his will would, he reasoned, be inclined to remain in his room and sulk, rather than explore his new surroundings and seek acquaintances amongst his fellow sufferers. And so it was that, when the gong sounded on the floor below summoning Mr. and Mrs. Danvers and their "guests" to dinner, he chose to ignore it. A few minutes later, he heard a light scratching on the door.

"Mr. Pickett?" called an anxious voice, obviously a member of the reduced staff; he suspected the redoubtable Mrs. Danvers had never sounded so timid in her life. "It's time for dinner, sir, if you'd care to come downstairs."

"I'm not hungry!" Pickett shouted in sullen accents.

"It's a very nice rack of veal, sir, along with mushroom gravy and—"

"I said *I'm not hungry!*" In fact, he was very hungry indeed, having not eaten since breakfast that morning, but that was all the more reason not to be obliged to listen to a litany of foodstuffs recited through the keyhole.

"Yes, sir! Beggin' your pardon, sir!" the voice said breathlessly, and the faint echo of hurried footsteps assured Pickett that he would not be burdened with further admonitions.

Still, his failure to appear at dinner did not mean he intended to remain shut up in his room all evening. He waited a full fifteen minutes (as indicated by the tinny chime of the long-case clock in the hall below marking the quarter-hour) before making his next move. Then, having judged that everyone else in the house would be occupied in appeasing the demands of appetite, he opened his door and peered out, glancing down the corridor in first one direction and then the other. It was fully dark by now, and tallow candles in wall sconces cast circles of soft yellow light at intervals, their flames flickering slightly in a draft of air too weak to be felt by human senses. Feeble as it was, the light was sufficient to assure him that the corridor was empty, so he slipped out of his room and carefully pulled the door closed behind him, wincing at the faint *snick* that sounded as loud as a gunshot.

He intended to do a bit of exploring while he could be reasonably certain of being uninterrupted; if he could determine which room was Miss Bonner's, he could perhaps communicate with her before ever encountering her face to face. A piece of paper torn from his notebook with a penciled message—*I've come to help you escape*, or something along those lines—might at least serve to assuage the lady's fears; in any case, she would have the comfort of knowing she was no longer alone. He could slip it under the door, if only he knew which room was hers. As he recalled, Julia had said that Miss Bonner, as the sole female resident aside from Mrs. Danvers, had been given a room on a separate floor from the men, in order to satisfy the demands of propriety. That should prove useful, since the other "guests" would be less likely to catch him in the act of absconding with the lady; however, against this slight advantage must be set the fact that Mr. and Mrs. Danvers—the only other people on the same floor as Miss Bonner—might make it a practice to retire to bed with one ear cocked for the sound of any man who might think to approach Miss Bonner's chamber with amorous intentions.

He dared not climb the broad, once-grand staircase at the center of the house, lest any of the residents finish their meal early and repair to their respective rooms, thus catching him out. But a house this size would surely have more than one way to access the other floors—wouldn't it? There was one way to find out. He set out soft-footed in the opposite direction of the main stair, in the hope of finding a narrower, less ornate set of stairs at the end of the corridor. He had traversed less than half its length when he glimpsed a light out of the corner of his eye. With an audible gasp (another faint noise that somehow seemed preternaturally loud), he whirled about to identify its source, then let out a shaky laugh, feeling more than a little foolish.

One of the doors along the corridor stood ajar, leaving a six-inch gap through which shone the candlelight that had caught Pickett's attention. Upon closer inspection, he could see that one of the residents had not extinguished his candle before going down to dinner, but instead had left it still alight on top of the chest of drawers, the counterpart to a similar piece of furniture in Pickett's own bedchamber. Had its occupant perhaps been reluctant to return alone to a dark room? Pickett could sympathize with such an impulse; at the moment, he was feeling none too courageous himself.

There was, he reflected afterwards, absolutely no justification for his next action. He had no reason, no reason at all, to enter that room, for it could not possibly be Miss Bonner's. And yet, almost of their own volition, his legs took him unhesitatingly to that partially-opened door, his hand rose to push the panel wide enough to allow him access.

He wasn't quite sure what he'd expected to find, but he had to admit the room was a disappointment. It was very much like his own: a bed, a chest of drawers, a washstand in one corner supporting a bowl and pitcher, a writing desk and ladder-backed straight chair placed beneath the window…

His mind drew up short at the thought. Unlike his own window with its view of the neglected lawn and reed-choked pool, this window looked over the back of the property. He recalled the open back gate and the glimpse it had afforded of the working heart of the house: the collection of outbuildings, the greengrocer's wagon drawn up to a door set into the back wall of the house, through which, presumably, one might access the kitchen.

How well-lit was this side of the house at night? How many people might be moving about there after dark?

He was unlikely to have a better opportunity to find out. Crossing swiftly to the window, he twitched the curtain aside and peered out. His own face stared back at him. With a huff of annoyance, he elbowed the curtain out of his way, then cupped his hands about either side of his face, blotting out the candlelight that turned the glass panes to mirrors.

Yes, this was better. From this distance, he could see a splash of light illuminating the front of the stable, the bright pinpoint at its center indicating the exact position of the lamp mounted just outside the stable door. The other outbuildings were dark, but quadrangles of light on the ground directly below indicated windows where candles were burning inside the house. Unfortunately, he was not familiar enough with the arrangement of its rooms to determine which ones were occupied.

A dark shape moved against the shadows, and a moment later a large black dog—no, two large black dogs—emerged into the light of the stable lamp, gamboling like puppies as the door of the stable opened and a man stepped out. A moment later, both dogs were head-down in their dinners, tails wagging. Pickett frowned thoughtfully at the sight of this new obstacle. He hadn't expected dogs. We they pets, or were they kept as guard dogs for the purpose of preventing just such escape attempts as he intended to make? Granted, there was nothing particularly terrifying in their manner at the moment, but then, they were eating. Dogs, he knew, could be bribed; it might work to his advantage to get upon terms with them.

His gaze shifted back to the lamp outside the stable door. In a pinch, he could break the glass and use the flame to start a fire, creating a distraction to keep the household occupied while he spirited Miss Bonner out by another way, but only if the stable was unoccupied. He wanted no witnesses to his act of arson, but more than that, he didn't want anyone, man or beast, to be unable to escape the fire once it caught. Pickett was no great lover of horses—his few attempts at riding had not been unadulterated bliss—but having once been trapped in a burning building himself, he knew it was a fate he wouldn't wish on his worst enemy, even a four-legged one.

Since the stable, however depleted from the family's glory days, was unlikely to be completely uninhabited, he would have to sacrifice one of the other outbuildings. But which one? A bit of exploration was clearly in order, and besides, he could hardly remain in his room for the duration. He would make a survey of the grounds the following morning, and should he encounter Miss Bonner while on this mission, perhaps even contrive to have a private word with her, so much the better.

Having settled upon his next course of action, he backed out of the window and let the curtain fall back into place, then turned…

And found himself staring into the rigid, angry face of a man he'd never seen before. Presumably, the resident had returned to his room, and was even now advancing upon the trespasser with one claw-like hand reaching out. It occurred to Pickett that this man did not look like one who would be fearful of returning to a dark room, but he had no time to ponder this curious discrepancy. Some explanation was clearly in order—and he had no possible excuse to give.

"Hallo, is this room yours, then?" he asked a bit too heartily. "I hope you'll forgive the intrusion—my name is Pickett, John Pickett—I just arrived today, and I'm afraid I got turned around a bit—mistook this room for my own—" Although how he'd thought to find it by staring out the window, he couldn't begin to say.

The man offered no reply to this disjointed speech, but grabbed Pickett's sleeve. In the same instant that Pickett tensed, bracing himself for a fight, he realized that what he with his guilty conscience had read as fury was in fact fear. And not just fear, but stark terror.

"Coming for me—they're coming for me," the man said, his voice low and urgent.

"Oh, are they?" responded Pickett, utterly bewildered. "Who—?"

"Don't let them get me," he pleaded, clutching Pickett's sleeve. "Don't let them—"

"Look here, there's no need to take on so," Pickett said, trying without success to extricate his arm from the man's grasp.

"They're coming! Don't let them get me!"

He leaned closer, and Pickett saw that the pupils of his eyes were mere pinpricks, tiny points of black within circles of pale blue. Clearly, this poor fellow had contrived to obtain the very substance whose hold he had come to the Larches to break. Pickett was not familiar with all the effects of opium use, but he had never heard that the substance could instill in its users morbid fears and imaginary terrors. Then again, he supposed it might not be so very different from alcohol; the same draft that inspired one man to bestow his coin purse upon a total stranger might lead another to beat his wife black and blue. In any case, it would probably be better to humor the poor fellow than try to reason with him.

"No, I, er, I won't let them get you," he said placatingly, prying the man's fingers one by one from his sleeve. "But now I'd best be going—"

"They'll come for you, too," the man predicted darkly. "They come for you in the night."

"Yes, well, thank you for warning me," Pickett said, inching his way toward the door. "Good night."

On this note, he ducked into the corridor and swiftly closed the door behind him.

* * *

Back in his room, however, the cryptic words were not so easily dismissed. Pickett told himself that it was foolish to set too much store by the rantings of a man who was obviously not in full possession of his faculties. And yet there had been two recent deaths here, and at least one of the people currently in residence (two, if he counted himself in his assumed rôle) was quite possibly being held under duress. Given those circumstances, the words seemed to hold some sinister meaning far beyond the incoherent ramblings of one clearly in thrall to the poppy.

What you need, Pickett told himself sternly, *is a good night's sleep*. He'd lain awake for much of the previous night, alternating between tenderly assuring his anxious wife that she was worrying over nothing, and lying on his back thinking about the task ahead and its importance not only to Mr. Poole and Miss Bonner, but to his own future as well. Another such night, and he would be no good to anyone.

Determined to remedy the deficiency, he stripped off his clothes and hung them over the back of the chair, recalling as he did so that the matter of how to launder one's clothing had not been addressed. No matter; Julia would be coming to visit in a few days, and if nothing else, he could send his clothes back with her. It would give Thomas, his valet, something to do in his absence. Having satisfactorily resolved this problem, he looked in the chest of drawers for a clean nightshirt—a garment he often dispensed with back in Curzon Street, but one which was very likely necessary, now that he no longer had the warm body of his wife beside him. He pulled the nightshirt over his head, extinguished his candle with a pinch, and slid between the patched and darned sheets.

He was obliged to shift positions several times before he found one that was comfortable; as he had noted earlier, the mattress provided by Mr. and Mrs. Danvers was a far cry from his feather-stuffed bed back in Curzon Street. *What a snob you've become*, he scolded himself, squirming into yet another position.

The comparison to his bed in Curzon Street led, not unnaturally, to thoughts of Julia, who was at that very moment lying in it alone. *And I hope she's having a better time of it than I am*, he thought, rolling over onto his other side. He recalled how she'd looked as he'd last seen her, climbing into the carriage without so much as a glance in his direction, and felt again the same sense of abandonment that had assailed him at the time. He raised himself up on one elbow in order to plump up his pillow. It was unfair to blame Julia for doing the very thing that he himself had urged her to do, he chided himself. In any case, it wasn't as if he would never see her again; she would be coming to visit him in only a few days—and he did *not* intend to waste what little time they would have together in airing baseless grievances. Fully resolved on this point, he pulled the counterpane up over his ears and closed his eyes.

It was perhaps inevitable that his belly should choose that moment to punish him for his earlier neglect. There was no ignoring its rumblings, for in the silence they sounded loud enough to awaken anyone who might be sleeping in either of the rooms adjacent to his.

"Oh, the devil," he muttered, throwing back the covers. Sleep was clearly out of the question, so he might as well do a bit of exploring while everyone else was still abed. He'd intended to investigate that door at the rear of the house at some point, and this was as good a time as any. If he was discovered, he could claim to have got lost. As this excuse would become less credible the longer her remained in residence, he might as well take advantage of it while he could. He would try to locate that back door, and if he was lucky, he would find his way to the kitchen, where he could procure something—bread and cheese, or perhaps an apple—to stave off the demands of his stomach until breakfast.

He groped in the darkness for the top of the chest of drawers, where he'd last seen the candle and flint. After providing himself with some illumination, he opened the bottom drawer and pulled out the banyan which Thomas had seen fit to pack along with his more practical garments. There were times, he admitted, shrugging the banyan on over his nightshirt, when a valet was a very useful person to have.

He picked up the candle and slipped out of the room, closing the door behind him. Then, cupping his hand about the flame as a shield—a protection against drafts as well as prying eyes—he stole silently down the corridor to the narrow staircase at the end of the hall.

13

In Which John Pickett Engages in a Battle of Wits, and Comes Off the Worse

Upon reaching the end of the corridor, Pickett looked speculatively at the steps going up to the floor above where, according to Julia, Miss Bonner had been assigned a room. Although it was tempting to climb the stairs and determine, if he could, which room was hers, he resisted the urge; aside from the risk of being discovered there by his hosts, who occupied a suite on the same floor, he thought it unlikely that Miss Bonner would look with favor upon a strange man who saw fit to wake her in the middle of the night, no matter how noble his intentions.

And so he began his descent, holding the candle before him to light his way. The hand he had cupped protectively about its flame was now needed to grip the banister; a fine thing it would be if he were to alert the entire household to his movements by tumbling down the stairs.

He reached the ground floor without incident, pushed

open the green baize door that separated the servants' domain—and froze where he stood. In the blackness beyond the feeble light of his candle, a pair of glowing yellow eyes stared back at him. As he stood rooted to the floor, the eyes blinked.

"*Mrowr?*" A tortoiseshell cat leapt down from her high perch atop a stack of wooden crates, and stepped daintily into the light.

Pickett gave a shaky laugh. "Well, puss, I hope you're happy," he said softly. "You just scared ten years off my life."

"*Mrowr?*" repeated the cat, unrepentant.

He supposed he should have expected it; cats were welcome in most kitchens, provided they were good mousers. Although to judge by the expectant look on this one's face, that night's hunting must have been a disappointment.

"If it's food you're looking for, I haven't got any," he informed his four-footed companion *sotto voce*, not without sympathy. "In fact, I'm on a bit of a hunt myself. You won't give me away, will you? There's a good cat."

But it soon became apparent that this particular feline had no interest in being a good cat. It much preferred rubbing against Pickett's legs and making a general nuisance of itself. It had been Pickett's observation that animals usually liked him—most animals, anyway, although there had been one dog that had bitten his hand, and he and horses tended to regard one another with mutual antipathy—but he could think of few less helpful accomplices than this one, which he seemed all too likely to trip over in the dark. He gave the cat a nudge with his foot and continued down the dark passage, testing first one door and then another.

In this manner he discovered the butler's pantry and then the wine cellar, this latter, surprisingly, left unlocked—a circumstance no doubt made possible by the fact that there were no resident house servants to whom it would present a temptation. Finally, he opened a door that gave onto a large room with a heavy deal table in the center, flanked on one side by a deep basin set against the wall and, on the other, an enormous fireplace bristling with hooks, cranes, and other accoutrements to meal preparation.

The kitchen, he recognized with some satisfaction, and although he had not spoken the words aloud, a *mrowr* of agreement sounded immediately behind him.

"You again?" He turned, and sure enough, the cat stood right behind him, its tail curved up like a question mark. "I'm not going to feed you," he said, softly but (he hoped) firmly. Turning his back on it, he made his way through the kitchen toward a door on the far side which, if his suspicions were correct, would open onto the back of the house, or at least onto a passage that would lead him to a rear exit.

Not for the first time, he silently blessed the case that had taken him to Yorkshire the previous summer, where he had conducted his investigation while incognito as a footman; the knowledge he'd acquired there of the inner workings of an English country house had proven invaluable on more than one occasion. It was there, too, that he'd first kissed Julia, Lady Fieldhurst (although it had actually been she who had kissed him), a fact which had done nothing to make the memory of that case abhorrent to him.

Perhaps if his mind had been less taken up with cats and kisses, Pickett would have noticed the faint glow of light visible from the passage down which he had just come, a glow that grew steadily brighter as it neared the kitchen. Alas, he did not, his attention being wholly occupied in extracting the cat's claws from the hem of his banyan, to which garment it had unaccountably taken a fancy, and so had no idea another person was on the premises until a voice called out, "Hallo? Who's there?"

The cat took off like a rifle shot and disappeared into the shadows.

"Coward," Pickett muttered after it, then straightened and turned to address Mr. Danvers, who stood just inside the kitchen door. The man had obviously dressed in some haste: the tail of his nightshirt had been stuffed into the waist of his breeches, and his nightcap sat askew on his head. His feet were bare, and must have been cold against the stone flags that made up the kitchen floor.

"I'm sorry if I frightened you, sir," Pickett said. "I couldn't sleep—a bit peckish, you know—so I thought I would see if I couldn't look out a bite to sustain me until morning."

Mr. Danvers shook his head sadly. "Aye, it's no more than you deserve for shutting yourself up in your room and refusing to eat your dinner."

Too late, Pickett remembered that he was supposed to be resentful of, if not outright hostile toward, his current living conditions. He made no reply, but tried to look sullen, in the hopes of staving off any awkward questions his host might be inclined to ask. Alas, his was not a countenance that could easily assume a quelling aspect.

"Ah, well," said Mr. Danvers, apparently deciding to take pity on him, "it's often difficult to sleep in a strange bed. Have trouble that way myself sometimes. I've got something here that ought to fix you up in a trice."

"That's very kind of you, but it won't be necessary. I'll go back upstairs to my own bed, and allow you to return to yours. Goodnight; I'm sorry to have troubled you," Pickett said, and made as if to retrace his steps through the kitchen and down the passage to the back stairs.

"Nonsense!" chided Mr. Danvers, detaining him with a grip on the sleeve of his banyan as inextricable as the cat's had been on its hem. "You've come this far; no sense in leaving empty-handed—or empty-bellied, as the case may be," he added, winking broadly.

Releasing Pickett's sleeve, he opened the door of a cupboard set into the near wall, and for a moment Pickett thought the man was going to offer him the sustenance which had been his whole purpose—well, half of his purpose, anyway—of stealing down to the kitchen in the first place. But no; it was not the remains of that evening's dinner that Danvers produced from the cupboard, but a large bottle and a small glass tumbler, the latter of which he handed to Pickett.

"A drop or two of this, and you'll be sleeping like a babe newborn," he predicted confidently, decanting a good deal more than a drop or two from the bottle into the tumbler. "Just see if you don't."

Pickett recalled wondering if he might enlist Mr. Danvers

as an ally, taking advantage of the fact that they'd both married above themselves as a point upon which they could find some common ground. With this end in view, he somewhat reluctantly accepted the proffered tumbler, even as he looked askance at its contents.

"Obliging of you, but I'd better not," he said regretfully, trying to present the inner struggles of a man torn between duty and inclination. "The missus wouldn't like it—and it's she who rules the roast," he added with a tolerable imitation of resentment.

"Don't I know it!" sympathized Mr. Danvers, casting a speaking look up at the ceiling, as if he could see through it all the way up to the second floor, and the bed upon which his wife at that very moment lay. "But we'll show them, aye? Drink up, and assert your manly spirit."

Before Pickett could make any reply to his host's urgings, Mr. Danvers exclaimed, "I say! Did you hear that? Assert your *spirit* by drinking *spirits*! Clever, what?"

"Brilliant," agreed Pickett with perhaps more tact than honesty. Still, Mr. Danvers's self-congratulations had at least given him time to formulate a plan. He would raise the glass to his lips along with his host, but not actually imbibe any of its contents.

He encountered the first setback to this plan when Mr. Danvers closed the door of the cupboard without taking down a second tumbler.

"Aren't you going to join me?" Pickett asked, not at all pleased with this discovery.

Mr. Danvers gave a visible shudder. " 'fraid not. *Your*

wife is back in Mayfair; *mine* is just upstairs."

When his host had first fetched down the bottle from its shelf, Pickett had wondered if Mr. Danvers, like himself, had thought to enlist an ally, a clandestine partner with whom to share habits that must be hidden from his wife during the daylight hours. Now, however, it occurred to him that some more ominous purpose might be at play. What the devil was in that bottle, and why was the man so eager for him to drink it? The fact that Mr. Danvers did not intend to join him in imbibing added weight to his suspicions, and the more his host urged him to partake, the more perversely resolved Pickett became to resist his entreaties. Alas, he had accepted the empty tumbler when Mr. Danvers had first offered it, and now he discovered the man wouldn't take it back.

"I'd best not," Pickett said apologetically, holding it out to Danvers with every appearance of regret. "Empty belly, as you say."

"So much the better, if it's a soporific you're wanting," his host insisted, pushing the tumbler, and the hand that held it, back in the direction whence it had come.

Pickett might have pointed out that he did *not* want a soporific, but feared that to do so might raise uncomfortable questions as to what, exactly, he *did* want, wandering the house in the middle of the night. He was suddenly seized with the absurd notion that they were engaged in a silent battle of wills, with Mr. Danvers determined that he should drink the—the whatever it was—and he himself equally determined that he would not. Perhaps, he thought, a change in tactics was in order.

"I'm obliged to you," Pickett said, with the air of one allowing himself to be persuaded against his better judgment. After all, someone admitted to the Larches to overcome an attachment to opium might, in its absence, welcome a reasonable substitute, and to put up too much resistance could only raise his host's suspicions. If he could fob the man off long enough to return to his room, he could examine the concoction at his leisure and then dump it into the chamber pot. "I'll just take this upstairs with me, and—"

"No, best drink it here," Mr. Danvers insisted. "That way you can leave the tumbler for the daily girl to wash in the morning."

Pickett gave a little laugh, as if his host could not possibly be serious in suggesting that he consider the convenience of the hired help, and said with a great deal more confidence than he felt, "Oh, but if it works as well as you claim, I'm likely to tumble down the stairs before I reach my room!"

Mr. Danvers laughed heartily in response to this claim, and for a moment Pickett thought he had won.

But no. "Never fear, Mr. Pickett," Mr. Danvers assured him. "I can accompany you as far as your room—I'll be going that way myself, since mine is on the floor directly above—and between you and me and the banister railing, we'll contrive to keep you on your feet. Come, now! Surely it can't hurt to try it?"

Suddenly Pickett saw his way out, a way so obvious he could only wonder why he hadn't thought of it before. He would take a small sip—a *very* small sip—and then profess, truthfully or not, to dislike it. That way, he could discover exactly what was in the bottle without being obliged to down its entire contents beneath his host's all too watchful eye.

He wasn't sure what he'd expected. In his defense, however, few people would have anticipated so brazen an act of deliberate subversion.

For Pickett had been dosed with too much laudanum following the Drury Lane Theatre fire not to recognize it now: the bitter taste of opium that even the strongest of alcoholic beverages could not completely disguise. Why would a man who ran an asylum for opium-eaters deliberately press upon a resident a concoction containing that very substance? Was it possible that Mr. Danvers didn't realize the bottle was contaminated? Pickett rejected this possibility at once. Everything in the man's demeanor suggested one who had just got the better of an adversary.

"Well, Mr. Pickett?" he prompted, regarding Pickett with a rather smug smile. "What do you think?"

"This is laced with opium!"

Mr. Danvers's head bobbed up and down as if on a spring. "Yes! I *knew* you would like it!"

"Whether I like it or not is beside the point," Pickett said impatiently. "I'm supposed to be giving it up, remember?"

His host's face fell. "Aye, but a man needs something to sustain him through the lean times ahead—a last fling, so to speak."

Pickett hesitated, trying to decide what his attitude should be. Any man truly in thrall to the stuff would be only too glad to drink it all the way down to the dregs. If he had the strength of will to resist such an offer, he need not have come to the Larches at all. By refusing to drink, he ran the risk of demolishing the history he and Julia had concocted for him, or being dismissed from the establishment, believed to have overcome his habit, before he had even made contact with the lady with whose rescue he was charged.

He had no choice, really. Still, he was not prepared to go down (literally or figuratively) without a fight. Mr. Danvers might beam with pleasure as Pickett once again raised the tumbler to his lips; he might nod in approval as the level of liquid remaining in the glass decreased; he might even smile with satisfaction as he retrieved the empty tumbler from Pickett's hand, saying, with a distinct note of triumph in his voice, "There's a good lad!"—a designation Pickett would not tolerate from anyone except Mr. Colquhoun, who had known him at the age of fourteen.

Mr. Danvers could not, however, force him to swallow.

"There, now!" exclaimed his host, all but purring with satisfaction. "That wasn't so bad, was it?"

Pickett responded with a rueful, but close-mouthed, smile.

"In fact," Mr. Danvers continued enthusiastically, "I should go so far as to say it's quite good, wouldn't you?"

Tilting his head to one side, Pickett appeared to consider the matter for a moment before giving a thoughtful nod, as if he were a wine connoisseur weighing the merits of a particular vintage. He suspected that, were he to dispute this claim with a shake of his head, his host would express dismay and press him for some explanation as to its failure to please, and that would never do; until he could dispose of the doctored drink—by spitting it into the chamber pot beneath his bed, if no earlier opportunity presented itself—he was limited to nonverbal, yes-or-no responses.

"A courteous answer, Mr. Pickett," Mr. Danvers observed, "but I'm afraid it may not be an entirely honest one."

Pickett gave a careless shrug of his shoulders, but his hackles rose. He had no very clear idea of what the man was about, but he was fairly certain he was not going to like it—a suspicion that was confirmed with his host's next question.

"Very well, Mr. Pickett, I'm sure I can find something that would be more to your liking. What would you prefer?"

There it was, then, the question that he could not answer without first swallowing the mouthful of opium-infused port—he rather thought it was port, although the bitter taste certainly did nothing to improve it. He gauged the distance to the opposite wall, and for a moment considered the possibility of rushing past Mr. Danvers and ejecting the mouthful into the basin situated there. But he would certainly have to offer some explanation for ridding himself of the very substance which he supposedly craved.

Still, all was not lost, at least not quite. He lifted his shoulders and spread his hands, indicating that he had no particular preference, or that he had never given the matter much thought; he didn't really care how Mr. Danvers chose to interpret the gesture, as long as he didn't ask for enlightenment.

"Come now, Mr. Pickett," his opponent chided almost

jovially, as if he knew he'd won, "I'm well aware that tastes differ, so you need have no fear of giving offense. If you would prefer to partake of the poppy in some other form, you have only to say the word. Neither your wife nor mine will ever know."

During this heartening speech, he had moved closer to Pickett and even put a reassuring arm about the younger man's shoulders. And then, as Pickett struggled for some response that would not require speech, the man's hand slid from Pickett's shoulder to the spot between his shoulder blades, where it delivered a firm, convivial *whack.*

The blow was so unexpected that Pickett almost uttered an exclamation, an involuntary reaction that would have sent the dose in his mouth spewing across the kitchen floor, had he not managed to gulp it down just in time.

Panic gripped him as he realized what he had done—what, he was certain, Mr. Danvers had intended him to do.

He had swallowed it.

14

In Which John Pickett Suffers the Consequences of Defeat

He had done it. He had swallowed a mouthful of opium, or at least something generously laced with it, and it was only a matter of time before he began to feel the effects. At the moment, however, he felt only disgust at his own stupidity for being outwitted in such a way, and by one whose intellect he would, if asked, have rated as inferior to his own. He recalled Mr. Danvers's scurrying retreat from his room earlier in the day, and wondered how much of the man's timorous demeanor was genuine, and how much was an act. Either way, Pickett thought, his downfall had been perhaps no more than he deserved, for becoming so puffed up in his own conceit.

His pulse quickened at the thought, and he could all too easily imagine the narcotic he'd been duped into ingesting being pumped throughout his body with every beat of his racing heart. *Breathe slowly*, he told himself. *In…out. In…out.*

There was no need to panic. All he had to do was regurgitate it into the chamber pot under his bed—not so far removed, really, from what he'd already been planning to do. The only difference was that instead of ridding his mouth of it, he would be ridding his stomach instead. Not a pretty sight, perhaps, but there would be no one to see him anyway. He did not need to waste time, though; the sooner he could put this rough-and-ready remedy into practice, the more effective it would be.

"Well, that should help me sleep," he said, much more cheerfully than he felt. "I'll bid you goodnight, then, and—"

"No need to rush," protested Mr. Danvers. "Give me a minute here, and I'll go with you, as I said. Saves the candles, too, which will please my wife to no end," he added bitterly, and, before Pickett had a chance to object, reached out and pinched the wick of the candle Pickett still held, extinguishing the flame and leaving nothing to show for it but a curl of smoke.

Pickett almost ground his teeth in frustration. Since his only alternative was to grope his way up the stairs in the dark—and that with a bellyful of opium which would very soon be making its presence known—he had no choice but to await Mr. Danvers's pleasure.

And the man seemed to be taking a prodigiously long time. Whistling under his breath, he returned the bottle to the cupboard, but not before rearranging the other dozen or so bottles that occupied the same shelf; Pickett could not help wondering if they all contained opium and, if not, how Mr. Danvers would ever identify that particular bottle again out of so many.

Eventually, his host apparently had the cupboard

organized to his satisfaction, for he closed the door and took the empty tumbler from Pickett's hand. Instead of taking up his lantern and leading Pickett toward the stairs, however, he shuffled across the kitchen to the basin, where he spent several minutes in rinsing it so as (he said) to make things a bit easier for the daily girl when she arrived in the morning. This explanation was followed by a rambling monologue in which he described for Pickett's edification not only the girl herself, but her entire family as well, along with the misfortunes which had obliged her to seek work in the Larches' kitchen. Pickett, whose sympathies would usually be fully aligned with the hired help, thanks in large part to his own experiences below stairs, found himself wishing the man would get on with it and let the daily girl bloody well fend for herself.

By the time Mr. Danvers pronounced himself finished, however, Pickett's attitude had mellowed considerably. Unlike his days at Ludlow & Ludlow, or even before that, at Bow Street, he had no need to arise early the next morning, so he might stay up as late as he wished. At the thought of his emancipation from the counting-house, he felt a surge of elation so intense that it had to be shared.

"I'm not going back there," he informed Mr. Danvers, as the latter collected his lantern and steered Pickett out of the kitchen and back up the passage toward the stairs. "Not ever again."

"I'm sure you don't have to go anywhere you don't like, Mr. Pickett," Mr. Danvers said soothingly. "Where is it you don't want to go?"

"Ludlow & Ludlow," he said. "Importers," he added

darkly, feeling some further explanation was called for.

"I see." Mr. Danvers nodded sagely, as if a great mystery had been solved. "No, you'll never have to go back there again, I promise. Have a care, Mr. Pickett, the stairs are this way."

Having reached the foot of the stairs, Pickett looked up. He had only come down two flights, but from where he now stood, they seemed to stretch upward for miles, with only a pinpoint of yellow light to mark the top. He took a deep breath, grabbed the banister, and began the long climb. She was up there somewhere, the lady he had come to rescue. He could picture her sleeping serenely in her bed, her tousled golden curls splayed over the pillow…

No, that was Julia. He had no idea what Miss Bonner looked like. Surely she must be beautiful, though, or at least reasonably attractive, for Mr. Poole to pay so handsomely for her safe return.

But thoughts of ladies, beautiful or not, were driven from his brain as the tiny point of light grew, gradually becoming larger and brighter until it resolved itself into the hideous face of a gorgon swimming before them on the staircase above, challenging them to pass.

"*There* you are!" the loathsome creature exclaimed. "What took you so long?"

"He was harder to manage than I expected." Mr. Danvers sounded somewhat breathless, a fact Pickett found puzzling; he himself felt as if he might have floated up the stairs to his room, had not this harpy blocked the way.

"I should've thought he'd jump at the chance," Mr.

Danvers complained.

In spite of his labored breathing, his host seemed unperturbed by the ghastly vision, and as it drew nearer, Pickett discovered the reason why. This was no gorgon, but only a woman clad in a dark dressing gown and bearing a candle—a candle whose flame, bobbing just below the level of her chin, cast her angular features into harsh and unflattering relief. He had just been thinking about a woman; who was it? Julia, waiting upstairs for him to join her—no, not Julia, but the lady he'd been sent to rescue. But that lady was younger than this—wasn't she? Unless, of course, the fellow had conceived a grand passion for a woman fully two decades his senior…

No, he decided. It was impossible. Not *this* woman, in any case.

"You're not her," he said ungrammatically. "You can't be."

"Does he suspect anything?" the gorgon—no, the woman—asked.

"Not a thing," Pickett assured her, glancing at Mr. Danvers, who seemed to be regarding him uneasily.

"Are you sure we should—?" Mr. Danvers began.

To Pickett's surprise, he sounded almost nervous. "It won't hurt us," he told his drinking companion. "It's only a woman."

As if to give the lie to this statement, the woman leaned toward Pickett, raising her candlestick in a manner suggestive of violence. Uttering a faint protest, he threw up a hand to ward off the blow as well as blot out the light that was now shining directly into his eyes.

"Perfectly safe, so far as this one is concerned," she pronounced. To Pickett's relief, she removed the blinding light that was surely brighter than any one candle had a right to be. "I should be surprised if he remembers coming downstairs at all. Still, one never knows who else might be stirring, so I suppose we'd best wait until—"

The last of this speech was lost to Pickett as she turned and led the way up the stairs, holding the candle aloft like a beacon to guide the two men trailing after her. To his surprise, both she and Mr. Danvers accompanied him down the corridor to the door of his own room.

"Here we are," Mr. Danvers said soothingly, opening the door and allowing Pickett to precede him.

Pickett was slightly annoyed when the pair entered the room in his wake, closing the door behind them as if they had every intention of staying. He had only the one bed, and he did *not* intend to share it with the gorgon. Besides, there was something he needed to do, something to which he rather thought it was important that he have no witnesses. What was it? He couldn't *think*, not with the pair of them speaking in low whispers behind his back, and certainly not with the bed looking so very inviting…

The murmured sounds behind him seemed to grow louder, and he could now distinguish the words with almost superhuman clarity. Stranger still, he felt as if he were somehow detached from his own body, looking down at a young man with tousled brown curls and a banyan of crimson and gold brocade sprawled facedown across the mattress. Nor was Pickett the only observer, for the man and woman stood at the foot of the bed, regarding the sleeper with clinical detachment.

"Yes, perhaps, but we mustn't leap to conclusions," the woman was saying, her voice amplified as if heard through an ear trumpet. "How can you be certain he hadn't gone down to the kitchen in search of food, as he claimed? If you'll recall, he did refuse to come down to dinner."

"I know," the man answered impatiently. Pickett knew who he was—knew the woman, too, for that matter—but could not think of their names. "But by the time I reached the kitchen, he was almost all the way through to the other side. If all he wanted were a bite to eat, it stands to reason he would've stopped to have a look-see through the cupboards. But if he'd done any such thing, he left no trace of it. And powerful reluctant he were to drink that port, I'll be bound," he added darkly.

"No doubt," the woman agreed, "but a man who has come here to overcome a dependence on opium would certainly put up at least a token protest at being given a drink laced with it, would he not?"

"Aye, but this weren't no token protest," insisted the man. "Kept the whole thing in his mouth to the very last, he did, and would've spat it out if he'd had half a chance."

They're talking about me, Pickett thought, not quite sure whether to feel flattered or insulted.

"What, exactly are you suggesting?" For a moment he thought the woman was demanding an answer of him, but it was the man who replied. Which was just as well; Pickett knew he ought to tell them he could hear every word they said, but he couldn't seem to make his tongue obey his brain's commands.

"I think he knows," the man was saying. "He knows, or at least suspects, and he was trying to escape."

There was no response from the woman, but the man apparently felt she was still in need of convincing, for he said, "Then, too, I heard voices."

"Voices?" she echoed sharply.

"One voice, anyways. His."

"That is…troubling," the woman admitted. "Have you any idea who he was talking to?"

It was the cat, Pickett thought, resisting the urge to giggle. *It was only the cat!*

"No. I couldn't hear what he was saying, neither. Still, I don't like it. I don't think we ought to wait too long," he concluded.

"Perhaps not, but we must take care of Mr. Tomkins first," the woman said firmly. "It won't do for it to happen twice, too close together. Still, it was my impression that she wants the business settled before her confinement."

The man looked at the sleeper, still lying motionless on the bed. "I'll bet you all of Lombard Street that he ain't the father, and that's why she's so anxious to get him out of the way."

He's talking about Julia! Pickett realized in indignation as the couple turned away, preparing at last to depart. *Come back here, you bastard! I dare you to say that to my face! I dare you…*

But the young man still lay sprawled facedown across the mattress, his left arm hanging over the side of the bed, the tips of his fingers just grazing the floor.

Then the door closed, darkness fell, and Pickett knew no more.

15

Which Finds John Pickett Unsuitably Dressed for Polite Company

Pickett awoke the next morning heavy-eyed and lethargic, with a mouth so dry it might have been packed with cotton wool. Sitting up somewhat unsteadily, he discovered with some surprise that he was still wearing his banyan over his nightshirt, and that he had fallen asleep lying on top of the covers rather than beneath them. He'd expected to have trouble sleeping in a strange bed, especially one so different from the one he shared with Julia, but evidently he'd been so exhausted that he hadn't even troubled to turn down the counterpane, much less get undressed. What had he done last night to wear himself out so completely? Gradually it began to come back to him. Something about a cat, and a hideous apparition blocking the stairs…

No, he thought with growing conviction, not an apparition. It had been Mrs. Danvers, her sharp features distorted by the flame from the candle she'd held. She'd been coming down the stairs to meet the pair of them: him and the cat. No, not the cat. There had certainly been a cat, but that had been earlier, and the cowardly feline had bolted when someone else had come down the passage to the kitchen. Mrs. Danvers? No, she had been on the stairs above them. It had been her husband—Mr. Danvers. He'd come down to the kitchen, and they were going to find something to eat, since he himself was so hungry, having foregone dinner. At least, that had been his own plan; Mr. Danvers, however, had opened a cupboard and produced, not the bread and cheese Pickett had come to the kitchen to search for, but a small glass tumbler and a bottle of port.

And the port—he knew it with absolute certainty—the port had been laced with opium. The bitter taste had given it away. He'd tried not to swallow it, but Mr. Danvers had tricked him (there would be time enough later to berate himself as a fool for having been so easily bested) and he had wanted only to reach his room and rid himself of it before it took effect. Had he succeeded?

His lethargy banished, Pickett leapt up from the mattress, then dropped to his knees and reached beneath the bed frame for the chamber pot. He knew what he would find even before he caught a glimpse of the ceramic vessel. The lack of any telltale odor provided evidence enough of the chamber pot's emptiness, but even without this proof, there were also his strange impressions of that night: the stairs that had seemed to climb upwards through the darkness to infinity; the weird and frightening impression of what had proven to be nothing more sinister than a woman of late middle age holding a candle; the vague and unsettling dreams of the Danverses, man and wife, standing at the foot of his bed, discussing him in whispers that had somehow sounded as loud as shouts. What had they been saying? He couldn't remember, but he had the impression that it might have been important.

One thing was certain: his recollections, already vague, were unlikely to grow clearer with the passing of time, so it behooved him to commit them to paper before they were lost entirely. He reached beneath the mattress and pulled out his notebook and pencil, then spent the next quarter-hour attempting to reconstruct the night's activities and writing them down. There were far too many gaps for his liking, but aside from leaving blank spaces that might (he hoped) be filled in later, it was all he could do.

No, he decided, there was one other thing—more mundane, perhaps, but one that might prove to be useful. Already, time was becoming distorted in his mind; it hardly seemed possible that scarcely twenty-four hours had passed since he'd watched from the window as Julia departed, leaving him to continue his investigation alone. After a week, maybe even less, he would have lost all sense of the passage of time. He lay down full length on the floor and made two tick marks—one for each day he spent at the Larches—on the baseboard underneath the bed, where no one would see them but himself.

Having finished this task and returned his writing materials to their hiding place, he pulled open the top bureau drawer, where he received an unwelcome surprise. The drawer, and the one beneath it, and the one beneath that, were almost completely empty.

His clothes, down to the last pair of stockings, were gone.

He stared at the empty drawer for a long moment, unable to believe the evidence of his own eyes. Then he closed and opened them all again one by one, as if he might somehow conjure his clothes through sheer disbelief in their absence. When this exercise failed to produce any result, he glanced about the room. A more thorough search would be pointless, for there was literally nowhere for them to hide; in fact, that was why he'd been obliged to conceal his notebook and pencil beneath the mattress. There was nowhere that one could put anything larger—and certainly nothing as bulky as a pair of breeches or a tailcoat—that would not be immediately visible to anyone who entered the room.

He turned his attention back to the bureau and took a quick inventory of his other possessions. He hadn't brought much with him, so it didn't take long. And yet he couldn't help feeling that something was missing. He went over the little collection again: comb, tooth powder and toothbrush, shaving kit—

That was it.

His razor was missing.

The absence of this one item seemed more ominous than the loss of his entire wardrobe. The removal of his clothing might be indicative of nothing more than a misunderstanding with the laundress or, at worst, a prank in very poor taste. The idea of someone deliberately taking his razor, however, filled him with foreboding, whispering as it did of premeditated violence.

It was this possibility, and the fear that the blade had already been put to just such a purpose, that compelled Pickett to swallow his pride and go down the main stairs to the public part of the house clad in nothing but a nightshirt and a banyan that bore all the appearance of having been slept in. What if Miss Bonner was the intended victim? Worse yet, what if the deed was already done? That might account for the theft of his clothing, as well. Her lifeless body might already be awaiting discovery somewhere within the house or its grounds, hastily dressed in male clothing to confuse matters and throw investigators off the scent, at least temporarily.

Heedless of any curious looks cast in his direction by the asylum's residents or staff, he ran Mrs. Danvers to ground in her office, where she sat at her desk entering figures into a calf-bound volume.

"A word with you, ma'am," he said, not wasting time on such trivialities as courtesy.

She looked up from her account book, and although she adjusted her spectacles, her face registered no surprise at Pickett's unorthodox attire. "Yes, Mr. Pickett? What is it?"

"*What is it?* Good God, surely you don't think I make a habit of capering about in my nightshirt! I've just discovered that my razor and all my clothes are missing."

"They aren't missing," she assured him calmly. "They're really quite safe."

He stared at her. "*You* took them?"

"Yes. Well, strictly speaking, it was my husband who took them, but he was acting on my instructions." As Pickett struggled for words that might adequately express his indignation, she continued in the same unruffled tone. "It was a very good thing Mr. Danvers found you when he did. Had you fallen down the stairs while walking in your sleep, you might have done yourself a serious injury."

"I wasn't walking in my sleep!" Pickett insisted. "I've never walked in my sleep in my life!"

"In that case"—her tone hardened—"your presence in a part of the house where guests are strictly barred from entering can only be seen as an attempt at a clandestine departure. We cannot allow our guests to slip out and indulge the very habits they have come to us for help in overcoming."

"Maybe you should have told your husband that before he forced a tincture of opium down my throat!" Granted, it hadn't happened exactly like that, but the end result had been the same.

" 'Forced,' Mr. Pickett?" Mrs. Danvers regarded him skeptically over the top of her spectacles. "Somehow I doubt it took much effort on his part, given the purpose of your presence among us."

For an instant Pickett feared she had discovered the truth about his mission at the Larches, and frantically tried to recall everything he had said the previous night while not in full possession of his faculties. Then he realized she was referring to the supposed fondness for opium that should have made him only too eager to drink the concoction he'd been offered. Apparently he'd said nothing indiscreet, or at least not so indiscreet that he'd wrecked the story he and Julia had concocted. Still, the momentary fright reminded him of the other, more urgent reason he'd sought out Mrs. Danvers.

"And what about my razor? I suppose you were afraid my beard would attempt a clandestine departure, too?"

Her expression grew wintry. "I would be more likely to suppose it had yet to arrive. Yes, what is it?"

This last was not directed toward Pickett (thus depriving him of the chance to protest the inevitable observation on his age, or lack thereof), but at some point beyond his right shoulder. He turned and saw Mr. Danvers hovering in the doorway bearing all the appearance of one who knows himself to be bringing unwelcome tidings.

"Pray forgive the interruption, Mrs. Danvers," he began in trembling accents, and Pickett, noting the formal honorific by which the man addressed his wife, recalled the early days of his own marriage, when he'd struggled to accustom himself to calling Julia by her Christian name after thinking of her as "my lady" or "Lady Fieldhurst" for almost a year.

"It's Miss Bonner," Mr. Danvers went on. "She—well, I'm afraid she was discovered in the old smokehouse. Again," he added with a nervous glance at Pickett, as if reluctant to discuss a delicate matter before a third party.

His reticence was well-placed, for at the mention of the familiar name, Pickett was instantly on the alert. Still, it would not do to give the Danverses reason to suspect his interest in the lady, so he made as if to reclaim Mrs. Danvers's attention. "About my razor, ma'am—"

Mrs. Danvers closed her ledger and rose from her desk, visibly annoyed. "Very well, Mr. Danvers, I shall speak to the wretched girl. I'm sorry, Mr. Pickett, but I've no more time for you. Suffice it to say that, given your conduct up to this point, we have deemed it best not to leave a potentially deadly weapon in your possession. Now, if you will excuse me—"

Pickett would have vehemently objected to this assessment of his character, but it was clear that his hostess had already dismissed him from her thoughts as well as from her presence. Resolving to broach the subject again at the first opportunity, he left the room at her signal, only to discover Mr. Tomkins, whose room he had invaded the previous night, in the hall. Not wishful to engage in social conversation while dressed in his nightclothes, Pickett would have stolen up the stairs unobserved, but he saw the light of recognition dawn in the man's eyes, and when Mr. Tomkins lifted a hand slightly as if to detain his nocturnal visitor, Pickett knew he had no choice.

"Good morning," he said, nodding in a manner that was (he hoped) polite but uninviting.

"Good morning, Mr.—Pickett, is it?" He ducked a head in an approximation of a bow that was, Pickett supposed, as formal a greeting as anyone clad in his nightshirt could expect. "I trust you slept well?"

Pickett was not quite sure how to answer this, but the man's hurried speech gave him to understand that the question was purely rhetorical.

"I hope"—his eyes darted from Pickett to the Danverses and back again—"I hope you won't set too much store by what—by anything I might have said last night. I fear—I fear I was not quite myself, you see, and—"

"It's quite all right," Pickett assured him. "The fault was all mine."

"What's this?" Mrs. Danvers asked sharply. "Has Mr. Tomkins been annoying you, Mr. Pickett?"

"Not at all," Pickett insisted, taking pity on his clearly mortified companion. "Last night I accidentally wandered into his bedroom by mistake, so if one of us was annoying the other, I'm afraid it was the other way 'round."

"Have you been neglecting your medication again, Mr. Tomkins?" Although it was a perfectly reasonable question, especially in such an establishment as this, it seemed to Pickett that there was something vaguely menacing in her tone.

"I—I didn't—I haven't—"

She didn't wait for an answer. "Go up to your room, and Mr. Danvers will be there directly. Now, Mr. Pickett," she continued, after Mr. Tomkins, still stammering disjointed excuses, had obeyed these instructions, "exactly what took place last night between yourself and Mr. Tomkins?"

Pickett shook his head dismissively. "Nothing of any importance. As I said, I entered Mr. Tomkins room by mistake. When he returned to the room a few minutes later, he seemed—confused."

"Confused?" she echoed, regarding him through narrowed eyes. "In what way?"

Recalling the man's fear that someone was coming for him with some sinister purpose—Mrs. Danvers, perhaps, or her husband, or both?—Pickett was reluctant to betray him. Fortunately, his own conduct on that occasion was not above reproach, and a seemingly reluctant attempt to explain it might serve to distract her attention from the hapless Mr. Tomkins.

He shrugged his shoulders in a vague gesture intended to convey indifference to the mental state of his fellow resident. “I really couldn’t say. In fact,” he added with the air of one forced to reveal a guilty secret, “I was too conscious of my own transgressions to pay much attention to his ramblings. Earlier in the evening, I had refused to come down to dinner, but later I was hungry, and wondered if there might still be time to join the others at the table. I haven’t a clock in my room, and so when I stepped out into the corridor and saw Mr. Tomkins’s door ajar, I thought I would have a look in and see if he could tell me the time. I didn’t realize he wasn’t in—he’d gone down to dinner, I suppose—and when he surprised me there, I was too aware of having trespassed to pay much attention to anything he said.”

He might have saved his breath.

“And what, exactly, did he say?”

“I really don’t remember—I wasn’t really listening—”

“Come, Mr. Pickett! You must have been listening to some extent, if for no other reason than to be sure he wasn’t berating you for your presence there. So *what did he say?*”

Pickett’s first thought had been to spare the man from having to own up to behavior that seemed to embarrass him now, in the light of day. It occurred to him, however, that he might find it much more useful to tell Mrs. Danvers of Mr. Tomkins’s inexplicable fears, and see what reactions this disclosure might provoke.

“He was—afraid,” Pickett said somewhat reluctantly, in the manner, not entirely feigned, of one forced to betray a confidence.

"Afraid?" Her voice sharpened. "Afraid of what, pray?"

"It was hard to tell; he was barely coherent. He seemed to think he stood in some kind of danger. Exactly what, he didn't say, at least not in a way that made any sense."

If he had hoped to surprise some expression of guilt or fear on the woman's face, he was doomed to disappointment, for aside from a slight thinning of her lips, her countenance remained impassive.

"I shall have Mr. Danvers tend to the matter," she promised.

Pickett couldn't help wondering if Mr. Danvers's method of "tending to the matter" would entail compelling the recalcitrant resident to ingest copious amounts of some opium-infused beverage.

"In the meantime," Mrs. Danvers continued, "if Mr. Tomkins troubles you again, I hope you will let me know at once."

Before Pickett could voice either acceptance or refusal of this desire (which had, in fact, sounded more like a command), she turned and walked away in the direction of the stairs. Clearly, he was dismissed.

16

In Which John Pickett Hears Startling News

Since Pickett had slept late, thanks to the machinations of Mr. Danvers, he arrived at the breakfast table to discover that the other residents had already eaten and gone. This was good news insofar as he was spared the curious looks which his state of undress must have provoked, but it also meant that the flames heating the chafing dishes had been allowed to die out. As a result, the eggs looked clammy and the fat on the bacon was congealed. Pickett didn't care; his belly was vehemently protesting its empty condition. In any case, he had eaten far less-appetizing meals in his life, and been grateful for them. He picked up a plate from the depleted stack and set about filling it with whatever food remained.

He lingered over his late breakfast in the hopes of contriving a meeting with Miss Bonner, but by the time he finally finished, she had yet to put in an appearance. He wondered if she was being confined to her room as punishment for her foray to the smokehouse and, if so, how long such an isolation might last.

For that matter, why the smokehouse? Mr. Danvers had said she'd been discovered there "again," as if she made a practice of visiting that particular site. And he'd called it the "old" smokehouse, which seemed to suggest that the building was no longer in use, at least not for its original purpose. Had she been keeping clandestine assignations with one of the other residents? A secret lover—assuming she had one—might explain why she refused to see Edward Poole on those occasions when he'd come to visit her only to be turned away. Unfortunately, if that was indeed the case, she might be all the more unwilling to leave if it meant abandoning a lover in order to escape with a total stranger. And that she would have to leave him behind was certain. It would be difficult enough for two persons to escape without being caught; bringing along a third would increase the difficulties exponentially.

Was it possible that her partner in the intrigue was someone from outside, someone who had found a way to slip in and out at will? It would be useful to know the method of entrance and egress the intruder employed. For that matter, it would be useful to know why the devil the fellow didn't rescue her himself. *Either way,* he thought, *if she's playing some deep game of her own, she won't thank me for shoving a spanner into the works.*

There was very little he could do until he actually met the lady and got from her own lips the answers he sought. And since such a meeting appeared unlikely to occur spontaneously, it was up to him to contrive one.

Having delayed as long as possible, Pickett finally rose

from the breakfast table, albeit not before encountering more than one glowering look from the daily girl who had been obliged to wait until he had finished before she could remove the dirty dishes from the table and convey them to the kitchen for washing. Pickett, unmoved by these silent expressions of disapprobation, contented himself with wandering about the dining room examining the paintings adorning the walls. As these were few, he was soon finished with his inspection, and still Miss Bonner had not come downstairs.

He broadened his scope to include all the paintings in all the public rooms, keeping a weather eye out for a female form descending the stairs, but this exercise, too, proved to be in vain. Desperate for some reason to remain downstairs, he entered the library, and found someone was there before him: a silver-haired gentleman of about sixty sat comfortably ensconced in a wingback chair upholstered in threadbare crimson velvet, an open book on his knee. He looked up at Pickett's entrance, and the two men exchanged nods, the younger surprised but relieved to find that his unorthodox apparel excited no curiosity, much less disapproval. He was still wondering what to make of this discovery when his fellow guest spoke, and Pickett soon realized that his deshabille had not gone entirely unnoticed.

"Good morning, young man. I don't believe we've met, have we? Sir Anthony Moring, at your service." Sir Anthony rose and, marking his page with one finger, stretched out his other hand in greeting.

"Pickett, sir. John Pickett," he said, accepting the proffered handshake. "No, we haven't met. I only arrived yesterday."

The bibliophile gave a knowing chuckle, as his gaze dropped from Pickett's face to his banyan and the collar of his nightshirt showing beneath it. "And thought to make it a very short stay, I've no doubt."

"Beg pardon, sir?" asked Pickett, all at sea.

Sir Anthony inclined his head toward Pickett's undress. "The penalty for attempting to leave the premises without permission. I daresay most of the people here have been obliged to partake of breakfast in their nightclothes at one time or another. Dinner too, for that matter. Never fear; they'll be returned eventually," he added, and although the words were clearly intended to reassure him, the reference to dinner gave Pickett to understand that he could not expect to be properly dressed anytime soon.

"How long will *that* take?" he asked with a trace of impatience he could not quite suppress.

Sir Anthony shrugged his shoulders. "It depends on the severity of the infraction. Or, as is more likely, on how long it takes for one to become resigned to his fate."

"You appear to have done so, in any case," remarked Pickett, taking envious note of his companion's well-cut tailcoat, tastefully patterned waistcoat, and biscuit-colored breeches.

"Oh, but I never displayed the slightest interest in escape. Indeed, why should I?"

"Begging your pardon, sir, but a better question might be why you should not," Pickett observed dryly.

The older man chuckled. "I see you have come to the

Larches at someone else's urging."

"My wife's," interpolated Pickett.

"There you are, then. I, on the other hand, am here at my own instigation."

"You're an opi—you've made a habit of opium use, sir?" Pickett asked in some surprise. He had no very clear idea of how an opium-eater ought to look, but this well-dressed, self-possessed gentleman was surely not it.

"An opium-eater?" Sir Anthony voiced the unflattering designation Pickett had bitten back. "I'm afraid so. Hence my need to avail myself of Mr. and Mrs. Danvers's hospitality."

"I understand it's a very difficult habit to overcome," Pickett allowed.

"On the contrary; giving up opium is easy." His blue eyes twinkled over the rims of his spectacles. "I've done it half a dozen times, at the least reckoning."

Pickett acknowledged this jest with a grin, but saw his chance to garner information from this candid, to say nothing of engaging, source. "You said almost everyone has appeared at breakfast in his nightclothes at one time or another," remarked Pickett in a tone that he hoped indicated nothing more than idle curiosity. "Not Miss Bonner, surely? I understand she's the only female currently in residence. Aside from Mrs. Danvers, that is."

Sir Anthony frowned in concentration. "No, at least not that I can recall—and I suspect the sight of Miss Bonner *en déshabillé* would be a sight not easily forgotten. But then, she has never shown the slightest desire to leave the premises. I can only assume that she, like her poor brother before her—to say nothing of your humble servant—must recognize the need for help in overcoming the opium habit. We comprise a very small minority. Most people don't give it up so readily."

Most people aren't afraid their guardians' next attempt might be even worse, Pickett thought. He proceeded to ply Sir Anthony with questions in the hope that the amiable gentleman might prove to be a valuable source of information regarding Miss Bonner, at least until he could make the young lady's acquaintance himself, but this hope was destined to be dashed. It appeared that Sir Anthony knew very little about her, as he had done little more than bow to the lady when meeting her in the dining room or on the stairs.

"Mrs. Danvers is very careful of Miss Bonner's rather precarious position as the only lady here, save for herself," Sir Anthony explained. "And one can hardly blame her for an excess of caution, can one?"

Pickett owned that one could not, although he personally found Mrs. Danvers's vigilance on behalf of her only female guest more than a little inconvenient. He lingered in the library long enough to select a volume from its shelves and, more importantly, to allay any suspicions Sir Anthony might harbor as to his interest in the lady, then returned to his room with his book.

Any hope he might have entertained that he might encounter Miss Bonner on the stairs were doomed to disappointment. When he reached the floor where his own chamber was located, he regarded with a speculative gaze the turn in the stairs that led upward to the next floor, where the lady herself was housed. Did he dare climb them and knock on her door? Would she open it to him, if he did? He couldn't quite banish the image of her lying insensible on her bed, drugged into obedience. That might account for her prolonged absence; heaven knew there was little enough in the sparsely furnished bedchambers to keep one occupied for long.

Upon reaching his room, he closed the door and turned the key in the lock, then withdrew the little notebook and pencil from their hiding place beneath the mattress. He sat down on the ladder-backed chair before the writing table, and spent the next ten minutes mentally reconstructing the events of the morning: his confiscated wardrobe and razor, his hostess's peculiar interest in his encounter with Mr. Tomkins on the previous night, and the tidbits he'd gleaned from his recent exchange with the charming opium-eater Sir Anthony Moring.

Having finished this task, he rose from the table and would have returned the tools of his trade to their hidey-hole when he stopped, gazing thoughtfully at the notebook in his hands. Obeying a sudden impulse, he tore out a blank sheet of paper, sat back down, and began to write.

Miss Bonner, he wrote, *you don't know me, but a mutual friend has enlisted my aid in extracting you from a situation that he fears may place you in considerable danger. I realize you have no reason to trust me, but I offer as my credentials six years' employment at the Bow Street Public Office, the last two as a principal officer, as well as my recent marriage to the former Lady Fieldhurst, whose husband's killer I was charged (successfully, I may add) with bringing to justice. I would like to speak privately with you at a time and place of your choosing, during which I hope to formulate some plan for your escape. Awaiting your convenience, I am, respectfully,*

John Pickett

Tucking his pencil behind his ear, he read back over the words he had written. Not, perhaps, a missive to fill any gently bred lady with confidence, but until he could make his case in person, it was the best he could do. Now he had only to deliver it into the hands of the lady herself. He folded the sheet in half, folded it again, and wrote *Miss Lydia Bonner* on the outside.

After hiding his notebook and pencil once again beneath the mattress, he tucked the note into the pocket of his banyan, then opened the door of his chamber, stepped out into the empty corridor, and sauntered down the passage in the direction of the main staircase. He would have much preferred to take the narrower back stair he'd employed the previous night on his sortie to the kitchen, but to do so now would suggest a furtiveness of manner he was trying to avoid. Nevertheless, he stole a quick glance down the stairs to ensure there were no witnesses before commencing his climb to the next floor, where Miss Bonner's bedchamber was located.

He recalled what Julia had said about Mrs. Danvers's self-appointed position as guardian of Miss Bonner's virtue, a claim that had been confirmed only half an hour ago by Sir Anthony Moring. Was it truly her virtue that concerned Mrs. Danvers, or was she merely determined to set a barrier between the young lady and the other residents, lest Miss Bonner take one of the men into her confidence, perhaps even enlist his aid? Pickett thought it very likely; few men, isolated and with too much time on their hands, would be able to resist the appeal of playing knight-errant to a damsel in distress, even—or perhaps especially—one several decades younger than themselves. Still, Mrs. Danvers's excuse would serve him quite well; if he were caught in the act of slipping the note beneath Miss Bonner's door, he had only to assume the manner of one hoping to lighten the burden of his incarceration with a bit of dalliance. He was sure Julia would forgive him, under the circumstances.

His confidence suffered a setback when he reached the landing and found himself standing in the center of a corridor punctuated at intervals by no fewer than a dozen doors—six on each side of the passage, half to his left and half to his right—any one of which might belong to the chamber that housed Miss Bonner. As he stood staring at the seemingly identical panels, however, he gradually began to notice subtle differences. The locking mechanism of the door nearest him appeared to have been completely removed; given Mrs. Danvers's stance regarding her only female guest's virtue, it was highly unlikely that she would have placed the young lady in a room so easily accessible by anyone who might have designs upon breaching it. The door adjacent to it appeared to be standing very slightly ajar; he would certainly peer inside to be sure, but he was reasonably certain that this one, too, could be ruled out. Finally, the door at the very end of the corridor appeared to be somewhat wider than its fellows, and the panel bore traces of faded gilt trim. This was most likely the door to the suite occupied by the master and mistress of the house. It stood to reason, then, that Mrs. Danvers would have placed Miss Bonner in the chamber nearest her own.

Having come to a decision, Pickett strode down the corridor with the air of one who had every reason to be there. Casting a quick glance up and down the corridor in both directions, he stooped and slipped his clandestine correspondence beneath the door, then rose and, feeling he had pushed his luck quite far enough for one day, stole down the narrow staircase nearest at hand.

It was not until he was once again safely ensconced in his own room that he realized he had given Miss Bonner no instructions as to how she was to communicate her preferences to him. Left to her own devices, would she scribble her choice of time and place on the bottom of his own missive and return it to him in similar fashion, or would she seek him out in person? Still worse, now that he thought of it, he'd given her no indication of which room was his, and no way of identifying him if she saw him.

Lord, what an idiot he was! He had been a resident at the Larches for more than twenty-four hours, and had nothing to report to Mr. Poole thus far except evidence of his own incompetence. He did not look forward to the prospect of wandering about the place in his nightshirt and banyan, but at this point he had very little alternative. Remaining cloistered in his room all day would be fruitless, and sounded tedious, besides. Miss Bonner might not recognize him, but *he* would certainly recognize *her*.

Seeing no alternative, he left his room (albeit with some reluctance, given his present state of undress) and once again trooped down the central staircase to the common areas of the house. There was once again no sign of her, so he expanded his search to the grounds. If he was lucky, he would come across her making the most of what appeared to be a relatively mild November morning; if he was not, well, at least he could make a more thorough examination of the property, and possibly determine the most promising escape route.

Pickett exited the house through the front door but, seeing nothing of interest on the lawn beyond the same ornamental pool he could see through his window any time he chose, he circled around the house to the rear, where the more mundane operations of daily life took place.

A wagon was drawn up before the back door—the same door he'd hoped to discover the previous night, before he'd been interrupted first by a cat and then by Mr. Danvers. This particular wagon appeared to have come from the greengrocer's, for a man and a youth were busily unloading crates of onions, cabbages and potatoes, which were then carried inside by a second boy, with assistance from a man who appeared to belong to the house; Pickett wondered if he might be the gardener of whom Julia had spoken.

He watched this process for some time, speculating as to the possibility of climbing aboard the wagon and concealing two adults—one a rather lanky six feet three inches, the other a lady whose proportions were as yet unknown to him—beneath piles of sacking without the driver, the greengrocer's boys, or the household staff being any the wiser. He could not be optimistic, and so dismissed the idea with some reluctance.

"Don't remember seeing you here before, young fellow."

The voice interrupted Pickett's thoughts, and he turned

to see a man regarding him curiously, his head tilted in seeming puzzlement, although this might have been due to the lumpy burlap sack balanced on his shoulder. Pickett rather thought he was the same man whose silhouette he'd seen from Mr. Tomkins's window, feeding the dogs—a theory that appeared to be confirmed when one of the two bounded up to him, nudging the man's hand with its great head as if issuing an invitation—or an order—for him to pat it.

Whoever he was, he must have mistaken Pickett's moment of hesitation for disapproval of his own presumption, for he added quickly, "Begging your pardon, sir. The name's Ned—Ned Stubbing. I'm the gardener, not but what I don't lend a hand here and there, seeing as how there's little enough I can do for the place without staff to—but never mind that. I thought you might be lost, you being new and all."

Recalling his rôle as reluctant inmate, Pickett acknowledged the introduction with a nod and answered grudgingly, "I've only been here since yesterday. I figure if I'm going to be stuck here for a while, I might as well have a look about my prison."

He concluded this speech on a bitter note, and the man responded with an uncomfortable cough. "You may not find it so bad as all that, sir."

Pickett neither agreed with nor disputed this statement, but held one hand out to the dog, allowing it to sniff him or, if it preferred, to help itself to a finger or two. With the other hand, he gestured in the direction of the building he and Julia had determined must be the stable. "See here, you might as well help me learn my way about. What is that building, pray?"

"That's the stable, sir, though I won't deny it's but a shadow of its former self. In my old da's day, now—"

"And that building?" Pickett interrupted brusquely, pointing at random to another of the outbuildings.

"That's the henhouse, and beyond it's the dairy," the man answered, regretfully keeping any further reminiscences to himself.

Pickett asked a few more questions, then indicated the building he'd been interested in all along, a round, windowless structure of red brick, its conical roof punctured at the peak by a metal pipe, presumably a vent. "And that?"

"Er, that's the smokehouse, sir. It's not much used nowadays, so it need not concern you." His gaze slid away from Pickett's as he spoke, and he toed a tuft of grass at his feet with great concentration.

The man's sudden diffidence aroused all Pickett's suspicions. He asked a few more utterly pointless questions in whose answers he had not the least interest, and as soon as he could make his escape without attracting undue attention, he abandoned the workers to the unloading of the wagon and made his roundabout way to the smokehouse.

Seen at close range, it bore the unmistakable signs of disuse. A few shingles were missing from the peaked roof, and the mortar between the bricks was beginning to flake. Pickett ducked inside the single low doorway, blinking as he waited for his eyes to adjust to the darkness within. Gradually the interior features came into focus: the brick pit in the floor where the fire would be lit; the furred boards of the wooden framework, their pale, fuzzy fibers standing out in stark contrast to the thick, blackened beams overhead; the hooks, as thick as his thumb, driven into this last, from which would be hung the carcasses of sheep, pigs, and cattle slaughtered at nearby Smithfield and brought to the estate for smoking.

A shadow suddenly blotted out the light, and Pickett turned to see Ned Stubbing silhouetted in the open doorway. "You'd best come along now, sir," he said uneasily. "There's naught here to interest a young gentleman such as yourself."

Jarring as it was to hear himself referred to as a gentleman (young or otherwise), Pickett let this pass. "And Miss Bonner?" he asked. "I understand she comes here often."

"Aye," the man conceded with obvious reluctance, "but that's hardly surprising under the circumstances, is it?"

"Is it?" Pickett echoed noncommittally.

"If you only just arrived yesterday, I reckon you haven't yet heard." He was obviously torn between reluctance to gossip and eagerness to divulge lurid secrets, and Pickett would have found the man's moral dilemma amusing, had not the man's next words driven from his thoughts all traces of humor. "It was in the old smokehouse only a few weeks ago that her brother hanged himself."

17

In Which John Pickett Witnesses a Curious Spectacle

Her brother hanged himself.

Pickett pondered the significance of those simple words, paired as they were with Miss Bonner's predilection for visiting the scene of her brother's last minutes on earth. It occurred to him that his task might require an even more delicate touch than he'd thought. It was bad enough that he had to persuade the lady to entrust her safety to a complete stranger; now he had also to consider the possibility that she might feel it a betrayal of her brother to abandon the place where that unhappy young man had met his end. Should that prove to be the case, Pickett feared it must test his powers of persuasion to their limits, for he would not resort to the hypocrisy of glib assurances that it was what her brother would have wanted for her; he would not insult the lady, or her brother's memory, by claiming to know the sentiments of a man he'd never met.

He recalled his search through the coroner's files for the

report of the inquest, and his frustration upon discovering that most of the pertinent pages were missing. It was possible that their absence was perfectly innocent. They might have been lost, or misfiled—either one of which was all too likely, given a filing system that would make Mr. Ludlow of Ludlow & Ludlow, Importers go off in an apoplexy—and they might still turn up years from now, having been put to use lining the bottom of a bird cage or wrapping fish. And yet, he did not think so, especially now that he knew exactly what it would have said as to the ruling of the coroner's jury; the death of a man found dangling from a rafter could hardly be written off as "misadventure," no matter how sympathetic the jurors might have been.

Could the record have been deliberately removed in order to spare the family the scandal of suicide? Granted, Mr. Bagley hardly seemed possessed of so exquisite a sensibility to do such a thing, but someone might have greased his palm sufficiently to overcome any professional scruples the coroner might harbor. The Bonner siblings' guardians—the uncle and aunt of whom Mr. Poole had spoken—might have done so, especially if they were already making plans to install the surviving Bonner within the same establishment to which her brother had evidently preferred death.

Failing Miss Bonner's guardians, it was always possible that Edward Poole had obtained the damning report himself, in order to fix his interest with Miss Bonner. Granted, Mr. Poole had not mentioned such a thing, but then again, he had not said that Philip Bonner was a suicide, either. Had he thought the manner of the young man's death insignificant?

Surely not! It was more likely that he had not been present at the coroner's inquest, and the family had chosen not to confide in him, in spite of his claims of intimate friendship.

Of course, Pickett could not overlook the possibility that Miss Bonner herself had persuaded the coroner to part with the records of the trial, given the fact that she was following in her brother's footsteps, even to the point of developing a morbid fascination with the place where he had drawn his last breath.

Pickett sighed. There was no way of knowing for certain until he put the question to the lady herself.

If he could find her.

He spent the rest of the morning and most of the afternoon wandering about the grounds, returning to the house only when the sharp November wind became too uncomfortable for anyone so sketchily attired as himself, but if Miss Bonner made any further attempts to visit the smokehouse, she must have been intercepted before she'd contrived to escape from the house.

Nor did she put in an appearance at dinner that night. If Pickett had not had it on good authority that such a lady existed, he would have suspected Mr. Poole of having him on, although for what purpose he could not begin to guess. Since her residence at the Larches had been confirmed more than once—first by Mrs. Danvers during Julia's initial interview, and more recently by both Sir Anthony Moring and Ned Stubbing—Pickett supposed he must absolve his client of perpetuating an elaborate hoax. Still, he didn't dare appear to take too keen an interest in the establishment's only female guest by inquiring as to her absence, particularly in view of fact that the lady in question, whose virtue Mrs. Danvers considered it her duty to safeguard, was much the same age as himself. Thus, he was profoundly relieved when Sir Anthony raised the question for him.

"I see Miss Bonner doesn't join us tonight," the older gentleman observed from his place at his hostess's right. "I trust she is not unwell?"

His "trust" notwithstanding, the tone of Sir Anthony's voice made it clear that this was not a simple statement as to his feelings, but a question for which he clearly expected some response. Pickett took a bite of roast beef drenched in a heavily flavored sauce whose components he could not identify, and tried to act as if he had nothing more than a polite interest in a conversation whose subject was a person with whom he was unacquainted.

"Not unwell, precisely," Mrs. Danvers replied, "but I fear her exertions this morning have sadly overset her nerves. I suggested she might prefer to rest quietly in her room for the rest of the day."

To Pickett's disappointment, Sir Anthony seemed to accept this explanation, acknowledging it with a nod before lifting his wineglass to his lips. Mr. Tomkins, seated directly opposite Pickett, licked his lips nervously, his gaze darting from Mrs. Danvers at one end of the table to her husband at the other. Pickett hoped he was about to make some contribution to the conversation, but when it became clear that the man did not intend to speak, Pickett felt himself obliged to fill the silence before some other topic could be raised, putting an end to a potentially useful dialogue.

"Is Miss Bonner so frail, then?" he asked, feigning mild surprise. "I haven't yet made the lady's acquaintance, but I was under the impression that she was quite young."

Mr. and Mrs. Danvers, facing one another down the length of the table, exchanged a look Pickett saw but could not interpret. Unsurprisingly, it was Mrs. Danvers who took it upon herself to offer an explanation.

"In fact, Miss Bonner must be very nearly your own age," she said, addressing herself to Pickett. "The sad truth is that her brother suffered a tragedy during his stay here not long ago. His body was discovered in the smokehouse, and Miss Bonner appears to have conceived a morbid obsession with the spot where young Mr. Bonner met his end."

Pickett could not deny a certain grudging admiration for his hostess; she had managed to answer his question without giving the slightest hint that Mr. Bonner's death had been anything but a tragic accident. Still, he had no intention of letting her off so easily.

"It sounds like a very sad business," he said, his tone suggesting nothing more than polite curiosity. "What was he doing in the smokehouse?"

"Hanging from the rafters," put in Mr. Danvers, who had heretofore allowed his wife to do the talking.

Mrs. Danvers frowned at her husband, but conceded his point. "I'm afraid Mr. Danvers is quite correct," she said, although there had certainly been murder in her eye when she'd silenced Mr. Danvers with a look. "You must understand, Mr. Pickett, that when it comes to giving up one's opium habit, some people have a harder time of it than others. In the worst cases, the opium user finds the idea of life without it insupportable. We must hope that your own habit is not so deeply ingrained."

To Pickett's chagrin, he found himself suddenly the center of attention. Everyone else at the table, even the usually incoherent Mr. Tomkins, wanted to know how he had first come into contact with the substance, and how he had developed so great a dependence on it that he had been obliged to come to the Larches to seek a cure. He was obliged to offer an expurgated account of the "accident" on the night of the Drury Lane Theatre fire that had resulted in his being given laudanum to ease the pain in his head resulting from what he contrived to imply was simply an unlucky blow from a falling beam. As he recounted the events of that night to an enthralled audience, he was doubly glad that he and Julia had agreed to stick to the truth as nearly as possible; the fire was a matter of public record, having been described in detail by the *Times*, the *Morning Post*, and the *Morning Chronicle*, along with a host of smaller newspapers. Anyone curious (or suspicious) enough of his account to investigate would find nothing to contradict it.

"Lord, how I've run on!" he said at last, only too glad to let someone else be interrogated for a while. "I've bored poor Mr. Tomkins senseless."

Sure enough, Mr. Tomkins was sound asleep, his chin sunk onto his chest. Perhaps more to the point, Pickett was aware, with a certain detached interest, that a feeling of lassitude had stolen over him, and though it was not unpleasant (in fact, it was quite the opposite), he feared he might not have guarded his tongue as carefully as he ought.

"Run on? Not at all," Sir Anthony assured him, then turned his attention to his hostess. "Mrs. Danvers, if you will excuse me for not waiting for you to withdraw, I believe I shall seek my bed. It appears Mr. Tomkins would be wise to do the same," he added in some amusement, just as Mr. Tomkins emitted a soft snore.

As if on cue, the entire party rose from the table, pushing back chairs with enough noise that Mr. Tomkins was jerked from slumber. "What?" he asked urgently. "Have they come? Are they—"

"It's quite all right, old fellow," Sir Anthony told him, shaking him gently by the shoulder. "You've been dreaming. Come along, you'll be much more comfortable in your bed. Goodnight, all. Mrs. Danvers, pray give my compliments to your cook. The roast beef was excellent, and the sauce even more so."

The sauce, Pickett thought. That heavily spiced sauce, all the better for concealing the bitter taste of opium. Suddenly it all made sense: his own feeling of detached wellbeing; Mr. Tomkins's falling asleep at the table; Sir Anthony's particular appreciation of the sauce that had dressed the beef.

But why? He'd had the distinct impression that Mr. Danvers's determination to make him ingest an opium-infused beverage had been intended to put a stop to his midnight wanderings—a punishment, of sorts, for his presence in a part of the house where he had no business being. Although how his host could consider this a punishment when Pickett had supposedly come to the Larches for the express purpose of overcoming a dependence on that same substance, he could not imagine.

Still, Miss Bonner's absence from the dinner table seemed to lend credence to this theory. She might well have been given opium as a preventive measure, to discourage her fixation on the site of her brother's suicide. In that case, the opium might be seen as—not a punishment, exactly, but a means by which the Danverses could exercise control over their clients. He could readily imagine Mrs. Danvers compelling Miss Bonner's obedience by plying her with opium and then threatening to withhold it. He recalled, too, Mr. Poole's despondent claim that he had not been allowed to see that elusive young woman, and his own rather cynical suspicion that it had been Miss Bonner who had not wished to see him; now he wondered if Mr. Poole indeed had the right of it, and she'd been lying on her bed drugged into unconsciousness, having never been informed of her suitor's visits at all. As for his own recent experience in the kitchen, Mr. Danvers might well have been testing the limits of his resistance, preparatory to gaining just such a hold over him.

But to what end? Try as he might, Pickett could see nothing in this scheme that would be of use to anyone looking to develop sufficient strength of purpose to resist the siren song of the poppy, either during their residence at the Larches or later, after they had returned to the wider world. Was it possible that the couple's motives were mercenary? Presumably, the longer it took one to overcome a supposed predilection for opium, the more he—or she—would be obliged to pay.

Moreover, no one truly in thrall to the narcotic would be fool enough to raise any objections to a situation that allowed him—or her—to eat his cake and have it, too.

And Miss Bonner, Pickett recalled, was heiress to a fortune…

Whatever their reasoning, there was no denying that for an establishment dedicated to aiding its paying guests in overcoming an excessive attachment to opium, the proprietors of the Larches certainly had strange ways of going about it. He wondered if the other residents were aware that they were being surreptitiously fed the very substance they were trying to give up. At least one, he decided, must be: Sir Anthony's habit was of sufficiently long duration that he must surely recognize the taste of the substance, whatever the vehicle through which it was administered. Mr. Tomkins, on the other hand…

Pickett frowned thoughtfully as he considered Mr. Tomkins. The man was certainly frightened of something—or someone—but his ravings were so vague that it was impossible to determine exactly what, or who, it was that he feared. In fact, Pickett doubted very much that Tomkins knew it himself. It was curious, he reflected, that opium should have such a distressing effect on the poor fellow, when his own experience had been quite the opposite: one dose of laudanum—or a swig from Mr. Danvers's black bottle—and he soon felt as if he hadn't a care in the world.

"Oh, well," he said aloud to no one in particular, dismissing the conundrum with a shrug that never quite reached his shoulders, "it's not my problem." All he had to do was get

Miss Bonner well away, and the rest— Mr. and Mrs. Danvers, Mr. Tomkins, even the engaging Sir Anthony Moring—could all go to perdition.

I'll do it tomorrow, he decided, climbing the stairs on leaden feet. *Tomorrow will be time enough.*

* * *

Pickett awoke in the middle of the night to find himself in a prison cell. Thick black bars striped the wall opposite the window, closing him in so tightly that they even blocked access to the bowl and pitcher that stood out sharply in the moonlight, the white porcelain vessels crisscrossed by prison bars that prevented him from even such rudimentary ablutions as washing his face and hands.

No, he thought, blinking in confusion as his befogged brain struggled to make sense of the vision. *That can't be right.*

Iron bars wouldn't bend to follow the curved edge of the bowl, to say nothing of the irregular shape of the pitcher. What he'd taken for imprisonment was nothing more threatening than the shadows of the narrow strips of wood within the window frame—there must be a name for them, but he had no idea what it was—that separated the individual panes of glass. He'd been so lethargic by the time he reached his room after dinner that he'd forgot to draw the curtains; the moonlight shining through the window had done the rest.

Still, the sense of being imprisoned had worked so strongly upon his mind that he was compelled to throw back the counterpane and drag his weary body to the window, just to be certain. Sure enough, when he turned to look at his room from this new vantage point, the "bars" were interrupted by the shadow of a man's head and shoulders.

"Am I glad to see you," Pickett addressed the newcomer. "If only you were real," he added with a sigh, and turned back toward the window.

The moon was at the full, and the lawn that sloped down to the London Road was bathed in a pale light that concealed the signs of neglect and made the rundown property look almost beautiful. A wind had risen in the night, and the larch trees that had given the property its name shook their bare limbs in a dance mirrored by their shadows on the ground. Even the ornamental water, in daylight nothing more than a stagnant pool, was stirred by the breeze, sending glints of silvery moonlight winking over its rippling surface.

Perhaps strangest of all, distance itself seemed to be distorted, so that the expanse of lawn appeared to stretch out to infinity, while at the same time seemed so close that he could almost reach out and dip his fingers into the water.

A movement caught his eye, and a moment later a ghost emerged from the copse of larch trees, a pale form that flitted across the lawn toward the ornamental water with its arms spread wide. As the figure stepped out of the shadows, Pickett realized it was no ghost, but a man in his nightshirt. His outstretched arms were in fact draped across the shoulders of the men flanking him; dressed as they were in dark clothing, these two had been very nearly invisible until they had abandoned the shadowy grove for the moonlit lawn.

Pickett frowned thoughtfully. The trio should have presented the very picture of masculine camaraderie, and yet to his heightened senses it appeared that something was not right. The steps of two of the three were oddly businesslike as they strode across the expanse of lawn in the direction of the water. The third, however, seemed to glide over the ground—a fact that no doubt explained his ghostly appearance—with his two companions bearing his weight between them.

Upon reaching the ornamental pool, one member of his escort ducked beneath the man's arm and bent as if reaching for something hidden by the overgrown reeds along the water's edge. When he straightened up again, Pickett was astounded to discover that he held the fellow's feet by the ankles. In the meantime, the third member of the group had shifted his own grip so that he now supported his companion under the arms.

To Pickett's horrified gaze, they swung their unresisting burden out over the water and released him. They were too far away for Pickett to hear the splash, but the newly disturbed water, evidenced by the moonlight that sparkled like diamonds on the choppy waves, told its own tale. Somewhere in the distance, a dog bayed mournfully at the moon, the only sound to break the eerie silence.

Don't leap to conclusions, Pickett thought, hearing his magistrate's—his former magistrate's—voice echoing in his brain. It was quite possible that his two companions had thought to give their fellow a midnight dunking as a lark. And yet, surely not even the most good-humored of men would submit to such rough-and-ready treatment with no response at all.

As he watched, the two men—harder to distinguish, now

that the pale nightshirt of the third was no longer visible—turned and retraced their steps to the grove of larches, where they were so completely swallowed up by the shadows that they might never have existed at all. Farther away, the water gradually stilled until it was once more a quiet pond, disturbed by nothing more threatening than the restless wind that stirred the reeds fringing its banks. The scene was so placid that he might have imagined the whole thing.

That's it, he thought, seizing with heartfelt relief upon the only explanation that made sense. That was what came of having opium for dinner.

Turning away from the window, he staggered back to his bed, and was soon sound asleep.

18

In Which John Pickett Receives a Pleasant Surprise

Pickett awoke the following morning to a pale November sun that cast a quadrangle of light onto the wall opposite the window in almost the very same spot where the previous night's "prison bars" had been. Here, too, strips of shadow crisscrossed the wall, but now the effect suggested nothing more sinister than the promise of a relatively mild autumn day. Recalling the bizarre illusion of the night before, Pickett rose from his bed, crossed the floor to the window, and looked out. The view was once more the leaf-strewn expanse of weed-infested lawn, the ornamental water once again a stagnant pool choked with reeds.

Had he dreamed it all? Had it been nothing more than the natural result of the opium he'd unwittingly ingested at dinner? Granted, there had been a certain dreamlike quality to the scene; he'd been aware of it at the time. And yet it had seemed so incredibly real…

But perhaps this, too, was a common effect of opium.

When he'd taken laudanum to relieve the pain of injuries sustained in the aftermath of the Drury Lane Theatre fire, he'd had the most realistic impressions that Lady Fieldhurst was truly his wife, and had taken up residence in his shabby flat—but this was nothing to judge by, since it had turned out that those impressions were entirely correct.

He wondered if he might ask Sir Anthony Moring—without, of course, going into any detail about the specifics of his dream, or illusion, or whatever it had been. Surely that gentleman, by his own admission, had been an opium-eater long enough to know whether such vivid images were no more than what one might expect. Of course, he would have to probe very carefully, for Sir Anthony would assume that he himself would have sufficient experience to know without being told. Resolving to put the matter to Sir Anthony at breakfast, Pickett washed his face and pulled his banyan on over his nightshirt, thinking what a pity it was that the opium could not have manifested his clothing while it was about it.

He had almost reached the door of his spartan bedchamber when he recalled one more task still undone. He returned to the bed and slipped the notebook from beneath the mattress, then detached the small pencil. Dropping to his knees, he ducked under the bed and made a third tick mark on the wall beside the first two. Had it really only been three days? It seemed like a se'nnight at the very least, and he was no nearer to rescuing Miss Bonner than he'd been when he'd first arrived.

Upon reaching the breakfast room, Pickett was surprised to discover the household at sixes and sevens. Mrs. Danvers was holding forth in some indignation upon the subject of Ingratitude, while the daily girl, busily employed in removing empty serving dishes from the table and replacing them with full ones, cast nervous glances at her mistress, and Mr. Danvers, in between making soothing noises to his wife, focused on his plate with a concentration that seemed excessive, be he never so hungry.

Pickett claimed the empty chair beside Sir Anthony, asking *sotto voce* as he took his seat, "What's happened?"

"Mr. Tomkins," the gentleman replied in like manner. "He's gone."

"Gone?" echoed Pickett in some alarm.

"Done a bunk in the middle of the night, apparently."

Pickett glanced at Mrs. Danvers for confirmation, and found that lady still in full spate. "…And after all we've done for him here, feeding and housing him, and a great deal more besides, what must he do but go off in the dead of night without so much as a by-your-leave…"

Or had he? Pickett wondered, recalling again that unresponsive figure in the white nightshirt, offering little or no resistance to the two black-clad men bearing him inexorably down to the silent, waiting water… Mr. Tomkins, who was terrified of some unspecified person or persons… *They're coming for me…Don't let them get me…*

Was this—whatever "this" was—what he had been afraid of? Had they all, by failing to take his fears seriously, been complicit in the man's death? Assuming, of course, that Mr. Tomkins was dead, which was by no means certain; after all, why would anyone want to murder a man whose only fault—aside from a fondness for opium—appeared to be an excess of sensibility?

Although, if Tomkins had indeed been done away with during the night, it would explain the addition of opium to their dinner only a few hours previously. Besides ensuring that Mr. Tomkins would be in no condition to resist, it would have guaranteed that everyone else in the house would sleep soundly while the murder was being carried out. Everyone, at least, except himself; he'd been so relentlessly plied with questions about his experiences on the night of the Drury Lane Theatre fire that he'd only been able to snatch a bite here and there, and consequently had ingested a smaller quantity than he might otherwise have done.

His first obligation might be to Miss Bonner, Pickett thought, but now it appeared that another had no less a claim on his efforts. He was going to discover exactly what had happened to Mr. Tomkins, and if anything sinister was going on behind the locked gates and bricked-up walls of the Larches, he was going to put a stop to it. The most pressing problem, as far as he could see, would be finding some excuse for going down to the water for a bit of poking about.

This dilemma was soon solved for him, and in the best possible way. He had scarcely risen from the breakfast table when Mr. Danvers, coming from the front of the house, jerked a thumb in the direction of the front door and said, "You've got visitors, Mr. Pickett."

Pickett could think of only one person—well, two—who might call on him here. In his eagerness, he brushed past Mr. Danvers without pausing to utter a word of acknowledgement, much less thanks. As he emerged through the door of the breakfast room into the hall, a small figure barreled into him with sufficient force to knock the breath from his body. Or perhaps it was the sight of Julia that produced much the same effect. He put his arm about Kit, but it was Julia who drew his gaze like a magnet. She looked so fresh and lovely and—yes, so *normal* that he couldn't tear his eyes away. And if any further proof were needed that something strange was afoot at the Larches, the idea that his marriage to such a woman was "normal" must surely be it, he reflected, disengaging himself from Kit's fierce hold.

"Julia," he said, advancing upon her. "I didn't expect to see you so soon."

"I hope we haven't interrupted you at breakfast." She took his hands and gave them a little squeeze that held the promise of a more satisfactory greeting once they were alone. "I hadn't thought to visit for a couple of days yet, but Kit was pining for you so pathetically that I took pity on him and—"

"*Me?*" Kit put in indignantly. "*You're* the one who—"

Pickett withdrew one of his hands from her hold and ruffled his brother's hair. "That's enough, Kit. It's not nice to contradict a lady."

"I knew you would make an excellent husband!" Julia exclaimed, looking admiringly up at him.

"Let's go outside, shall we?" Pickett took her arm and steered her toward the front door through which she had entered, with Kit bringing up the rear.

"Can we go down to the water?" the boy asked, all but dancing in impatience.

"In a minute," Pickett said. "There's something I have to do first. Why don't you go play in the woods there, and Julia and I will join you directly?"

"Now," Julia said after they'd watched Kit set out at a run for the little copse of larches, "what is it you—*oh!*"

She broke off abruptly as Pickett pulled her up against the wall and kissed her soundly.

"Oh John, I have missed you," she sighed when at last he released her. "Can it really have been only forty-eight hours since I left you here? It seems like an eternity! Still, I could have waited long enough for you to shave and dress," she added, stroking his prickly jaw.

"You'd have been waiting a long time." He recounted his midnight foray downstairs to the kitchen and the punishment that had resulted from it, concluding with, "I'm sorry I couldn't look a bit more presentable for you."

"On the contrary," she said, regarding him critically, "it gives you a certain rakish air that makes me want to drag you under a bush and debauch you."

Pickett considered this tempting prospect, and found a flaw. "If I'm the rakish one, shouldn't I be the one doing the debauching?"

"We shall try it both ways and decide which one we like best," declared Julia. Putting a hand to her distended abdomen, she added, "at least, we *would*, if I could fit under a bush."

"Not much longer now," Pickett said with somewhat warily, torn between the desire to reassure her and the dread of having his own words flung back at him with an irritable (and yet perfectly accurate) “Easy for *you* to say!”

On this occasion, it seemed, he was in luck, for his wife had more pressing concerns. “John, you will be home in time, won’t you?”

“I’ll be home in time,” he promised. “Even if I have to leave Miss Bonner to fend for herself.”

She smiled gratefully up at him. He took her hand and drew it through his arm, and together they set off after Kit. They had not gone far when she suddenly stopped and turned to him.

“John, why the kitchen?”

“I beg your pardon?” asked Pickett, all at sea.

“Why were you poking about the kitchen in the middle of the night? They must have given you dinner, did they not? They certainly charge enough for both room and board!”

“Since I’m supposed to be here under duress, I thought it might be best to stay in my room and sulk, at least for the first night. Then, too, if I was discovered in the kitchen—as proved to be the case—I would have an excuse sufficient to divert suspicion from my real purpose.”

“Which was?”

“Learning the configuration of the house in order to determine the best way to escape from it.”

“And have you?”

He sighed. “Not yet. But then, I haven’t contrived to speak with Miss Bonner, either, so much good it would do me, even if I had.”

“In other words, I’d best not look for you to come home any time soon,” she observed, crestfallen. “How much longer do you expect to be here? I seem to recall someone telling me it would take two days, three at the most."

"I'm afraid it's going to take a bit longer than I'd imagined," he confessed somewhat sheepishly. "The situation appears to be rather more complicated than I thought."

"Oh? In what way?"

He told her about the scene he'd witnessed from his window, and the opium-laced dinner that might have inspired such a dream—if dream it had been. "But given the fact that Mr. Tomkins apparently 'escaped' sometime during the night, it looks rather sinister, to say the least," he concluded. "That's why I wanted to take you and Kit outside. Besides giving us privacy to talk, it will give me a chance to have a look around while I'm supposedly showing the two of you about the place."

"What are you looking for?" she asked.

"I don't know," he said, "but I'll know it when I see it."

At that moment Kit came up to them, cradling something in his cupped hands. "Look what I found!"

Pickett and Julia bent to examine his prize. In his rather grimy palms rested a fluffy white feather, its short length curled so tightly as to almost form a complete circle.

"What kind of bird is it from?"

The question was addressed to his elder half-brother, whom he seemed to consider the font of all wisdom. Pickett was just about to admit his ignorance when Julia saved him from disgrace.

"It's eiderdown—the inner feathers from the eider duck," she said. "The very same thing your pillow is stuffed with, in fact."

Pickett, having little knowledge of ducks and still less interest, had turned away to survey the copse of trees through which the three men—and, more recently, Kit—had come, but at this he turned his suddenly sharpened gaze upon her.

"Why would anybody have a pillow out here?" asked Kit.

Leave it to Kit to put his finger on it, thought Pickett, then answered the question with one of his own. "May I keep this for a little while?" he asked, removing it carefully from the boy's hands lest it blow away.

"*I* found it," Kit said mulishly.

"Yes, I know you did." Pickett readily conceded the point. "But it might prove to be—important."

Kit's brown eyes, so like his brother's, grew wide. "D'you mean it might be a *clue?*" he breathed.

Pickett was rather taken aback, as he and Julia had been careful to speak softly enough so as not to be overheard. Then he realized the boy was thinking of Mr. Poole, and the case that had originally taken him to the Larches.

"Yes, that's it," he agreed readily, unwilling to disabuse his young brother of this comfortable notion.

"I'll see if I can find some more!" Kit announced, then turned and ran off to make good on this declaration.

Julia turned a speculative gaze upon her husband. "What are you thinking, John?"

"I'm thinking," he said with great deliberation, "that anyone smothered in his bed in the middle of the night might very well end up with down from his pillow caught in his nose, or mouth, or fingernails—"

Julia shuddered at this last, conjuring as it did images of frantic hands clawing in effectually at what surely must be the softest of murder weapons.

Pickett, seeing her reaction, quickly apologized. "I'm sorry," he said hastily. "I tend to forget I shouldn't burden you with such things."

"On the contrary, you could pay me no greater compliment," she assured him. "But here comes Kit. That was surely the quickest search on record!"

"I didn't see any more," the boy reported, panting slightly. "Can we go down to the water now?"

"Yes, but don't get too close," Pickett cautioned. "I have no intention of diving in after you!"

This last was directed at Kit's retreating back, as he had lost no time in acting upon his newly granted permission. Pickett followed at a more sedate pace with Julia on his arm, stopping at the spot where, as nearly as he could recall, the two men had tossed their nightshirt-clad companion.

"Look at that," he said, directing Julia's attention to the bent and broken reeds leading to the water's edge. "Someone's been here."

"And quite recently, too," Julia agreed. "It wasn't like that the day Mrs. Danvers showed me about the grounds."

"Are you sure?"

She nodded. "Positive. I took special notice, for I was thinking what a pity it was that it had been so neglected. I imagined clearing all the reeds away except for a little patch there at the far end where the overflow drains—or ought to drain—and putting in new plantings, including one lone willow on the little island in the middle, with its branches trailing in the water."

This picturesque image was overshadowed by the sight of Kit some little distance away, picking his way through the tangle of reeds to peer into the water.

"Kit!" Pickett bellowed, cupping his hands about his mouth. "Not so close!"

They watched as Kit obeyed with obvious reluctance. As he trudged toward them, Julia remarked to her husband, "How shocking it would be if one were to fall into the water and discover the body of a man in a nightshirt! Can you imagine?"

"Vividly," Pickett said without enthusiasm. "Because that's exactly what I intend to do."

19

In Which Julia Makes a Progress Report

John!" exclaimed Julia, wide-eyed with horror. "You cannot be serious!"

"I'm perfectly serious," Pickett said, somewhat taken aback by her response to what seemed to him a logical, albeit an unsavory, action. "It's a bit hard to prove a murder when you can't produce a body."

Julia cast an uncertain glance toward Kit, who had discovered a horse chestnut tree in the copse and was now throwing conkers one by one into the water, each hitting the surface with a very pleasing splash followed by a pattern of ever-widening circles on the previously still surface. "Not now, surely?"

Pickett caught that glance and knew exactly what it meant. "Not in front of Kit, no," he assured her hastily. "Tomorrow, probably. If you can come back the day after that—without him, if possible—I'll give you a letter to take to Mr. Colquhoun. He'll know what to do from there."

"Or," put in Julia, "you could abscond with Miss Bonner tonight, hand her over to Mr. Poole, collect your fee, and wash your hands of the matter!"

"Sweetheart, you know I can't do that," he chided her gently.

"No," she conceded with a sigh. "Not if Mr. Tomkins was indeed murdered. But John, what if he wasn't? What if it was only a dream? It wouldn't be at all surprising, given that Mrs. Danvers had chosen to serve the roast beef with a side of opium. Or"—her eyes widened as a new interpretation of the event occurred to her—"what if you saw *something*, but what you took to be a murder—an effect of the opium, no doubt—was in fact Mr. Tomkins making his escape, just as Mrs. Danvers claimed? The two men in dark clothing may have been there to assist him, but your imagination, clouded as it was by opium, provided the rest."

Pickett shook his head. "It's the fact of the opium that puts paid to that idea."

"Oh?" asked Julia, nonplussed. "In what way?"

"Any man intending to make his escape in only a few hours would surely lay off the stuff, at least until he'd got well away. The taste of opium is practically impossible to hide. Mr. Tomkins must have known it was there, but not only did he *not* lay off it, he was falling asleep at the table."

"Not everyone has your force of will, darling," Julia pointed out, tucking her hand into the curve of his arm and giving it a squeeze.

"That man has been terrified; you saw that much yourself, the first day you came here," Pickett insisted. "If he'd finally seen an end in sight, surely something of that must have been evident in his demeanor. Then, too, there's the question of the opium itself. Why would Mr. and Mrs. Danvers be forcibly feeding residents the very substance they're supposedly helping the residents to overcome?"

"I give up," Julia said, lifting her hands in surrender. "Why?"

"If they did intend to murder Mr. Tomkins last night, the opium would have made him too lethargic to resist. As for the rest of us, I think it was to make sure we would all be sound asleep so there would be no witnesses."

"None except you," put in Julia.

"Only because all throughout dinner the other residents peppered me with questions about the Drury Lane Theatre fire. I barely had a chance to eat at all—which may have turned out to be a good thing. And now," he added briskly, "we'd better head back toward the house. It won't do for anyone to decide I'm taking entirely too much interest in the water."

He called to Kit, who flung his remaining conkers into the water in one great splash, and the trio began trudging up the sloping ground toward the house. Julia slowed as they drew abreast of the copse of larches, allowing Kit to move some little distance ahead and forcing Pickett to slow his pace in order to match his steps to hers.

"Tired, love?" Pickett was instantly all solicitude, even as he gauged the remaining distance to the house and mentally assessed his ability to carry a very pregnant lady in his arms uphill all the way.

She shook her head. "No. At least, not much. It's just that—John, don't you think I should go to Mr. Colquhoun today? I daresay he would send someone, if he knew—"

"Oh, I'm sure of it. And that's exactly why you mustn't go to him, at least not yet. I dare not tip my hand too soon, lest Mr. and Mrs. Danvers get the wind up."

"But what if I return in two days' time and they don't allow me to see you?"

"Why shouldn't they? Mrs. Danvers said you could visit whenever you wished, didn't she?"

"Yes, but she also warned me not to visit you too frequently, as it might interfere with your supposed course of treatment, whatever that may be. Then, too, I haven't forgotten Mr. Poole's telling you he'd been asking for Miss Bonner in vain."

"I'm still not entirely convinced it wasn't she, and not Mrs. Danvers, turning him away," Pickett said with a good deal more confidence than he felt. In fact, he thought nothing he might find at the Larches would surprise him anymore. Still, he had no intention of allowing his wife to dwell on horrors, no matter how much she might claim to be flattered by his sharing them with her.

"But you can't know that!"

"Not until I can ask the lady herself," he conceded. "Although I have to say that she appears to have a rare gift for playing least in sight."

"Still, can we not arrange some sort of signal? Perhaps you could hang one of your cravats from the window."

"My cravats were confiscated along with the rest of my

clothes," he reminded her.

"A bedsheet, then," she suggested, undaunted.

He shook his head. "Sweetheart, even if I could prize the window open—and I can't; I've tried—it would be plain as a pikestaff to anyone who chanced to set foot out the front door. I couldn't announce my intentions any plainer if I took out an advertisement in the *Times!*"

Her face fell. "We shall have to think of something more subtle, then."

Seeing she would not rest easy until some such provision was made, he bent and, following Kit's example, snatched up one of the conkers that littered the ground at the base of the horse chestnut. "Look here," he said, pointing toward the brick wall that surrounded the property. "Do you see how far it is from this tree to the wall? It would take a gale wind to blow these things that distance, do you agree?"

"I suppose so," Julia said, baffled by the sudden *non sequitur*.

Pickett drew his arm back and hurled the conker toward the wall. It sailed over the top and disappeared as it descended on the other side, presumably landing in the lane beyond.

"If you come to visit me and Mrs. Danvers turns you away, you have only to look at the ground as you leave the premises. If I've run into any trouble, I'll throw a couple of these over the wall. What do you say?"

"John, they're tiny! How could I possibly see them from a moving carriage?"

"You wanted something subtle," he reminded her. "But you don't have to stay in the carriage; have the coachman set you down, and you can walk along this short stretch. Dr. Gilroy said a little exercise is good for you, and since the wall will prevent your being seen from the house, you can take as much time as you like."

"I suppose it's better than nothing," Julia conceded grudgingly.

She only wished she could make herself believe it.

* * *

It was a very subdued pair who entered the portals of number twenty-two Curzon Street some time later, passing through the door opened to them by Rogers, who glanced past Julia's shoulder as if expecting to see a third person bringing up the rear.

"He isn't here, Rogers," she said, correctly interpreting this look.

"Yes, ma'am," he said, closing the door behind them. "I confess, I had hoped you would be bringing the young master home."

"So had I, but it appears he will be gone a little while longer." She dared not say more in front of Kit, having no desire to fill the boy's head with gruesome images of dead bodies lurking in the green depths of the water. "The matter proved to be a bit more complicated than he had originally thought."

"Yes, ma'am," repeated Rogers, and she wondered how much he understood of what she had not said—an idea which seemed to be confirmed when he added, "I believe Cook has just removed a batch of apple scones from the oven, if you would like a tray brought up—"

Kit's quick intake of breath and brightening eyes gave Julia to understand that, whatever her own views on the subject, he would like very much for a tray to be brought up. Julia readily agreed; however little her own appetite, it could only be good to give her young brother-in-law's thoughts a more positive direction.

Once these treats had been disposed of, however, a melancholy silence descended on the drawing room. It was a curious thing, Julia noted, that although she had lived here alone for almost a year following her first husband's murder, the house had never seemed so empty as it did now.

It soon became apparent that Kit, too, was conscious of the void left by his half-brother's absence, for after ravaging the tea tray, he left the drawing room only to return a few minutes later with a long flat box containing a chess set. Julia recognized it at once; it was one of only a very few luxuries her husband had allowed her to bestow upon him in the very early days of their marriage. She smiled a little at the memory as she watched Kit arrange the pieces on the board apparently at random. Obeying a sudden impulse, she picked up the sketchbook and charcoal that lay on the little table at her elbow and began describing a series of long, curved lines.

"He was going to teach me how to play," Kit said without looking up.

"And so he will, for I expect he will be home very soon," Julia predicted confidently, ruthlessly banishing the little voice in her head that whispered otherwise.

"Do you know how to play?" the boy asked, bending a keen gaze upon her.

She recalled certain evenings spent stretched out on the floor before the fire with the chessboard between them. "A little," she admitted. "I know how the pieces are supposed to move, anyway."

"Will you teach me, then?"

"I think you would do much better to wait for John," she said. "He is much better than I, you know." In addition to the likelihood that he would be disappointed to discover that Kit had already learned the game (and under the tutelage of a player to whose skill his own was far superior), there was the fact that their games had tended to devolve into moves which would almost certainly *not* be found in Hoyle's.

"Would you like to read another chapter of *Gulliver* instead?" she asked, feeling the offer of some alternative activity was called for. "John has read it many times before already, so he won't mind us reading ahead."

Kit considered this for a moment. "Can I read the short para—para—?" he asked at last.

"The short paragraphs? Certainly, if you wish."

He darted upstairs to retrieve the book from his bedside table, and when he returned with it a short time later, Julia patted the seat beside her on the sofa. As Kit sat down, however, he noticed the sketch book still open on her lap, and stared, opcn-mouthed.

"That's me!" he breathed in amazement.

"Yes. At least, it's supposed to be. Do you like it?"

He tore his gaze away from it to look into her face. "Can I have it?"

"If you like."

"Can we put it in a—a—" His fingers described a rectangle in the air.

Julia was rather surprised that he could not recall quite a simple word, until she recollected her visit to the house where he had spent the first ten years of his life. No, the children of St. Giles would not be overly familiar with the concept of framed artwork.

"A picture frame? Of course, if you would like. Would you prefer to hang it in your bedroom, or here in the drawing room?"

He pondered this question for a long moment. "Down here," he said at last. "That way Rogers can see it, too."

"Very well," agreed Julia, smiling a little at the bond that had formed between her butler, whose son had perished on the Peninsula, and her husband's young half-brother, whose father had been transported to Botany Bay before he was born. "Let's see now, where were we?"

"Gulliver had just got away from the pirates," Kit reminded her.

"Oh, yes, and he had come upon an island, had he not?"

She found the page, but before she could see Gulliver off on his next adventure, Rogers came into the room bearing a few letters on a silver salver.

"Begging your pardon, ma'am, but the post is here," he said, proffering the tray.

Julia removed the letters and sorted quickly through them: a letter from Claudia, an invoice for the most recent shipment of coal (a good deal more expensive than last month's, no doubt, now that autumn was well advanced) a letter bearing the crest of the Fountainhead Academy—

"Julia drew a picture of me, Rogers," Kit announced. "Do you want to see it?"

Without waiting for an answer, he leaned across her—no mean feat, now that her lap was full of baby Pickett—and snatched the sketchbook from the small side table. He flipped through it until he found the page he wanted, then presented it for the butler's inspection.

"Very nice, Master Kit," said Rogers with a nod of approval. "It looks very like, if I may say so."

Kit, struck by a sudden thought, turned wide eyes on his sister-in-law. "Can you show me how?"

"You want to learn to draw?" Julia asked, rather taken aback not only by the question, but also the eagerness behind it.

"Aye, that's it. You could show me how to draw now, and we can wait about reading Gulliver 'til John comes back home."

It occurred to Julia that it might be good for the boy to have something to occupy his thoughts besides the prolonged absence of the brother he was well on the way to idolizing. For that matter, she reflected, it would be good for her to have something to occupy her own thoughts as well.

"I can try," she said, honesty compelling her to add, "but you must know that it takes time to learn a new skill. So you mustn't become frustrated if you can't draw as well as you would like, at least not right away."

Kit avowed in the most enthusiastic terms that his supply of patience was more than equal to the task (a promise which, she suspected, children far more well-behaved than he would strive in vain to keep), and Julia bade him take his book back upstairs. While he was gone, she sifted once more through the day's post. The coal merchant's invoice must be paid before the end of the month, of course, and the letter from Claudia, she decided, she would save to read later that night, when she was alone in her bedroom. It was by far the worst part of the day, lying alone in a bed which seemed much too empty, wondering what he was doing and if sleep eluded him the same way it eluded her; the fact that he had been awake and peering out his window in the middle of the night would seem to suggest that it did. Claudia's letter would at least give her something to look forward to, although it made an admittedly poor substitute for the warm weight of her husband's body beside her.

There remained the letter from the Fountainhead Academy. She broke the seal and unfolded it, fully expecting to see the headmaster's blunt avowal that there was no place at the school for any pupil of young Christopher Pickett's ilk, neither for the upcoming Hilary term nor at any other time. To her surprise, the letter was cordial—indeed, almost warm—and claimed that the Fountainhead Academy would be pleased to welcome any young scholar who carried with him the endorsement of that highly respected magistrate, Patrick Colquhoun, Esquire. There followed a list of the textbooks Kit would require and where these might be purchased, along with a delicately worded suggestion that used textbooks might be available at a greatly reduced price. However well-intentioned this recommendation, Julia rejected it at once; Kit's adjustment to public-school life would be trying enough without giving his more well-born classmates further reason for treating him like a charity-school pupil—never mind the fact that a charity-school pupil was exactly what he was, or at least had been, just like his brother before him.

Her unborn child chose that moment to kick, and she laid a protective hand on her abdomen. The challenges Kit faced would serve as a preliminary glimpse of the trials that lay ahead for their own child—the spawn (as her husband had noted) of a Bow Street Runner and a viscountess. She wondered if the lofty social status that had once been hers would ease her child's way, or make matters worse.

Reminding herself not to borrow trouble, she turned her attention back to the letter, and saw that the headmaster's next suggestion raised a question she had not anticipated, and to whose answer she had not the slightest idea.

"Kit," she addressed the boy who was at that moment returning to the drawing room, "have you ever been inoculated against smallpox?"

Kit looked at her in utter bewilderment. "Have I ever been in—in—"

"Inoculated." Julia repeated the unfamiliar word, then explained, choosing her words with care. "It's when they give you a small bit of cowpox, to ensure that you won't get smallpox, which is a great deal worse, in the future."

"Cowpox," echoed Kit, wrinkling his nose in revulsion. "I bet that tastes awful."

She might have assured him that he would not be expected to eat it, but suspected he would like the alternative even less. Still, the fact that he had no idea how the dose would be administered seemed to suggest that he had no personal experience of it.

She shook her head and laid the letter aside. Keeping her voice carefully neutral, she added, "Never mind. I daresay your mother will know. I shall call on her tomorrow and see what I can discover. Would you like to go with me?"

Kit could not have looked any more dismayed if she had slapped him. "You're gonna give me back to Mum?"

"No, no, my dear, I would *never* do that!" She took his arm and drew him down to sit beside her on the sofa, her arm about his thin shoulders. "I only thought you might miss her, and want to see her again. Or she might miss you," she added, although privately she doubted this. From what she'd seen of the woman, Moll's maternal instincts wouldn't fill a teaspoon.

"If you take me back to Mum, she might not let me come back to live with John and Rogers," Kit insisted, and Julia noticed with some amusement that she herself had disappeared entirely from the household.

"Very well, then, I shall go alone," she declared, and heard the boy let out a long breath of pure relief. "You may stay here and help Cook prepare something special we may take to John when next we visit him."

Too late, she remembered his request that she come alone on her next visit. Ah well, she reasoned, she would fight that battle when the time came. In any case, she had little time to dwell on the matter, for she heard the sound of the door knocker, and a moment later (during which she chided herself that even if her husband had contrived to escape from the

Larches, with or without Miss Bonner in tow, he would hardly knock upon his own front door) Rogers entered the drawing room.

"Mr. Edward Poole, ma'am," the butler announced, and that gentleman entered the room with his hand held out.

"I fear I must beg your pardon, Mrs. Pickett," he said, shaking her hand with a firm grip. "I seem to have a knack for calling at the most inopportune times. Your man here tells me Mr. Pickett is absent, and you don't know when he may return."

"That is true, but if you should care to sit down, I shall do my best to act as his surrogate. Rogers"—she turned her attention to the butler—"the tea tray, if you please, and if Kit has left us any of the apple scones, we shall have those, too."

"Very good, ma'am," said Rogers, and betook himself from the room.

"My husband will be sorry to have missed you, Mr. Poole," Julia said, as the visitor settled himself on the sofa adjacent to hers. "Kit—"

"*I* know," the boy grumbled, rolling his eyes. " 'Go upstairs so we can talk.' "

"Thank you," Julia told him. "I daresay we shan't be so very long."

With a noise indicative of the deepest skepticism, Kit trudged out of the drawing room into the hall, and a moment later they could hear heavy footfalls as he climbed the stairs.

"I hope you will not judge him too harshly," Julia told her guest apologetically. "He has made his home with us for the last month, but his upbringing before that was shockingly neglected. He is my husband's half-brother, you see, and misses him terribly."

"Has Mr. Pickett been away so long, then?" asked Mr. Poole in some surprise. "I confess, I had hoped to have some report of his progress, but if he has been obliged to be gone from home, I don't suppose—"

"Oh, no! I fear you quite mistake the matter," Julia protested hastily. "It is on your own account, or rather, Miss Bonner's, that he is away from home."

"Oh?"

At that moment, Rogers reentered the drawing room bearing the tea tray, and conversation was briefly suspended while the butler arranged everything to his mistress's liking. Julia could not be sorry for the interruption, as it gave her time to consider exactly what, and how much, to tell Mr. Poole of her husband's progress in the case. She had not known how badly she wanted—no, *needed*—to tell someone of his courageous yet (she could not but feel) hasty actions on his client's behalf until now, when that client sat on the drawing room sofa willing, perhaps even eager, to listen while she unburdened herself. Still, she knew better than to tell everything she knew. And so after the butler had gone, she put on a brave face and answered with a confidence she was far from feeling.

"Yes, in order to determine the best way to spirit Miss Bonner out of the house, he bade me commit him to the Larches as an opium-eater in need of a cure. He felt he could learn the configuration of the house and the routine of its inhabits more thoroughly from the inside than from—why,

Mr. Poole, what is the matter?"

For as she had spoken, her visitor's expression had changed from polite interest to perturbation to something akin to horror.

"Mrs. Pickett, are you saying your husband is currently *in residence* at the Larches?"

She confirmed that this was so, adding, "I confess, I could not quite like the scheme, but I could not argue with his reasoning, so in the end I was obliged to do as he asked."

"Do you think that was wise, given the fate my young friend Philip Bonner met there, the fate against which his sister may be struggling even as we speak?"

The fate John will *persist in tempting, no matter how convincingly I may urge caution...* Mr. Poole's misgivings fed her own, and Julia found herself saying, "If you fear Miss Bonner's life is in imminent danger, perhaps it would be wise to call in Bow Street."

Of course, her husband would never forgive her if his client were to follow such a course of action, and at her own recommendation, so she could not deny a certain feeling of relief when Mr. Poole rejected this suggestion out of hand.

"I know you mean well, Mrs. Pickett, but please believe me when I say it would be impossible. Whatever their sins against her, Miss Bonner's aunt and uncle are the only family she has left. She would not want their name blackened by scandal."

Six years of marriage to a viscount had given Julia an intimate knowledge of the lengths to which members of the *ton* might go to avoid a scandal; indeed, it was that very trait that would eventually (she hoped) make it possible for her husband to earn a tidy income by resolving the problems of the aristocracy while simultaneously keeping those problems out of the public record. She did not, therefore, attempt to overcome Mr. Poole's scruples by pointing out that Miss Bonner's "accidental" death would surely be scandal enough in itself, but sought a middle ground by trying to reassure him and, at the same time, giving her husband more time to conduct an investigation that had unexpectedly grown to encompass matters far more portentous than his original commission.

"Young Mr. Bonner's death was certainly a senseless tragedy, and scandal enough for any one family to endure," she began, choosing her words with care, "but—forgive me, Mr. Poole, but what makes you so certain Miss Bonner must meet the same end? Perhaps, having witnessed their nephew's struggles, her aunt and uncle entrusted her to the Larches in an effort to intervene before her own case becomes so desperate."

"I am not allowed to see her!" Mr. Poole shot to his feet as if fired from a cannon, and began pacing the room in long, restless strides. "Oh, there is always some new reason cited, some vague explanation given, but it always comes down to this: 'Miss Bonner is not receiving visitors today.' *Is* not, or *can*not? That is the question that keeps me awake at night."

Julia could sympathize. She, too, lay awake at night, unable to shake the conviction that her own visits would one day meet with the same response. Still, she recalled her husband's theory as to Miss Bonner's inaccessibility, and felt compelled to offer Mr. Poole some more palatable explanation; one of them, at least, might as well rest a bit easier.

"Mr. Poole," she began, summoning all of the diplomacy at her command, "have you considered that it might be Miss Bonner herself, rather than Mrs. Danvers, who is refusing to receive you?"

Clearly, he had not. "*Miss Bonner* refuse to—but why should she do such a thing? Why, I'm—I was—her brother's dearest friend!"

"Yes, and that is why I make the suggestion, for gentlemen would be unlikely to consider the matter from a female perspective. Few ladies would wish for their gentleman callers to see them looking less than their best, and bear in mind that Miss Bonner no longer has her lady's maid to dress her hair, or to iron the gowns that must have been sadly crushed after being packed for her stay, or any of the innumerable little things that mean so much to women. Surely you would not wish to put her to such a disadvantage!"

Mr. Poole appeared to be much struck by this hitherto unconsidered possibility, and so Julia gently expounded upon it. By the time he took his leave some minutes later, his anxieties seemed to be at least to some degree allayed.

She only wished she could say the same for her own.

20

In Which John Pickett Finally Runs His Quarry to Ground

Pickett spent most of the afternoon in his own room, lying on his bed staring up at the ceiling and formulating his plans for the night, or napping so that he would be well-rested enough to carry them out. When the residents of the Larches retired to their bedchambers for the night (following an interminable dinner which he dared not eat), he left his door slightly ajar so as to hear the tolling of the long-case clock in the hall below, and stretched out on his bed to wait.

And wait.

And wait.

When at last he heard the clock strike two, he judged it time to proceed. He pulled his nightshirt over his head and put on his banyan over bare skin; it would not do to have the white collar or cuffs of the former betray him. He collected his candlestick from the top of the chest of drawers, but made no attempt to light it. Instead, he dropped the flint into the capacious pocket of his banyan, then crossed the room to the door and inched it cautiously open, peering through the widening crack for any glimpse of light from a fellow wanderer.

Satisfied on this point, he slipped into the corridor and pulled the door closed behind him, wincing at the faint *click* that seemed to reverberate like thunder in the still, dark house.

He did not on this occasion head for the stairs as he had done before, but crossed the corridor on bare feet and knelt before the door of the room formerly occupied by Mr. Tomkins. He groped in the pocket of his banyan and extracted the paper into which he'd folded one of his wife's hair pins. To overcome the lock was the work of a moment, and soon Pickett opened the door and let himself into the missing man's room, pulling the door closed behind him.

Mentally reconstructing the arrangement of the furniture from memory, he groped his way in the direction of Mr. Tomkins's bureau, and was relieved when his outstretched hand met the smooth wooden surface; he'd managed to find it without stubbing his toe, or barking his shin, or doing anything else that might have made enough noise to bring the Danvers duo down upon his head. He set his candlestick on top of the bureau and extracted the flint from his pocket. Within seconds, a soft yellow glow dispelled the darkness, illuminating the clothing draped over the back of the room's single chair and glinting off the buckles of the shoes neatly lined up at the foot of the unmade bed.

Pickett supposed it was just within the realm of possibility that Mr. Tomkins, not wishing to slow his clandestine departure by burdening himself with superfluous clothing, would leave it behind, but would any man attempt an escape in his bare feet?

Turning back to the bureau, he slowly and cautiously pulled open the top drawer, gritting his teeth as if by doing so he could prevent it from making any noise. Just as he had suspected, it was filled with shirts, stockings, and a pocket watch whose gold case gleamed in the candlelight. It was this last that filled him with foreboding. Mr. Tomkins might deem his clothing expendable, but this? Pickett thought it unlikely.

He pushed the drawer closed, using the same caution with which he had opened it, and moved on to the next, and then the next. Finally, in the last of the four drawers, he made a discovery that put paid once and for all to Mrs. Danvers's claim that her guest had fled in the middle of the night. For here he found a knitted coin purse—and quite a full one, if the weight and bulk of it were anything to judge by. He tugged the drawstring open and slid two fingers inside.

Pickett had not lost the skills (many of dubious legality) learned in his youth, and he quickly identified a crown piece, a couple of shillings, a miscellany of pennies, ha'pennies, and farthings, and—his probing fingers grew still. He'd never actually seen one until he'd come to Bow Street, and even then not until his association with Julia had brought him into the orbit of persons to whom such things were commonplace; gold, after all, rarely found its way into the palms and pockets of the denizens of St. Giles. He spilled the contents of the coin purse into his cupped hand. A collection of copper, silver, and yes, two golden guineas winked in the candlelight.

He still had no proof, of course, not until he probed the

depths of the stagnant pool, but so far as circumstantial evidence went, this was fairly damning. No one, not even a man as frightened and desperate as Mr. Tomkins had been, would willingly leave such a sum behind, not when it might have paid for the hire of a hackney or covered the cost of engaging a Bow Street Runner.

At the thought of Bow Street, Pickett braced himself for the pang of regret that always accompanied the memory of his former position there, but to his surprise, it was not so strong as it once had been. In fact, he derived considerable satisfaction at the thought of Harry Carson, newly elevated to the position of principal officer, being assigned to the case only to discover that Pickett had beaten him, as it were, to the post.

He was still pondering the question of whether to return the coin purse to the drawer (where it would very likely be claimed by Mrs. Danvers or her husband) or retain it for safekeeping, when the rattle of the latch warned him that he was not the only one prowling about the premises. In one swift movement, he licked his finger and pinched the candle flame to prevent any telltale smoke from betraying his presence, then dove beneath the bed, the only hiding place the sparsely furnished room offered.

In the next instant the door swung open, and Pickett watched from his unique vantage point as a pair of slender bare feet entered the room, the lace-edged hem of a nightdress playing about the shapely ankles. The door closed again with a faint *click*, and then the feet padded soundlessly from the door to the bureau—the same route, in fact, so recently traced by Pickett himself. He heard the grate of wood against wood as first one drawer and then another was opened and, with some satisfaction, tightened his fist around the coin purse he still held. This pleasurable emotion was short-lived; in the next moment, the pink toes were headed straight for him, and Pickett knew with terrible certainty that their owner was about to search beneath the mattress.

He edged noiselessly toward the center of the bed as four well-manicured fingers curved around the corner of the mattress almost directly over his head. Just as they tightened and began to lift it from the bed frame, the latch rattled once again, and Pickett was saved.

Almost.

The light that had illuminated the shapely toes was instantly snuffed, and a generously curved form barreled into him with enough force that he was hard-pressed to prevent an audible *oof* of hastily expelled breath. At that moment the door swung open, and the lantern carried by this latest arrival cast enough light that Pickett was treated to the sight of wide, astonished eyes and indignantly parted lips all but nose-to-nose with him beneath the bed. Pickett made not a sound, but put a finger to his lips, entreating her to silence.

She obeyed, albeit with obvious reluctance, and they lay side by side as heavy footfalls crossed the room. For the third time that night, the drawers of the bureau were pulled open one by one, but this time the soft *whump* of piles of fabric hitting the floor indicated that their contents were being indiscriminately removed. When the ponderous footsteps retraced their route, Pickett turned his head toward the door and saw that the visitor now carried a bulging canvas sack. If he'd needed further proof of what it contained, he found it in the ruffled cuff of a cambric shirtsleeve that dangled from the mouth of the sack as if waving in farewell.

Pickett waited until the door was closed and the retreating footsteps indicated that they were alone before turning to address the woman at his side.

"Miss Bonner, I presume."

21

In Which John Pickett Goes for a Swim

Who are you, and what are you doing here?" demanded the woman lying beside him in the dark.

Pickett, who had been fully prepared to reassure a terrified young lady as to his honorable intentions, was perhaps understandably goaded into retorting, "I could ask you the same thing!"

She did not answer at once, but a soft rustling noise suggested she was abandoning their shared hiding place beneath the bed—a suggestion confirmed a moment later when the darkness was banished by the soft yellow glow of a candle flame. Pickett, following her example, scrambled out from under the bed and rose to his feet, taking care not to crack his head on the bottom of the bedframe.

His first sight of the lady he was charged with rescuing defied all his expectations. He'd thought to find a timid, frightened young woman whose trust he would be obliged to win; instead, he found himself confronting a veritable

Amazon fully six feet tall, whose dark hair lay over her shoulder in a single thick braid and whose eyes—probably blue, but appearing green in the yellow light of the candle she held—sparkled with fury. The fine cambric of her nightrail hinted at a voluptuous figure beneath, but even if he had been inclined to make a closer study of the lady's hidden charms, her wrathful expression would have cautioned him against so unwise a move.

Since she apparently had no intention of answering his question, at least not until he had answered hers, he sketched a slight bow (conscious at the same time of the absurdity of such a gesture under the present circumstances) and said, "John Pickett of—formerly of—Bow Street. I'm here to help you escape."

"*Escape?* You idiot! You're going to ruin everything!"

Of all the reactions with which Pickett had been prepared to contend, this one had never entered his head. "It was my understanding that you are being held here against your will, Miss—Bonner? You are Miss Bonner, are you not?"

She answered his question with one of her own. "And how, pray, do you know anything about me, much less come to the conclusion that I am in imminent need of rescue? Never mind; I think I can guess. It was Edward, wasn't it? Edward Poole?"

"Mr. Poole enlisted my services in extracting you from what he believed to be a dangerous situation, yes."

Her lip curled in derision, confirming his suspicions that she was not nearly so taken with Mr. Poole as that gentleman was with her. "And you, Mr.—Pickett, was it?— naturally jumped to do his bidding, like an obedient little lapdog."

"I'm no one's lapdog!" he retorted, stung by the injustice of this accusation. I 'naturally jumped,' as you say, to do the job I'm being paid for."

"I see. And what did you think to do, throw me over your shoulder and carry me out bodily like a sack of meal?"

"If you would prefer that I leave you to your fate—"

"Infinitely!"

"—I will be more than happy to do so," Pickett lied, with a hollow feeling in the pit of his stomach at the thought of the promised fee slipping through his hands.

"Thank you; I am much obliged to you," she said, although nothing in either her tone or demeanor struck Pickett as indicative of gratitude, much less obligation. "I only wonder how you think I came to be here in the first place. You will have noticed, I'm sure, that it would be very difficult to physically compel me to do anything I did not wish to do."

Pickett wisely forbore to make any comment concerning the lady's Rubenesque figure. "Then—you *chose* to come here?"

"Of course! What did you think?"

"Your aunt and uncle—" Pickett sputtered, feeling strangely as if the ground were giving way beneath his feet. "Mr. Poole said—"

She raised a hand to forestall him. "Pray do not quote Mr. Poole to me. If Edward thinks my aunt and uncle had me committed to the Larches, he is an even bigger fool than I took him for. No, Mr. Pickett, my aunt and uncle begged me to reconsider—as I'm sure you must be aware, if you spoke to them on the subject at all."

But he had not. Mr. Poole had urged him not to do so, and he, fool that he was, had given the man his word. It was a very good thing he was no longer with Bow Street, for Mr. Colquhoun would certainly have something to say about so glaring an omission.

"Then why did you—no, wait," he said, recalling the gardener's words regarding Miss Bonner's fascination with the old smokehouse. "It's your brother, isn't it? He died here."

The sympathy in Pickett's voice had the unexpected effect of disarming her, and when she spoke again it was without her earlier scorn. "He was discovered hanging from one of the rafters in the smokehouse. I don't believe he died by his own hand, but I have no way to prove it, much less to determine exactly what happened there, or who was responsible. So"—she shrugged—"I had myself admitted as a resident."

"I'm very sorry for your loss, Miss Bonner, but it still doesn't explain why you saw fit to break into this room in the middle of the night."

"Speaking of which," she began, her fine eyes narrowing in suspicion, "just what are *you* doing in this room? If you are—or were—a Bow Street Runner, you must surely know it isn't mine. But nor is it yours, unless you've taken to sleeping underneath the mattress instead of on top of it."

"So we're back to 'who are you and what are you doing here?' are we? No, I'm well aware that this is not your room. In fact, it was occupied by Mr. Tomkins, at least until sometime last night."

He strode past her and crossed the room to the bureau, then pulled open the top drawer. It was empty, just as he expected.

She clutched at his sleeve. "Do you know what happened to him, then?"

"Do you?" Pickett asked in return, deriving a wholly unworthy satisfaction from the novel sensation of possessing information to which she was not privy. He closed the drawer and pulled open the next. It, too, was empty.

"Mrs. Danvers says he ran off in the night," she said, her voice carefully neutral.

"So she says," he agreed noncommittally. "But that still doesn't explain why you decided to break into an apparently unoccupied room."

"I don't think Mr. Tomkins left it," she confessed. "At least, not voluntarily."

Having examined the remaining drawers with the same results, he turned away from the ransacked bureau to face Miss Bonner. "What gave you that impression?"

"He was so frightened. He kept saying 'they' were coming for him, whoever 'they' were. And you?"

He told her what he had seen—at least, what he thought he'd seen—from his window the previous night, culminating in Julia's visit earlier that day, and the feathers discovered quite fortuitously by his young brother.

"Speaking of feathers," put in Miss Bonner, interrupting this narrative to reach up and pluck something from Pickett's hair, "you're molting."

"I'm what?"

In answer, she held up her hand. A short white feather curled around her forefinger. His eyes widened in recognition, and he dropped to his knees and bent arse-upward to peer beneath the bed. He stretched a hand into his erstwhile hiding place and extracted one, two, three identical feathers, which he held out for her inspection.

She regarded them in silence for a long moment, then looked up to regard him with a puzzled expression. "I don't quite see—"

"I should think that anyone being smothered to death with his own pillow would struggle enough to dislodge a few feathers, wouldn't you?"

She let out a long breath, and the feathers in his hand fluttered in response. "You think that's what happened to Mr. Tomkins?"

"It would explain his lack of response last night when I saw him—at least, when I *thought* I saw him." Pickett sighed. "In any case, I suppose I'll know tomorrow."

"Why? What happens tomorrow?"

"I'll be going for a swim." Seeing her puzzled expression, he explained, "I'm going to see if Mr. Tomkins's body is at the bottom of the lake." A new thought struck him, and he added, "Look here, I can see how my coming and throwing a spanner into the works was the last thing you wanted, but now that I'm here, hadn't you might as well make use of me?"

One delicately arched eyebrow rose toward her hairline, and Pickett flushed, belatedly realizing how this suggestion might be construed, especially in light of the fact that she was clad in her nightrail while he wore only a banyan with nothing underneath.

"I only meant that we might help one another." Finding this proposition not much better than his original offer, he hurried into explanation. "I'll help you find out whatever there is to be discovered about your brother's death if you'll help me search for Mr. Tomkins's body. Then maybe we can both get out of this godforsaken place," he added, still harboring some small hope of receiving his promised fee.

"What exactly do you want me to do?" Her voice was wary, but at least she had not rebuffed the suggestion outright.

Emboldened, he outlined his plan. "I'll need a distraction sufficient to keep everyone—not just Mr. and Mrs. Danvers, but the staff and Sir Anthony Moring, too—away from the front of the house long enough for me to conduct my search and get back upstairs to my own room without being seen. Do you think you could create such a diversion?"

"I suppose so," she agreed, albeit without enthusiasm. "But to be honest, Mr. Pickett, I don't think there's anything to be discovered about poor Philip. Anything I might have found in the old smokehouse is long gone now. I suppose I should have known it must be, but I had to try."

"Are there no papers, then? Mrs. Danvers kept no records?" Julia, as he recalled, had been asked to sign something prior to his own admission.

"I daresay there are, but they're locked up in a cabinet in her office. And the key"—she gave a bitter little laugh—"is kept on a chain which Mrs. Danvers wears around her neck beneath her gown. So unless you intend to seduce our hostess—"

"No seduction will be necessary," Pickett said, suppressing a shudder at the very thought of it. "Create a diversion for me tomorrow, and at this time tomorrow night, we'll search Mrs. Danvers's office for any papers pertaining to your brother."

She regarded him for a long moment, then held out her hand. "Very well, Mr. Pickett," she said. "We have a bargain."

* * *

Shortly after noon on the following day, Pickett stood on the front portico, leaning against one of the pillars and idly watching the traffic on the London Road, just visible through the rusting ironwork of the elaborately scrolled gates. *By this time tomorrow*, he thought, *Julia will be here*. Was it too much to hope that when she returned to Curzon Street, he would go with her? Perhaps, if his midnight tryst with Miss Bonner succeeded in turning up the information she sought, that determined young woman would be willing to leave, and he would sleep the following night in his own bed, with his wife in his arms.

This promising train of thought was interrupted by a shriek, followed by a lady's high-pitched voice. "A snake! A snake!"

Pickett, recognizing his cue, did not hesitate. He ran down the sloping lawn to the ornamental pool and made straight for the point at which Mr. Tomkins had been thrown in, easily recognizable by the broken and trampled reeds that marked a rough trail to the water's edge. He cast a quick glance in the direction of the house, and noted that Miss Bonner was as good as her word: not another living soul was in sight, everyone having been pressed into service in the quest to find and kill her nonexistent serpent. At least, he hoped it was nonexistent; a pretty fool he would look if they actually found a snake and killed it, and the whole group rounded the corner of the house just in time to see his bare arse hitting the water.

Satisfied that he was quite alone, he pulled both banyan and nightshirt over his head in one swift movement, stuffed them down amongst the reeds so they could not be seen from the house, and dove.

He had known, of course, that the water would be cold; there was, after all, a reason why the month of November was not generally favored by sea-bathers. But he had not expected the bone-chilling cold that pierced his bare skin like a thousand knives, and it took all his effort not to gasp as the water closed over his head.

He opened his eyes onto darkness, and felt a vague sense of ill-usage. He'd wished he might have waited as late as two o'clock for his aquatic investigation, in order to give the feeble autumn sun more time to warm the water, but had thought it best to perform his underwater activities while the sun was at its zenith, allowing for as much light as possible to illuminate the murky green depths. Now, however, he doubted very much if any sunlight penetrated farther than six inches below the surface. How he was to find anything in this liquid hellhole—

Even as his brain formed the thought, his eyes adjusted to the darkness sufficiently for him to identify the long fronds of some aquatic plant just ahead on his left, swaying gently in rhythm to his strokes, while further ahead and considerably deeper, a patch of paler green glowed dimly, a hint of peridot in a sea of deepest jade. A few more strokes brought him near enough to identify it as a man's long-sleeved nightshirt. His gaze traveled from the hem of the garment up past the buttoned placket and collar and, finally, to the face of the wearer. The greenish-gray cast of the skin was not, he knew, entirely due to the condition of the water. The gray hair, worn longer than the current fashion dictated, stood up from the man's head and moved to and fro in a manner suggestive of the plants Pickett had noticed earlier. Most disconcerting of all was the way the man seemed to regard him through half-closed eyes, as if to say "I told you so."

Yes, you did, Pickett thought, acknowledging the truth of this silent accusation with some chagrin. Perhaps if he'd taken the trouble to discover exactly what, and who, Mr. Tomkins had feared, the poor fellow might be alive today. In his own defense, he reminded himself that when he'd tried to press the man for specifics, he'd got nothing—nothing coherent, anyway. How could he possibly have expected this? *You knew something wasn't right at this place,* the dead man, or perhaps his own conscience, accused him. *You knew it from the first.*

Pickett could not deny it. And yet…

His own account of dastardly doings on the Larches' grounds after midnight would never hold up in a court of law, not when half a dozen people could testify that the dinner he'd consumed a few hours earlier had been liberally laced with opium. A body in the water, on the other hand, discovered at the very spot where he claimed to have seen it thrown in, would not be quite so easily dismissed. Regrettable as it was, Mr. Tomkins's death might provide the evidence needed to expose whatever the Danvers duo was doing at the Larches.

I'm sorry to leave you here, old fellow, Pickett silently told the man, *but it won't be for long. You'll have justice and a proper burial, if it's the last thing I ever do.*

He had no idea how prophetic this promise was to prove.

22

In Which the Secret of the Larches Is Revealed

Having found what he'd been looking for, Pickett swam toward the bank as quickly as his rapidly numbing limbs would carry him. He dragged himself out of the water and shook himself in much the same manner as a dog might, considerably aided in this endeavor by the fact that he was trembling so violently his teeth were chattering. In fact, he was surprised that the entire population of the Larches did not hear them clacking together and come running to see what all the racket was about. He snatched up his banyan and nightshirt (trying not to picture the similar garment and its wearer lying unseen beneath the choppy water at his back) and pulled them over his head, then made for the house with all due haste.

Neither his sodden nightshirt nor the decidedly damp banyan covering it offered much in the way of warmth, but the exercise had the effect of bringing the feeling back into his lower limbs—a somewhat mixed blessing, as by the time he reached the house his legs and feet were aching with cold. Still, it appeared his luck was in, for he gained not only the house, but also the back stair and his own room without being seen.

The residents of the Larches were each provided with a modest measure of coal with which to heat their separate bedchambers, and Pickett had been reserving his own small store of fuel ever since he had first recognized the need for underwater exploration, even going so far as to make that morning's ablutions in a decidedly wintry atmosphere. Now that the deed was done, he did not spare the coal, but piled the entire supply onto the grate. His trembling hands fumbled with the flint, but at last the spark caught hold, and since the bedchamber was quite small, it was not long before the room grew wonderfully warm.

It was a pity that the fireplace was not furnished with a hob, as a kitchen hearth would be, for he would have liked to reheat the water which the daily girl brought up every morning before dawn while the residents were still abed; his hair, he was sure, was rather badly in need of washing, and he did not look forward to plunging his head into cold water for the second time that day. Still, it was possible that it had retained at least a little of its heat, and he could help it along by moving the pitcher and bowl from the washstand to the hearth, as near to the fire as possible. The ladder-backed chair beneath the writing desk could also be positioned before the fire, where it might serve as a clotheshorse from which he could hang his wet garments.

Having made these minor rearrangements to the

furnishings, he stripped off his banyan and nightshirt. The banyan, he decided, might suffice, once it had dried out a little. His nightshirt was quite another matter. Besides being soaking wet, it had a distinctly greenish cast, to say nothing of a decided odor of pond scum. Clearly, he would have to wash it as best he could, but as it would have to wait its turn behind his hair, his face, and the rest of his body, he had no very high hopes for the water being clean enough to make much of an improvement. He tossed the sodden nightshirt onto the hearth, where it landed with a splat, then knelt before the bowl, picked up the pitcher, and began pouring the water over his bowed head.

* * *

Half an hour later, he sat curled up in the room's single wing chair with the counterpane, which he'd stripped from the bed, wrapped around him like a cloak, and his notebook on his knee. He'd written a full account of the day's activities, as well as the previous night's, and was now composing a letter for his bride to take to his former magistrate. He thought fleetingly of writing one to her as well, but decided against it; he would see her tomorrow when she came to visit, and anything he might have written to her would be far more satisfactorily communicated in person.

Having described in as much detail as possible the location of the body within the ornamental pool, he signed his name and then folded the letter, realizing with a pang that this was the only rôle he would play in the recovery of the body; assuming he was still in residence at the Larches when the magistrate descended upon the establishment with a search warrant and a contingent of Bow Street men, he would be obliged to stay out of sight in his room lest one of his former colleagues unwittingly compromise the success of his own mission by betraying his incognito. Granted, he could still watch the proceedings from his window, but he wasn't sure that wouldn't make it worse, only serving to emphasize his status as an outsider.

Having completed his correspondence, he rose from the chair and, still trailing his counterpane cloak in his wake, knelt beside his bed and tucked the notebook back into its hiding place beneath the mattress. He had begun to back away when his gaze fell upon the row of tick marks on the wall. Had he added one this morning, or had his midnight encounter with Miss Bonner—to say nothing of the resulting lack of sleep, which was beginning to make itself felt—driven the matter from his mind? He retrieved the pencil tucked into the spine of the notebook and added another mark to the wall. Was that right? It was strange how being cut off from the outside world affected one's concept of time; it seemed like only yesterday since Julia—acting under his instructions, albeit with obvious reluctance—had left him here, and yet at the same time it seemed like an eternity. He frowned at the markings on the wall. That wasn't right, surely? He licked his finger and rubbed out the one he'd just made, then, still unsatisfied, wrote it in again. Of one thing, at least, he was certain: Julia would be coming tomorrow, and she would have been counting the days just as he was, and probably with greater accuracy. In the meantime, it behooved him to get what sleep he could now, during the afternoon, for he had another long and sleepless night ahead of him.

He stood up only long enough to collapse across the bed, still wrapped in the counterpane. *Tomorrow*, he thought, surrendering to the arms of Morpheus. *Julia will be here tomorrow, and everything will be right again.*

* * *

To Pickett, the rest of the day seemed to crawl by. He awoke to find his nightshirt had dried, although it was a very far cry from the snowy white garment his valet, Thomas, had packed for his sojourn. He thought wistfully of the clothes that had been taken from him following his exploration of the kitchen, and acknowledged that if their return was to be contingent upon his good behavior, they were unlikely to reappear any time soon.

Dinner that night was an ordeal. He lived in expectation that at any moment someone would comment on the faint odor that still clung to his clothing (and, he feared, his person), and ask questions to which he would be hard pressed to give answers. Then, too, there was Miss Bonner, sitting almost directly across the table from him and never betraying by so much as a blink that they had spent a good deal of the previous night together in Mr. Tomkins's now-vacant room—hiding under the bed, no less!—nor that they had another clandestine meeting planned for that very night. He supposed he should be grateful for the lady's discretion, but there was no denying that her seeming unawareness of anything out of the ordinary added to the sense of unreality that still made the murder of Mr. Tomkins seem like a dream, the corpse at the bottom of the pool notwithstanding.

After twenty-four hours of inactivity interrupted only by that bizarre search for the body of the missing man, it was a relief to hear the long-case clock strike two, the hour he and Miss Bonner had agreed upon. He rose from his bed—he hadn't allowed himself to fall asleep, lest he should miss the assignation—fumbled in the darkness with the flint until his candle flared to life, then took up the candlestick and slowly opened the door of his bedchamber. A quick look down the corridor in both directions showed no signs of life, so he slipped out of the room and closed the door softly behind him.

As he crept stealthily down the corridor, he wondered fleetingly how long it would be before he was able to enjoy an uninterrupted night's sleep. With any luck, Miss Bonner would find whatever she was looking for, and he could persuade her to evacuate the premises without further delay. He only hoped she had not overslept; he would feel very ill-used, if he were to discover that he'd forsaken his bed only to have his co-conspirator miss the rendezvous entirely.

In this, at least, he was not disappointed. As he approached the door of Mrs. Danvers's office, a voice spoke out of the shadows.

"What took you so long? I've been waiting this age!"

Pickett, who distinctly remembered seeing the time displayed on the clock face as he reached the foot of the stairs, objected to this implied accusation. "It's not yet five minutes past two!" he said indignantly.

She gave a shaky laugh. "Oh, is that all? It seems like twenty minutes, at the very least. Have you got the key?"

"No." He gave her the candle, whose flame was no

longer dipping and bobbing, now that it was no longer in motion. "Hold this, will you?"

She did as he asked, albeit not without protesting. "But how—"

"Shhh!"

Even as she spoke, he had dropped to one knee before the office door and inserted a hairpin into the lock with the ease of long practice, and now pressed his ear to the door, listening for the faint *click* as the locking mechanism yielded.

Her eyes widened as he pushed the door open. "How did you do that?"

He shrugged. "Just a trick my father taught me."

"And I suppose you carry a hairpin about for just such a purpose."

"Not usually," he said. He found he did not want to talk about Julia. His assignation with Miss Bonner might be perfectly innocent—well, perfectly innocent as to any amorous intention, anyway—but somehow it seemed wrong to discuss his wife while meeting clandestinely with another lady, both of them clad in only their nightclothes.

"Look here," he said, when it appeared her curiosity was not entirely satisfied, "now that I've got you into Mrs. Danvers's office, hadn't we best get started?"

Pickett once more sought recourse to the hairpin in order to open the doors of the large wooden cabinet, which proved to contain a number of pigeonholes in which various papers were stored. He chose one at random, reached inside, and drew out the document it contained. Finding that it detailed the course of treatment of a man he'd never heard of before, he returned it to its place and selected another. After four such fruitless attempts, he removed the document from another pigeonhole, and the name *George Daniel Tomkins* fairly leapt from the page. Without raising his eyes from the closely written lines, Pickett groped for the edge of the desk and lowered himself to the floor, then began to read.

It was apparently a legal document detailing the specifics of the treatment Mr. Tomkins was to undergo, signed by one David Edwin Tomkins, identified as the man's nephew. Pickett had no legal background—his only dealings with the law, at least in recent years, was concerned with apprehending those who broke it—but to his layman's eyes, some of the terms of the agreement seemed odd, to say the least. One item stated that the undersigned agreed to hold the Larches and its staff blameless in the outcome of any treatment administered. Pickett supposed this was only to be expected; one need only look at Sir Anthony Moring's inability to keep away from the poppy to recognize that the Danvers duo, whatever their faults, could hardly be blamed for the weaknesses of those who came to them for help.

Less easily understood, however, was the proviso giving the proprietors of the Larches permission to retain and dispose of any personal property left behind by the aforementioned, the profits of any such disposal going toward recouping the cost of treatment. Pickett supposed that must have been what the unknown visitor to Mr. Tomkins's room had been doing the previous night. Still, if the contract clearly gave the establishment the right to any such property, why had someone felt it necessary to exercise their claim in the middle of the night?

His brain immediately supplied the answer: *Because Mr. Tomkins was said to have run away.* It was unlikely that the man would have made his escape with nothing but the nightshirt on his back; therefore, his belongings must be spirited away, leaving the empty drawers of the bureau as evidence of his flight. Pickett wondered if someone had already been dispatched with the spoils to one of the secondhand shops with which London abounded. He thought it very likely; Mrs. Danvers would no doubt wish to be rid of the incriminating garments before someone—someone like himself, perhaps, or the equally inquisitive Miss Bonner—stumbled onto them and blew the gaff.

But this proviso, curious as it was, paled beside one brief notation at the bottom of the page. *Can't swim,* it said. That was all. Only those two words. So simple, so innocent—innocent, at least, until one questioned what the devil this observation had to do with overcoming an opium dependency.

"Here's mine," Miss Bonner said, pulling another document from yet another pigeonhole. "I remember signing it." She sat down next to him on the floor and adjusted the position of the candle so that its light fell between them equally.

She need not have bothered. Pickett had scrambled to his feet, and now plundered one pigeonhole after another until he found what he sought: a document very similar to the first, except that instead of George Daniel Tomkins, this one bore another name at the top: *John Pickett.*

He sank to the floor on legs suddenly weak, and scanned

the single sheet of foolscap until he came to the name of Julia Runyon Fieldhurst Pickett, and, further down the page: *Wife due to give birth in early December. Treatment must be completed prior to the end of November.*

"Mr. Pickett?" she prompted, when he made no response. "Did you hear me? I found my own record. What—?"

He looked at her then, but with an expression of such horror in his brown eyes that she broke off, leaving the question unasked.

"They're not helping people overcome opium dependence," he said in a voice curiously unlike his own. "They're committing murder for hire."

23

In Which John Pickett's Case Takes an Unexpected Turn

"*What?*" His co-conspirator leaned over to inspect the document in his hand. "You can't be serious!"

"I'm perfectly serious. Look at this: 'Can't swim,' " He pointed to the damning words as he read them aloud. "What else can it be, except a plausible method of doing away with the poor fellow?"

"I see how it might be interpreted that way," she said doubtfully. "But bear in mind that Mr. Tomkins was in the habit of taking opium. It could be nothing more than a precaution against a potential accident. If he were to wander down to the water while under its influence, he might well fall in and drown. In fact, something similar happened only a few weeks ago, when another resident fell to his death from the rooftop after—oh!" She broke off abruptly, her eyes widening as she realized the implications of that earlier death.

"Exactly," Pickett said. "Mr. Horace Lester, if memory serves. As it happens, the coroner's jury agreed with you, and rendered a verdict of death by misadventure. I wonder what his records would say—'Can't fly?' Perhaps more to the point"—he glanced down at the paper in his hand—"I wonder if David Edwin Tomkins is his uncle's heir."

"It's a tempting conjecture, Mr. Pickett, but I'm afraid it won't hold water," Miss Bonner insisted, albeit not without regret. "I shall always suspect that Philip's death was not a suicide, but I assumed he must have had a falling out with one of the other residents, or someone on the staff—perhaps even Mr. Danvers himself, which would explain Mrs. Danvers's unwillingness to tell me anything. But what you suggest is surely too fantastical! According to your reasoning, *I* should have been the one to admit Philip, or at least should have pressed my aunt and uncle to do so, for after his death our father's fortune, which was to have been divided between the pair of us, comes to me intact."

"And if you should have a tragic 'accident' or a 'falling out' while in residence?" Pickett asked. "What happens to your inheritance then?"

"It would go to my aunt—my father's only surviving sibling—and her husband, my uncle. And while it's true that they are the ones who admitted Philip to the Larches, they pleaded with me not to seek admission myself."

"Perhaps they lost their nerve after your brother's death. If you were to meet with a similar fate, it might draw a great deal of uncomfortable attention to your brother's apparent suicide."

She shook her head. "I realize you've never met my aunt and uncle, but what you are suggesting sounds absurd," she insisted, then grimaced. "Or it would, if one can describe murder in such frivolous terms.

Privately, Pickett wondered if perhaps the lady wasn't protesting a bit too much, but he realized that to argue the point would only waste valuable time. "I suppose we'd better keep looking, then," he said noncommittally, then rose to his feet and extracted another document from its pigeonhole. *Philip Henry Bonner* was written across the top of the paper in bold cursive. He glanced down at the subject's sister, who appeared to have dismissed the idea and was now deriving considerable amusement from reading about herself.

Satisfied that her attention would be engaged for some time, he turned his attention back to the paper in his hand. *Somewhat shorter in stature than the average*, it said, after stating the same provisos he'd noticed on the other contracts, followed by an additional notation reading *Prone to solitude*.

In other words, Pickett thought, the perfect candidate for stringing up from the low overhead beams of the old smokehouse, where his body might not be discovered for hours, or at least long enough for Mr. and Mrs. Danvers to have established suitable alibis.

It was the signature at the bottom of the page, however, that startled him into an exclamation that instantly commanded Miss Bonner's attention.

"What have you discovered?" she asked eagerly, making as if to rise.

"No, don't get up," protested Pickett, settling himself on the floor beside her. "I have a feeling you're going to want to be sitting down for this."

"Oh?" Her expression grew wary. "Why?"

"See for yourself," he said, holding the document between them so that it was fully illuminated by the candle on the desk.

Mrs. Arthur Conway, it read, and, inscribed directly beneath the lady's signature, *Referred by Mr. Edward Poole, 27 Wimpole St.*

"I don't understand," said Miss Bonner, staring at the cryptic notation. "If Edward was familiar with the Larches and thought highly enough of it to recommend to my aunt that Philip should be placed there for treatment, why was he so determined that I should not stay here, even to the point of engaging you to remove me bodily from the premises?"

"I give up," Pickett said. "Why?"

"Yes, I know what you think," she said impatiently. "But if your theory should be correct, then it means that all this time he—he—"

"He's paid court to you, having first concocted a scheme to make sure you would inherit the lot," Pickett finished for her. "I suppose he engaged my services to make sure you were removed from the scene of the crime before you discovered the truth—or at least enough of it to make his own position very uncomfortable," he added, nodding toward the paper she had snatched from his hand at the sight of the familiar name.

"Yes, but—Mr. Pickett, surely these contracts cannot be legal, at least not enough to hold up in court! It's not as if one could hand over to one's solicitor a document stating that one had paid a third party to commit murder."

"No," agreed Pickett, "but it would be enough to scotch

any attempt at blackmail. If, for instance, Mr. Tomkins's nephew should have any ideas about recouping whatever he might have paid the Danverses by threatening to expose them, they could produce the signed contract proving, or at least strongly suggesting, that the younger Mr. Tomkins was far from blameless—especially if I'm right in thinking he probably stands to inherit his uncle's fortune."

"Yes," she said slowly, "yes, I see."

Having won this concession from her, Pickett quickly pressed his point. "Why should Mr. Poole's name be mentioned at all, unless Mrs. Danvers realized during their initial interview that your aunt knew nothing about the scheme, while Mr. Poole very likely did? By the bye, was it Mr. Poole who made your aunt and uncle aware of your brother's opium use?"

She gave a snort of humorless laughter. "They could hardly have been *un*aware of it. By the—the end, Philip made no pretense of concealing it. He spent more nights in the opium dens of Limehouse than he spent at home."

"How did he first begin ingesting it?" The only answer he received was a look of blank incomprehension, and Pickett, realizing he'd given her a great deal to take in all at once, hurried into explanation. "My own experience with opium began with the laudanum I was given for pain relief following a head injury. I only wondered if your brother suffered from some painful condition of his own that led to his becoming dependent upon it long after the medical need for it had passed."

"No—at least, not that I know of. In fact, his condition

was already well established by the time I learned of it. There is a school of thought, you know, that claims the stuff opens one's mind and enhances the senses; I believe several of the poets currently in vogue subscribe to the notion. But Philip never moved in literary circles; in fact, although he never said as much, I was under the impression that he was introduced to the substance by a fellow member of his club."

"What club is that?" asked Pickett, knowing quite well that, should his investigation take him there, he would not be allowed past the front door, especially now that he no longer had the authority of Bow Street at his back.

"Brooks's. My uncle has been a member there for many years, and put Philip's name forward."

"Brooks's?" Pickett started at the familiar name. He had assumed Miss Bonner was speaking of some organization of students at Oxford or Cambridge. He had never entered its hallowed portals—he'd never even tried, having no fancy to be tossed out on his ear—but he knew that Brooks's, along with White's and perhaps one or two others, was one of London's most exclusive gentlemen's clubs, particularly favored by those men whose political views tended toward the Whig party. "I should have thought he was too young."

"Not necessarily. Charles James Fox was admitted at the age of sixteen, so Philip's status as a minor presented no insuperable bar to membership, especially since our father had belonged to the club. Edward is a member, too; in fact, it was there that Philip first made his acquaintance, for my uncle took special care to introduce Philip to some of the younger members." She frowned over this last statement. "Not that

Edward is young, precisely, although he must seem so compared to some of the greybeards."

"Miss Bonner, is it possible that it was Mr. Poole who introduced your brother to the joys of opium?"

"I suppose it might have been he," she said thoughtfully. "Although if he did, then that would mean he's been planning this for years: ingratiating himself with my uncle, cultivating a friendship with Philip, even feigning an amorous interest in me!"

"Exactly. It appears your devoted suitor has been playing a very long game. And I," he added bitterly, "I took his word for gospel on no evidence whatsoever, and ran to do his bidding just like the obedient lapdog you called me."

"Don't be so hard on yourself, Mr. Pickett," she said, leaning toward him to place her hand over his. "You had no way of knowing. How could you, when I, who have fended off Edward's importunities for a twelvemonth or more, never suspected him to be capable of such perfidy?"

Privately, Pickett feared that, having been unexpectedly presented with a case that appeared to be a godsend, he had seized upon it without asking a great many questions which in retrospect should have been obvious. Perhaps it was a good thing that he was no longer a principal officer at Bow Street; he would not want to have to answer to Mr. Colquhoun for his failings.

Aloud, however, he merely said, "Now that you know the truth about your brother's murder, you can return to your uncle's house with a clear conscience, knowing your suspicions were justified. I daresay you will know what, and how much, to tell your aunt and uncle, but I must ask you not to let Mr. Poole know you've found him out. You should be safe enough, so long as he remains in ignorance; after all, he won't wish to do away with you until he's got you to the altar, and his hands on your inheritance."

She stared at him. "You make it sound as if this is goodbye!"

"Well, isn't it?" asked Pickett, all at sea. "I mean, since you admitted yourself to the Larches, can't you pronounce yourself cured and leave?"

"Why, yes, I suppose so," she said. "But what about you?"

"I'm stuck here until my wife comes to release me. Eventually, I'll lay the whole matter before Bow Street—not only your brother's murder, but Mr. Tomkins's as well, along with whatever I can discover about that poor Lester fellow, who I strongly suspect was shoved off the roof. In the meantime, I'll continue to gather evidence until I've got enough to make a solid case against Mrs. Danvers and her merry band of murderers."

"All while dodging their attempts to kill you. No, Mr. Pickett, it seems to me that you had best take that gallant rescue you had planned for my sake, and use it for your own benefit."

Whatever Pickett might have said to this eminently sensible suggestion was destined to remain unspoken, for at that moment the doorknob rattled, and in the next instant the panel began to swing open.

24

In Which John Pickett Is Caught Out in Another Compromising Situation, and Julia Makes an Alarming Discovery

Somewhere in the back of his mind, it occurred to Pickett that he had played this particular scene before. That earlier occasion had taken place in the study of a Yorkshire country house, and Julia (still Lady Fieldhurst at the time) had seized the lapels of his coat of borrowed livery and kissed him; in fact, it was one of his fonder memories.

Miss Bonner, having no such convenient grip ready to hand, instead grabbed him by the ears and pulled, dragging him down with her as she pressed her mouth to his. They hit the floor with him sprawled atop her, his clothing (such as it was) disheveled and his lips joined to hers in what was to all appearances a passionate kiss. He had no doubts at all as to how they must have looked to anyone opening the door upon such a spectacle.

"*Mr. Pickett!*"

The voice of Mrs. Danvers, fairly quivering with outrage, confirmed his worst fears, and Pickett detached himself from Miss Bonner and faced his accuser as best he could; he dared not sit upright until his co-conspirator had had sufficient time to make any necessary rearrangements to her clothing.

Mrs. Danvers should have appeared ridiculous, standing framed in the doorway with a dressing gown of some pale hue thrown over her night-rail and her hair covered by a frilled cap, and yet somehow she conveyed the impression of an avenging angel—an impression heightened, no doubt, by the candle in her hand, whose light cast the planes of her face into strong relief and turned her mundane garments to gold.

"How dare you? For shame, sir!"

"I—I wasn't—this isn't—" Pickett stammered, torn between vehemently denying that he had ever played his wife false, or embracing (so to speak) the unflattering rôle into which Miss Bonner had cast him, taking what comfort he could in the knowledge that the diversion had, at least for the nonce, distracted his outraged hostess's attention from the open cupboard and the incriminating documents scattered about the floor. He felt a slight pressure against his thigh, and realized that Miss Bonner, still lying partially beneath him, had stuffed a sheaf of papers into the pocket of his banyan. He glanced down at her to communicate a silent acknowledgement of this maneuver, and was dismayed to discover that the hem of her night-rail was rucked up over her knees, while the pale-blue ribbon that gathered its neckline closed had come untied, leaving her left breast in imminent danger of exposure.

Mrs. Danvers silenced him with a lift of one imperative

hand. "I wasn't born yesterday, Mr. Pickett. I know very well what 'this' is. And *you!*" she said, turning the full force of her displeasure upon the young woman whose virtue she had guarded so diligently. "I am disappointed in you, Miss Bonner, although the word falls far short of expressing my sentiments. I had not thought you capable of such brazen conduct."

Miss Bonner grabbed Pickett's arm, a gesture so unexpected that it almost brought him toppling back onto her.

"But I love him!" she declared in throbbing accents that would not have shamed the great Mrs. Siddons. At least, that was what Pickett thought she said; his ears were still ringing from their rough treatment.

Mrs. Danvers was not impressed. "What you can find to admire in a married man who seduces innocents while his wife lives in daily expectation of her confinement quite escapes me. I can only say that he will not do so beneath any roof of mine. I fear I can do nothing more for you, Miss Bonner. You will leave us in the morning. You may partake of breakfast in your room, after which you will be conveyed to your uncle's house."

"Yes, ma'am," Miss Bonner mumbled with deceptive meekness, her eyes fixed upon the carpet beneath her feet.

"Now, go upstairs, pack your belongings, and get what sleep you can. I want to have a word with Mr. Pickett."

"Yes, ma'am," Miss Bonner said again, giving Pickett a speaking look before brushing past first him and then Mrs. Danvers on her way out of the room.

Alone with his accuser, Pickett felt strangely bereft; he had not realized how important it had become to him over the past twenty-four hours, to know he was no longer utterly alone in his mission. He was conscious of a renewed longing for Julia's coming visit. He would be able to tell her—with perfect truth—that he'd arranged for Miss Bonner's escape from the Larches (albeit not in quite the way he had expected) and that, having fulfilled the commission laid upon him by Mr. Poole, he was free to return to Curzon Street; he only wondered what, and how much, of the "rescue" he should divulge to her.

In the meantime, there was the interview with Mrs. Danvers to be got through.

"Well, Mr. Pickett?" she demanded, regarding him with a baleful eye. "Have you nothing more to say for yourself?"

"It was not what it appeared," Pickett insisted, having by this time had sufficient opportunity to construct a plausible explanation for not only the scene the offended lady had witnessed, but the papers scattered about the floor as well. "As you may be aware, Miss Bonner has a—an unhealthy fixation with her brother's suicide. She seems to have the idea that something is being deliberately withheld from her—I have no idea what—" he added, regarding his interrogator with a look of limpid innocence, "but something she said gave me the impression that she intended to search for the records of her brother's residence here. When I heard her footsteps on the stairs—I am a very light sleeper, you see—I had a very good idea what she was about."

He paused to gauge the effect of this combination of truths, half-truths, and outright lies upon his audience.

"Go on," Mrs. Danvers said curtly.

Pickett, nothing loth, obeyed. "I followed—from a safe distance, you understand—and found her here, sitting on the floor with papers spread out around her, just as you see them now. I tried to persuade her to give up a quest I feared could only cause her further distress, and in trying to comfort her, I, well, one thing led to another, and…" He broke off with a helpless shrug, rather pleased with the story he had fabricated. Mrs. Danvers might not believe it, but nor could she disprove it, which would serve almost as well.

Almost.

"Mr. Pickett, you have been nothing but trouble from the day of your arrival," she informed him bluntly. "For the remainder of your stay, a guard will be posted in the corridor just outside your room throughout the night, lest you have any more ideas about roaming the house under cover of darkness. Furthermore, Mr. Danvers or some male member of the staff will accompany you whenever you leave your room during the day. Do I make myself clear?"

Twenty-four hours earlier, Pickett might have raised a great many objections to the presence of a third party; now, however, he could think of only one. "But my wife is coming tomorrow!" He only hoped the designated watchdog was not offended by displays of marital affection, for he fully intended to kiss her with considerable fervor, and if the unwelcome observer didn't like it, he could jolly well lump it. Still, the presence of an audience would make it extremely difficult for him to communicate his findings to Julia, much less pass along the letter he'd written to Mr. Colquhoun or the incriminating files Miss Bonner had shoved into his pocket.

"Perhaps," said Mrs. Danvers, clearly unmoved, "you should have thought of that before attempting to seduce a defenseless young lady."

Privately, Pickett thought Miss Bonner was about as defenseless as a smallpox epidemic, but Mrs. Danvers's next words drove all thoughts of that strong-willed young woman from his head.

"Besides," she said, "are you quite certain Mrs. Pickett is coming tomorrow? I feel sure you must have mistaken the day."

* * *

Some time later in quite a different part of London, Julia awoke with a feeling of mingled anticipation and dread. In only a few hours, she would be reunited with her husband, if only for a little while. She wondered what, if anything, he had discovered in the green depths of the neglected pool, and whether the discovery might speed his return to Curzon Street. It was this happy prospect that spurred her to throw back the counterpane and roll (there was no other word for it, given the advanced state of her pregnancy) out of the bed.

On the other hand, today was also the day that she had determined to call on Kit's mother and inquire as to the boy's inoculation against smallpox. The Fountainhead Academy required that all its young scholars be immune to the disease, either by having suffered the dreaded illness and lived to tell the tale, or by having been inoculated against it. Kit's clear, smooth skin seemed to rule out the former condition; therefore, it remained to discover his status as to the latter.

She did not look forward to the visit. She had known, of

course, that Moll had expelled her nominal "stepson" from the house to fend for himself when he was only fourteen years old, and that was bad enough. But more recently she had added to her sins, first by selling the fruit of her own womb to a criminal gang and then attempting to seduce her now-adult stepson when he tried to rescue the boy. Still, something had been gained from her lack of maternal feeling, for she had been more than willing to surrender poor little Kit to his half-brother's custody, albeit for a price.

In fact, Julia feared Kit was still not entirely convinced that she would not take advantage of his brother's absence to return him to the slattern who had borne him, for when she had asked the boy if he would like to visit his mother, his response had been an emphatic negative. It stung a little to know that he did not yet fully trust her, but she had to own that his life, up to the point that John had entered it, had not been one likely to inspire him with trust of his fellow man—or woman, as the case might be.

Still, John had asked her to come alone on her next visit, and by combining the two errands into one, she had been able to oblige him in this request without much objection from Kit. And so it was that she set out alone from Curzon Street. As the carriage bowled northeastward, the vista from the window changed, the manicured residential squares of Mayfair giving way to the less genteel but more vibrant streets of Holborn, where residents and shopkeepers existed cheek by jowl. Lulled by the rhythm of the carriage wheels against the cobblestones, Julia leaned her head against the window, watching the shoppers and storefronts as she might have actors upon a stage moving against a painted backdrop.

Suddenly one detail emerged from the blur of commercial activity, one that made her sit upright, simultaneously rapping for the coachman's attention and demanding to be set down.

"Here, ma'am?" he asked in bewilderment.

"Yes, here!" she said impatiently. "You may circle the block, and by the time you return I shall be waiting for you."

The coachman did as she bade him, albeit not without a shrug of resignation, and a moment later Julia stood on the pavement before a secondhand clothing shop, regarding the article of clothing that held pride of place in its window. It was a man's double-breasted tailcoat of fawn-colored wool, and even when seen through the carriage window it had been obvious that this garment was of a better quality than would be within the means of the establishment's clientele—or it would have been, were it not for the brown smudge that stained the left lapel, as if its previous wearer had spilled some dark liquid—coffee, perhaps—and made an inexpert attempt to wipe it clean, succeeding only in smearing it further.

Surely, Julia thought, there could not be two men in London who possessed identical coats and had contrived to stain them in exactly the same place, with exactly the same substance. Could there?

There was only one way to find out. She strode into the shop, attracting the attention of not only the shopkeeper, but two women engaged in lively debate with him over the feasibility of paying all of sixpence for a small shirt of dingy white cotton that "my Tom" would very likely outgrow within three months. At the entrance of this new customer, the shopkeeper, sensing greener pastures, lost all interest in Tom's projected growth and hurried to meet her.

"Good morning, ma'am, good morning!" he exclaimed, rubbing his hands together in anticipation. "How may I be of service to you this fine day?" In fact, the day was far from fine, being much too cloudy and damp to deserve such an encomium, but any day that brought a member of the Quality through his door was surely deserving of all the praise he could give it.

Julia, meanwhile, had gone straight to the window, and was now subjecting the tailcoat to a close examination. She saw nothing to disprove her suspicions; in fact, they were substantially strengthened by the tailor's mark sewn into the lining that identified the garment as coming from the hand of Meyer of Conduit Street. Pressing the stained lapel to her nose, she could still catch the faint odor of coffee, although the familiar and beloved scent of the man who had once worn it had long since dispersed, overwhelmed by the myriad smells of the people and places that characterized the less refined parts of the Metropolis. She disliked intensely the thought of other, less worthy men pawing over her husband's garments, perhaps trying them on for size and peacocking before the large but faintly spotted mirror affixed to one wall for just such a purpose. As for how the coat had made its way from a discreet asylum in Islington to a secondhand clothing shop in Holborn, she could not even begin to guess, although she intended to demand answers of Mrs. Danvers before that lady was much older.

The shopkeeper, of course, knew nothing of the tumultuous emotions she struggled to hold in check; he saw only the potential for a very profitable transaction, and lost no time in extolling the tailcoat's many perfections—which, in his enthusiastically stated opinion, far outweighed its one rather glaring blemish.

"If you are looking to buy a coat for your husband," he hazarded, glancing at the lady's abdomen, "you could hardly do better outside of Bond Street itself. The wool, as you can see, is of a particularly fine quality, while as for the cut—"

"How much?" asked Julia, interrupting a catalog of the garment's virtues that threatened to be quite lengthy.

"Oh—er—" the shopkeeper stammered, not expecting to come to the point quite so soon. "You will say, of course, that it is stained, but a good laundress might well be able to remove it, and even if not, well, a bloom for the gentleman's buttonhole might very well conceal it. I'm afraid I couldn't possibly let it go for less than three and six."

A gasp from one of the women (both of whom were quite blatantly eavesdropping) suggested that this price was akin to highway robbery, but Julia paid no heed.

"I'll take it," she said, tugging open the drawstring of her reticule.

She left the shop a few minutes later with the coat draped over her arm, leaving to watch her departure a highly gratified shopkeeper and two women who regarded her with mingled contempt for one green enough to make no attempt to bargain for a lower price, and envy for one wealthy enough to have no need of it.

25

In Which Circumstances Conspire to Keep Mr. and Mrs. John Pickett Apart

Some half-hour later, having abandoned her plan to call on Kit's mother in favor of a more urgent errand, Julia was ushered into the office of the Larches, whereupon she strode boldly up to the desk and dumped a pile of fawn-colored wool onto its surface, causing the top few sheets of a stack of papers to flutter to the floor. Julia offered no apology, nor did she make any attempt to retrieve them.

"I should like you to explain to me," she commanded her hostess with no roundaboutation, "how my husband's tailcoat turned up in a secondhand clothing shop in Holborn."

Mrs. Danvers did not answer at once, but leaned down to pick up the nearest of the papers from the somewhat threadbare Turkey carpet. Not until she had returned to an upright position did she reply to the unspoken accusation.

"There must be dozens of coats of a similar color in London," she pointed out. "What makes you so certain this one belonged to Mr. Pickett?"

Julia noted her use of the past tense, but did not challenge it. Instead, she rooted through the folds of cloth until she unearthed the stained lapel. "This," she said, presenting it for the woman's inspection. "He spilled coffee on it the morning of his arrival here. Granted, there may be dozens of similar coats in London, even some with identical stains on their lapels, but surely few of them chance to turn up in secondhand clothing shops only days after being confiscated as my husband tells me his garments were, leaving him with nothing to wear but his nightclothes."

If she had hoped to catch the woman off her guard, she was doomed to disappointment. "Come, Mrs. Pickett, let us have done with these high-flown charges," Mrs. Danvers said coolly, refusing to be provoked. "If you will recall, you signed a contract when you entrusted your husband to our care, a contract that gives us permission to recoup any remaining costs of his treatment by disposing of his effects however we think best."

"His 'effects'?" Julia echoed in alarm. "Surely he is not—not *dead?*"

"He is not," responded Mrs. Danvers. "Needless to say, you would be notified at once in case of such an outcome. Still, there are always those who balk at paying any balance remaining at the end of treatment. We can hardly be expected to absorb such a loss."

"No, but you can certainly be expected to wait until the end of treatment to exercise your rights under such an agreement!"

"Clearly, a mistake was made in this case, and action was taken too soon. Still, is this not a storm in a teacup, given that the garment in its present condition is unwearable, at least by any gentleman worthy of the name?"

"As to its wearability I should think it is my husband's prerogative, not yours, to decide. Speaking of my husband, I should like to see him, if you please."

"I regret that I cannot oblige you, Mrs. Pickett," said her hostess, although Julia could detect no sign of regret, nor any other human emotion. "I fear he had a bad night last night, and is indisposed."

"A bad night?" Julia seized upon the words. "In what way? Surely not laudanum?"

"Er, no, not laudanum. It pains me to confess it, Mrs. Pickett, but he was discovered *in flagrante delicto* with the only female currently in residence."

"You cannot mean Miss Bonner!"

Mrs. Danvers inclined her head. "The very same."

"But—but there must be some mistake!" protested Julia.

"There can be no mistake," said Mrs. Danvers, albeit not without sympathy. "I discovered them myself, in this very room."

This very room, Julia thought, even as her brain reeled. The office, where any papers referring to Miss Bonner or her brother, or indeed Mr. Tomkins, would most likely be stored, probably in the wooden cabinet positioned against the wall at Mrs. Danvers's back. That must be significant, surely?

"Mrs. Danvers," she said, steeling herself, "will you tell me, please, exactly what you saw last night?"

The woman shook her head. "Come, Mrs. Pickett, it can do no good to torment yourself by dwelling on the matter. Suffice it to say there could be no other way of interpreting such a tableau as the one that met my eyes."

"If I could see Mr. Pickett and speak to him, then—"

"I'm afraid that is quite impossible." Mrs. Danvers's tone was scrupulously polite, but there was a hint of steel in her voice that made Julia recognize the futility of further argument. As if in confirmation of her reluctant surrender, Mrs. Danvers added, "As I told you on the day you brought Mr. Pickett to us, it is unwise to visit too frequently. You must be patient and give the treatment time to work."

With this Julia was forced to be content. But although she was obliged to take her leave without further protest, she could not quite forget one seemingly innocuous detail.

On one corner of Mrs. Danvers's desk had lain a single hairpin.

* * *

Julia called at the Larches again the next day, and the day after that, and the day after that. The response was always the same: Mr. Pickett had had a bad night, and was in no condition to receive visitors. On the fourth such day, Mrs. Danvers dropped all pretense of courtesy.

"I must ask you to cease these daily visits," the woman informed her. "I can assure you that it will all be over very soon, and you shall be notified when the time comes. Until then, you must be patient and have faith in the course of treatment that has proven so effective in the past."

"Yes, but—"

"But what?" prompted Mrs. Danvers, clearly annoyed.

But he isn't really an opium-eater, she might have said. *How can he be having "bad nights" when he has no such habit to overcome?* Of course, she could not say such a thing, for to do so would be to expose his real purpose for seeking admission to the establishment. As for inquiring into the particulars of this mysterious "treatment," Mrs. Danvers had already made it abundantly clear that this was a secret she refused to divulge.

And so she waited, and did her best to keep busy. She paid the dreaded call on Kit's mother, and even persuaded Kit to allow her to present Moll with a drawing of a slightly lopsided horse. Any art critic worthy of the name would have been quick to point out that, in addition to its tendency to list to starboard, this animal's eyes were rather too close to its ears, but in view of the fact that the artist was a ten-year-old with no formal training beyond a couple of very rudimentary lessons from his sister-in-law, that selfsame critic must also have admitted that it showed considerable promise.

Upon hearing from Moll's own lips that Kit had not been inoculated against the dreaded smallpox (Moll being firmly of the opinion that the introduction of cow pox fluid into the body of a human child would very likely cause her son to sprout horns on his head), she arranged for Dr. Gilroy, a friend as well as a physician, to administer the treatment—a procedure to which Kit responded by howling loudly enough to shake the rafters.

The following morning, the boy was discovered to be running a slight fever, and while her husband was never out of her thoughts, Julia was obliged to put away all thoughts of visiting him while she assumed the rôle of sickroom nurse, plying her young patient with chicken broth and bathing his flushed face with lavender water. On the third day, Kit's fever broke, and when he pleaded for apple tart instead of the chicken broth of which he was growing thoroughly sick—and, perhaps more to the point, complained bitterly that the hoped-for horns had never materialized—Julia knew her young patient was on the mend.

She finished embroidering the deep whitework border adorning the hem of the fine batiste christening gown she had made for the baby, and gave Kit another drawing lesson, and studied the Fountainhead Academy's brochure for any further preparations that needed to be made prior to his matriculating there.

And still there was no word from the Larches.

* * *

In the meantime, her husband was faring no better; in fact, it might even be said that Pickett's situation was a good deal worse. His breakfast had been brought to his room, just as Mrs. Danvers had ordered, after which an air of such oppressive silence fell that Pickett was emboldened to open his door and steal a quick glance down the corridor in the hope that, Mrs. Danvers having made her point with his breakfast, her other pronouncements would prove to be empty threats.

This hope, however, proved to be overly optimistic. As the door swung open, Pickett saw that redoubtable female's hapless spouse look up at him somewhat sheepishly from a chair positioned against the wall adjacent to the door. With a sigh of resignation, the man rose to his feet, clearly resigned to accompanying the prisoner wherever he intended to go.

Having no desire to go about the house or its grounds trailing his escort behind him like St. Anthony and his pig, Pickett closed the door, resolving to remain in his room until Julia came to release him from captivity. Until then, he told himself, he could bide his time. He picked up the book he'd chosen from the library three days ago, when he'd first met Sir Anthony Moring. Or had that been four days ago? He supposed it didn't much matter; one day at the Larches was very like another.

By late afternoon, he had finished the book, and there was still no sign of Julia. What could be keeping her? He considered going downstairs to fetch something else to read, and might have done so, had a quick peek into the corridor not informed him that he would be obliged to submit to an escort on even this brief excursion.

Abandoning this plan for his entertainment, he retrieved his notebook from its hiding place beneath the mattress. He had written no account of his and Miss Bonner's discoveries amongst Mrs. Danvers's papers; he had hoped to make this report directly to his former magistrate, and in person. Seeing that this meeting would not take place as soon as he would have liked, it behooved him to commit his findings to paper while they were still fresh. In any case, the exercise would give him something useful to do while he waited for Julia.

He was still waiting when the sun set and the moon rose. In fact, he was beginning to have second thoughts. He'd dismissed as pure spite Mrs. Danvers's earlier claim that he had mistaken the day, thinking she intended to punish him for his persistence in poking about in places he shouldn't, or his supposed indiscretion with Miss Bonner, or perhaps both. Now, for the first time, he wondered if she might have been telling the truth. He dragged the iron bedstead away from the wall, the better to examine the tick marks comprising his primitive calendar.

One…two…three…four… He'd rubbed that one out, thinking he'd miscounted, and then written it back in after deciding he'd been right the first time. Now it appeared he had been wrong. He started to rub it out again and then recalled that, in the turmoil following the little scene in the office, he had not yet made a mark to designate the day that was now ending. He left the mark as it was, and resigned himself to waiting another day for Julia, and his release. When his dinner was brought up to his room, he ate it in solitude—Mr. Danvers, still holding his vigil in the corridor, could not really be said to count—and then went to bed, determined to catch up on some of the sleep he'd lost over the past two nights.

He slept deeply but not restfully, his slumber disturbed by dreams in which Mr. and Mrs. Danvers stood once more at the foot of his bed, the latter saying something about a lady who was "growing impatient," and that they had best do "the thing"—whatever that was supposed to mean—sooner rather than later.

"He'll be too tall for the smokehouse," her husband observed. "It'll have to be the water again, or else the roof."

"No, not just yet," protested Mrs. Danvers. "We shall have to find another way. Has the new shipment come in?"

"The *Queen of the Orient* should've docked yesterday evening. If we haven't got our consignment by midafternoon, I'll go to the docks myself."

Pickett recognized the name. The *Queen of India* was one of Ludlow & Ludlow's ships. He'd never actually seen her—the *Queen* had still been on her months-long return voyage during his mercifully brief employment there—but a framed aquatint of the vessel had hung on the wall behind his desk. In spite of his unenviable position at the Larches, Pickett spared a thought of pity for the clerks who would have worked late into the night, cataloging her cargo.

"No, send Ned in your place," Mrs. Danvers was saying. "I have need of you here; someone must keep an eye on our client until the stock is replenished."

"Aye, but—" He broke off abruptly.

"Yes? What is it?"

"Nothing, I suppose. I thought I saw him blink, that's all."

She gave a skeptical snort. "I think it highly unlikely. His dinner contained enough to fell an ox. Depend upon it, he'll sleep the clock 'round." Her husband must have made some nonverbal expression of doubt, for she asked, more sharply this time, "What is it now?"

"I expect you're right, so far as the dosage goes, but that's only providing he's eating his dinner, and it's my belief that he's not. He's only pushing the food about on the plate, maybe putting some of it on the fire."

"If he persists in refusing to eat, he may resolve the problem for us. In the meantime, if he is putting it on the fire as you say, the smoke may have some effect. I shall send Ned to the docks to inquire after the shipment, and while he is gone, you can go up to the roof and block the chimney pot."

"Aye, but won't *he* notice when the room fills with smoke?"

"Certainly, he may notice," she agreed impatiently, then added, "although whether he will be in any state to do anything about it may be quite another matter."

"It won't do to take him too lightly," her husband cautioned. "This one's a fighter, he is."

"Then we shall have to take the fight out of him. You may leave everything to me."

Then slumber reclaimed him, and Pickett heard no more.

* * *

When he awoke the next morning with his head thick and stupid and his mouth as dry as cotton wool, he knew he'd been played for a fool. He'd allowed himself to eat very little since the night of Mr. Tomkins's murder, even though he'd detected no trace of the bitter taste that could not be completely hidden; instead, he'd put most of it onto the fire, a bit at a time to reduce the odor of burning food to a minimum, and pushed the rest around on the plate before sending it back to the kitchen. And having succeeded so far, he'd let down his guard when the tempting aroma of veal cutlets and rosemary gravy was too much to resist. He'd let himself let himself indulge, at least in part to lessen the sting of Julia's continued absence.

And now, too late, he realized his mistake. He made up his mind to eat nothing else prepared in the Larches' kitchens—nothing at all, not even a single bite, no matter how great the temptation.

He only hoped Julia would come soon, before he starved to death.

* * *

When there was still no sign of Julia by noon, Pickett decided a change of strategy was in order. Ignoring the complaints of his empty belly, he shrugged his banyan on over his nightshirt and left the room for the first time since his ignominious departure from Mrs. Danvers's office some thirty-six hours earlier. Mr. Danvers, still at his post in the corridor, fell into step behind him, but Pickett didn't care; he had more important things on his mind.

He led his escort down the stairs, across the hall to the front door (nodding a greeting to Sir Anthony Moring along the way), and out onto the portico. Here he paused and took a deep breath of chilly and decidedly damp autumn air. The clouds overhead threatened rain, but no matter; Pickett was on a mission, and he would have carried it out in the midst of a hurricane, if necessary.

He stepped off the portico and set out across the lawn with the slow, ambling gait of a man with no particular end in view, pausing at last near the horse chestnut tree that had provided Kit with such amusement the last time—the *only* time, in fact, at least so far—that he and Julia had come to visit. He idly rolled one of the conkers beneath his foot, then, as if on a sudden impulse, stooped and picked it up. He weighed it in his hand, tossed it up into the air and caught it once or twice, then scooped up two more and tossed them from hand to hand as he'd once seen a juggler do at

Bartholomew Fair.

"Would you care for a wager, Mr. Danvers?" he called to his guardian, having apparently tired of this amusement.

"What's that, sir?" asked that worthy, who, having hung back several feet, had been watching this display of skill with considerable interest.

"A wager," Pickett repeated.

Mr. Danvers shook his head. "I'd lose that one for sure. I can't do that—not but what it isn't fascinating to watch," he said with a trace of envy.

Pickett hastily demurred. "Oh no, I didn't mean that." He pointed toward the brick wall that surrounded the house and its grounds. "I'll wager you I can throw these things farther than you can."

His guardian's eyes gleamed with interest, but he saw one problem with the proposed scheme. "And what'll you wager? You've got no money, you've got no clothes—"

"I'll tell you what," Pickett said, with the air of one who has discovered the solution to a great difficulty, "if you win, I have to give you my pudding at dinner tonight."

Even without the prospect of signalling Julia, Pickett would have considered the contest worthwhile if only to see the expression on the man's face at the prospect of winning such a "prize." If he'd harbored any doubts that opium would be on the menu that night, that look would have settled them.

For the next ten minutes, the two men took turns hurling conkers at the wall. Pickett let his jailer win—he reckoned it was the least he could do, since Mr. Danvers had been so obliging as to help him leave a signal for his wife—and having settled this contest, they returned to the house, apparently in perfect charity with each other.

But when the rest of that day, and all of the next, passed with still no sign of Julia, he was considerably less smug.

It was not until the fourth day after Miss Bonner's departure that he began to admit to himself the possibility that Julia was not coming. The prospect brought with it a sense of panic. Had that witch, Mrs. Danvers, filled his wife's head with some nonsense about him and Miss Bonner? She might have tried—he certainly would not put it past her—but Julia surely must have known better! Even if Mrs. Danvers had described the scene in lurid detail, Julia would have recognized it at once as nothing more than a pretense to cover up, if not a botched escape attempt, then some other aspect of the case, which she knew had expanded to include the possible murder of Mr. Tomkins.

Now that he thought of it, he found it very likely that Julia would have heard the whole story from Miss Bonner herself, since the lady who had been both his quarry and his co-conspirator had been ordered from the premises in the aftermath of their discovery by Mrs. Danvers. Having gained her freedom (albeit not exactly in the way Pickett had intended), Miss Bonner would no doubt have gone straight to Curzon Street to inform Julia of his own predicament… wouldn't she?

Or was that it in a nutshell? Had Julia taken one look at the lady and, after hearing the story of their midnight rendez-vous from her own lips, drawn her own entirely erroneous conclusions? He supposed many men would find Miss Bonner attractive, especially if they liked their women cast in the battering-ram mold, but Julia must know better than to include him amongst their number. In fact, he pitied the poor sap on whom Miss Bonner eventually fixed her affections; the poor sap would find himself at the altar before he could say "Gretna Green." But Julia had somehow got into her head the ridiculous notion that her figure, increasingly rounded as her confinement drew nearer, made her unattractive. She was wrong, of course—nothing could be further from the truth, as he had assured her more than once—but feeling the way she did, the idea of his trysting with Miss Bonner even as a pretense might well have seemed a betrayal.

Depend upon it, he told himself, *she's getting a little of her own back by letting you stew a bit.*

The knowledge brought a sick feeling to the pit of his stomach. Mrs. Danvers thought Julia was paying a hefty sum to ensure that he did not survive the "cure" which admittance to the Larches supposedly offered. His being caught with Miss Bonner would only lend credence to this mistaken belief. And Julia, unaware of the true nature of the business conducted at the Larches, would not realize the need to correct the misunderstanding.

If she was trying to punish him for his supposed liaison with Miss Bonner, she just might succeed beyond her wildest dreams.

26

In Which John Pickett Receives a Shock

Of one thing Pickett was certain. He had no intention of meekly biding his time while Mr. and Mrs. Danvers decided how best to do away with him. Mrs. Danvers was certainly the dominant personality of that precious pair, and so it was with her that he intended to demand an audience. Any attempt to reach her by way of the corridor would, he knew, result in her hapless spouse trailing along behind and almost certainly remaining to make a third party in the conversation.

The Larches, however, had once been the private residence of a wealthy family, which meant there should be a jib door somewhere in the room that opened onto a concealed staircase by which, in more prosperous days, the servants would have accessed the various bedchambers without intruding upon the family or their guests. The daily girl (she must have a name, although he had never heard it mentioned) came and went by way of the corridor every morning when she brought up hot water and the day's supply of coal, but that meant only that the service stair was no longer in use, not that it didn't exist.

In fact, he felt a little foolish for not having remembered this useful architectural feature earlier; he had, after all, made use of just such a door almost every day during his investigation in Yorkshire the previous summer when he, in the guise of a footman, had slipped into Julia's room—rather, Lady Fieldhurst's room, as she had been at the time—almost daily, to report his findings and consult with her on their next course of action.

On second thought, it might be better that he had done nothing to betray any knowledge of a hidden stair; Mrs. Danvers would certainly have found some way to prevent his using it, and the fact that she had not taken such a precaution would now give him the advantage of surprise, allowing him to confront her unexpectedly while she thought him still confined to his room under her husband's watchful eye.

It remained only for him to find it. He was able to save some time by narrowing down to two the number of walls which might possibly contain the jib door; the wall containing the door to his bedchamber could obviously be ruled out, as any such door would of necessity open onto the corridor, and the wall into which the window was set could be likewise eliminated, as the outer wall was not thick enough to conceal such a feature. There remained only two walls, and as the fireplace took up most of one of these, Pickett began his quest on the one directly opposite.

He spent the next fifteen minutes with his ear pressed to

the wall, tapping upon the somewhat worm-eaten linenfold paneling and listening for the hollow sound that might indicate a cavity containing the service stair—a process that took longer than it should have, due to the necessity of conducting this experiment quietly enough that his guard in the corridor just outside would not hear and sound the alarm.

At last, just as he was conceding the necessity of sounding the fireplace wall, he rapped yet again upon the paneling and heard the faint reverberation that suggested an empty space on the other side. A few more taps in the same general area confirmed this theory, and Pickett turned his attention to finding the catch that would open the door. Relying more by feel than by sight, he ran his long, pick-pocket's fingers over the linenfold pattern carved into the wood until his sensitive fingertips found an irregularity. He pressed it, and heard the satisfying *snick* as the catch released. He pushed the panel inward, and the long-disused hinges groaned in protest as it swung open onto darkness.

Feeling more than a little pleased with himself, he turned back into the room only long enough to light his candle, then picked up the candlestick and returned to the service stair. He groped his way down the dusty and cobweb-strewn staircase one step at a time, holding his candle before him and ignoring the soft skittering noises that greeted his approach; clearly, the cat that had appointed itself his companion on his first such foray was not holding up her end of the bargain.

Upon reaching the foot of the stairs, he cautiously opened the door and peered around the corner into the kitchen. A stout woman in a white apron and cap stood at the deal table, briskly wielding a wooden spoon as she stirred the contents of a large bowl. Tonight's dinner, he assumed, wondering if it was she who added the opium, or if Mrs. Danvers did the honors herself.

Some slight noise must have betrayed him, for she abruptly looked up from her task.

"Lud, sir, you frightened me half to death! What are you doing down here? Look what a mess you've made of your fine robe!"

Pickett had no need to look, for he had been fully aware of the cobwebs that had clung to him as he'd made his descent. "Hallo, I seem to have lost my way." Pickett, trying to look the picture of innocent confusion, hoped she wouldn't stop to wonder how he had managed to get lost on what was essentially a hidden stair. "Can you tell me where I might find Mrs. Danvers?"

"She'll be upstairs, sir," the woman said, jabbing her spoon toward the ceiling over their heads. "She don't come downstairs to the kitchen, not much she don't."

In which case, Pickett thought, the cook very likely added the stuff to the dishes herself, before the butler took them upstairs to serve; in other words, he'd best not look to her for an ally.

He looked helplessly in first one direction and then the other. "Which way—how do I—?"

"Down the passage and to your left. Here,"—she left her spoon in the bowl and wiped her hands on a cloth—"I'll show you."

Apparently he'd overdone the confusion, and now she

thought he was a complete idiot.

"I don't want to put you to any trouble—"

"'Tis no trouble at all, sir. Only—"

"Only what?" he prompted, when she seemed disinclined to finish her thought.

"Only you might want to clean yourself up a bit first."

She handed him the cloth, and he wiped it across his face, feeling the scrape of the fabric against a jaw that had not been shaved in more than a se'nnight. Having made himself as presentable as possible, he followed the woman to the foot of a second stair that was wider and obviously more frequently used than the one leading down from the jib door in his room. He thanked her, and resolutely set his foot upon the first tread.

A very short time later, he rapped smartly upon the office door. Without waiting for an invitation, he opened it and strode into the room with the light of battle in his eyes. Mrs. Danvers sat at her desk bent over some papers, but looked up at his entrance.

"Well, Mr. Pickett?" If she was at all surprised by his sudden appearance, and without the watchdog she'd set over him, she didn't show it. In fact, her expression was more indicative of annoyance than distress. He would have to see if he couldn't do something about that.

"I want to send a message to my wife," he informed her in a voice that invited her to deny this request at her peril.

Alas, it was quite wasted. "Why didn't you say so? You had only to ask Mr. Danvers, and he would have furnished you with writing materials. I'm afraid today's post has already gone out, but if you will leave your letter on the piecrust table beside the front door when you've finished, I shall see that it is taken to the receiving office tomorrow."

Pickett shook his head. "Not tomorrow, and not by post. I want it delivered to her today."

"It may have escaped your notice, Mr. Pickett," she said coldly, "but we have a very small staff. I cannot spare anyone to run your personal errands."

"And,"—he continued as if she had not spoken—"I want an answer to my message, written in my wife's own handwriting, which I know by sight. Tell your man he is not to come back without it."

"I just told you why such a thing is impossible. Now, go back to your room at once before I—"

"Before you what? Pour laudanum down my throat? You told me I had been nothing but trouble since I came here; I can assure you, ma'am, I haven't even got started."

It was an empty threat. He could do very little without some link to the outside world—the link which Julia was to have provided. As matters now stood, Mrs. Danvers held all the cards in this particular game—and she knew it. He was trying to think how he might, if necessary, abandon an untenable position and still save face when, to his surprise, her demeanor completely changed. She regarded him with a look akin to pity, and rose from her chair with an air of resolution, as if she were determined to see a particularly unpleasant task through to completion.

"Very well, Mr. Pickett," she conceded, and it seemed to Pickett that her voice was almost gentle. Far from being reassured, the change made him doubly wary. "There is indeed more than I have seen fit to tell you, but we cannot discuss it here. Let us go for a walk, shall we?"

Pickett could only agree, and a short time later, they were traversing the same route across the lawn that he had taken with Julia a lifetime ago. It had rained in the night, and now a pale sun shone through the breaks in the dispersing clouds, turning to diamonds every drop of water clinging to each blade of grass. Less poetically, those same raindrops soon soaked the hem of his banyan halfway to his knees. He told himself this was a small price to pay, and made no complaint.

As they neared the ornamental pool where the body of Mr. Tomkins still lay in its watery grave, Pickett wondered fleetingly if Mrs. Danvers intended to shove him in, but dismissed this fanciful notion. Aside from the likelihood that a woman in her fifties would lack the physical strength to overpower a man half her age, there was the fact that Mrs. Danvers would have a very hard time explaining two bodies "accidentally" drowned in the same body of water within the space of a few days.

Sure enough, Mrs. Danvers did not lead him all the way down to the pool, but halted as they drew abreast of the copse of larches and the one lone horse chestnut, its vivid golden leaves, or what remained of them, now darkened to a shriveled brown.

"As you have surmised, Mr. Pickett," she began, "I have indeed been withholding information from you. I have been extremely reluctant to burden you with the unhappy truth when you have not yet finished your course of treatment, for I do believe you harbor some tender feelings for your wife in spite of recent evidence to the contrary."

Finished? Pickett couldn't tell any treatment had even begun. It was the reference to Julia, however, that caused his hackles to rise.

"Go on," he said tersely.

"Mr. Pickett, it pains me to inform you that your wife is dead."

27

In Which John Pickett Suffers a Relapse

Dimly aware of the pounding of his heart in his chest, Pickett could only stare at her.

It's the opium, he thought desperately, clinging to the thought as a drowning man might cling to a lifeline. *This isn't real; it's just the opium. None of this is real. Tomorrow Julia will come, and everything will be—*

"Mr. Pickett?" Mrs. Danvers's voice seemed to come from very far away. "Mr. Pickett, are you all right?"

She was clearly awaiting an answer, so he gave her the only one that made sense.

"You're lying."

"I realize this is hard to accept, Mr. Pickett—"

"How did she—" He couldn't bring himself to say the word, for saying it might make it so. "When did it happen?"

If he'd hoped to catch her in a lie by posing questions for which she would struggle to fabricate answers, he was doomed to disappointment.

"Three days ago, in childbirth. I'm afraid the infant died with her."

"The baby," he said, still struggling to make sense of it all. "Was it a—?" His throat closed, cutting off the question he'd intended to ask.

"A boy or a girl?" she suggested, guessing at the words that refused to come. "I don't believe I ever heard the baby's sex mentioned, but I can make inquiries, if you wish."

Pickett nodded distractedly, but his head was reeling. He had no reason at all to believe a single word this woman said. And yet, in a terrible sort of contradiction, it was the very vagueness of her answer that gave credence to her claim. If she was fabricating the tale out of whole cloth, it would have been easy enough for her to say either "boy" or "girl"; the fact that she had not done so suggested she was telling the truth.

"Mother and child were interred together at St. George's burial ground in Bayswater," she continued, just as if the world had not come to an end. "In your absence, I believe a family member took charge of making the arrangements."

"Her sister, most likely," he put in, marveling at the fact that his voice should be so steady when he wanted to curl up and howl like a wounded animal. She was gone—dead and buried—and he'd never even had a chance to say goodbye.

It's not true, his stunned brain insisted. *It can't possibly be true.*

And yet…

Julia had considered just such an eventuality from the very beginning, had even made provisions for the child's upbringing, given that the jointure from her first marriage which comprised most of their income would end with her death. Had she known something even then? Had she been trying to tell him something that he had refused to see, because he hadn't wanted to know?

"I know I've given you a great deal to think about, Mr. Pickett," Mrs. Danvers said soothingly, patting his arm. "I shall leave you in peace now. Pray take as long as you need before returning to the house. I believe we can dispense with Mr. Danvers's companionship for the nonce."

Peace? Pickett hardly heard the rest of this speech, focused as he was on the incongruity of the word. Did she really think it was *peace* he felt after such a revelation?

He watched without seeing as Mrs. Danvers retraced her steps back up the slope to the house. *It's not true. It can't possibly be true.*

And yet…

What else could explain Julia's prolonged absence? She had hated the idea of him coming here, had vehemently opposed the very suggestion. She would never have left him here—at least, not on purpose. Her prolonged absence was the most compelling evidence of the truth of Mrs. Danvers's claim.

But surely he would have known, would have *felt* it somehow, if Julia was no longer among the living. Three days, the woman had said. She'd been gone for three days, and yet life had gone on, just as if nothing had changed. A world without Julia in it should look different somehow. The sun should refuse to shine, and the birds no longer sing. And all the plants would die, he added mentally. He kicked at the dead leaves on the ground, and a glossy brown horse chestnut rolled beneath his foot.

I'll just throw a couple of these over the wall...

You had it all planned, didn't you? the memory accused him. *Nothing could be simpler. Just throw a couple of conkers over the wall, and Julia will come running to the rescue.*

Except that he had, and Julia had not come. And now she was gone and he was trapped here and no one would know to get him out, not if he were to throw a hundred conkers over the wall, and it didn't matter anyway, for even if he could return to Curzon Street that very minute it wouldn't be the same. Julia wouldn't be there, would never be there again.

On a sudden impulse, he snatched up a conker, and then another, and threw them one after the other over the wall. And suddenly, overwhelmed by mingled despair, remorse, and self-loathing, he was snatching them up by the handful and hurling them at the wall with all the force he could muster, more and more of them, until none were left and he was collapsed, exhausted and spent, upon the ground with his cheek pressed to the dead grass.

* * *

Pickett could not remember dragging himself to his feet and trudging back up the sloping lawn to the house. Nor could he recall stumbling up the stairs to his own room, or witnessing what must have been the startled expression on the face of his watchdog upon seeing his return.

Still, he must certainly have done all these things, for he awoke some time later to find himself lying on the bed. The sky beyond his window was growing dark, but the room was illuminated by the flickering light of a fire he could not remember lighting.

Pickett sat up so quickly that his head swam. *It was only a dream,* he thought, weak with relief. *It was nothing but a dream. Julia is perfectly well, and will be coming any day now to—*

His gaze fell on his banyan, draped across the laddered back of the straight chair drawn up to the hearth with its back to the fire. Both the garment and its makeshift clotheshorse appeared somewhat blurry, as if he were peering through a fog. No, not a fog; a haze of smoke. He'd never known the chimney to smoke before—certainly not so badly as this—but there was a distinct cloud hanging over the room that seemed to be emanating from the fireplace, giving the familiar scene an eerie sense of unreality.

One detail, however, was entirely too clear.

The hem of his banyan was fully twelve inches deep in soft wet earth to which tiny bits of dead grass and crushed leaves clung. A further dusting of grass and leaves covered the entire front of the garment, as though its wearer had lain down full length on his belly upon the rain-bedewed earth.

No.

But even as his brain shied away from the sight, he knew what it meant. Here was proof, beyond any hope of doubt, that the nightmare was real. Numbly, he turned away from the undeniable evidence and saw that, with the ladder-backed chair pressed into service as a clotheshorse, he had an uninterrupted view of the item that had been placed on the writing table, the item that had not been there before.

For in the center of the table stood an empty glass and a tall black bottle, the contents of the latter glowing deepest crimson in the firelight.

He could not simply give up and let the Larches have its way with him, tempting as the prospect seemed, for there were things he must attend to, things he could not do while he remained in residence here. Kit would have to be looked after, and the house in Curzon Street closed up and sold, for he could not afford its upkeep. The servants, whose wages he could no longer pay, must be dismissed, albeit not before he'd given them the references they would need to find positions elsewhere. Worst of all, he must go through Julia's personal belongings—her clothes, her jewelry, her silver-backed hairbrushes and toilet articles, and all the tiny garments she had so lovingly made in preparation for the birth of their child—and decide what to do with them.

Right now, though, he could not face the thought. Right now, he wanted only to forget—the recent past and Mrs. Danvers's horrible disclosure; the bleak present; and the once-promising future that now yawned before him, desolate and empty.

He picked up the bottle with shaking hands and poured a generous measure into the glass.

* * *

The corpse, in the meantime, was looking remarkably fit for a dead woman, albeit sadly pulled when compared to her previously blooming health. Kit's fever was gone, but it had left him weak and lethargic.

None of his previous ailments had been met with

sympathy, much less tenderness, and he found it a novel experience. It was really quite pleasant to sit up in bed braced with pillows at one's back while one's sister-in-law plied one with cups of chocolate or glasses of lemonade or even, on one occasion, a pistachio ice from Gunter's, served in its own little covered porcelain container to keep it from melting between Berkeley Square and Curzon Street. To do the boy justice, he did not intend to inconvenience Julia; it simply never crossed his mind that the procurement and delivery of these treats must require her to navigate two flights of stairs, at just the time when she was least equipped for so strenuous an activity.

Having left Kit listlessly marching his toy soldiers through a mountain pass somewhere in the Pyrenees (as represented by a blanket draped loosely over his drawn-up knees), Julia closed the door softly behind her and wondered whether she might have time to lie down for a bit before his next summons. As she was frequently plagued by backaches —the littlest Pickett had, she reflected, a great deal to answer for—even five minutes would be a welcome reprieve. Before she could put this plan into practice, however, she was interrupted by Rogers.

"Begging your pardon, ma'am, but there is a young lady below who wishes to see you," he said, then corrected himself. "That is, she wishes to see the young master, but upon being informed that he was not at home, she asked if she might see you instead."

"I understand," said Julia, who did not, in fact, understand why a young lady should be desirous of seeing her husband, and was not at all sure she liked them calling for such a purpose. "Does this young lady have a name?"

"Forgive me, ma'am," the butler amended hastily. "I should have said at once that she calls herself Miss Bonner."

"Oh!" Julia's eyes grew wide. Small wonder, then, that Rogers should appear discomposed. She did not question his recognition of the lady's name, or the significance it held for the Pickett household; servants, even those who would never stoop to such tactics as listening at keyholes, had an almost preternatural knowledge of the goings-on of the families they served. "Pray show her into the drawing room and tell her I shall join her there directly."

As Rogers departed on this errand, Julia hurried down the stairs to the next floor down, where her bedchamber was situated, and regarded with a critical eye her appearance in the mirror. Nothing could be done about the bulge of her abdomen (at least, not for a few weeks), but she could at least run a brush through her hair and re-pin it. Having made this repair to her appearance, she pinched her pale cheeks to give them color, then descended the stairs to the drawing room, and the young woman who owed her freedom to Julia's own husband.

Miss Bonner rose from the sofa as the mistress of the house entered the room, and Julia blinked at the most striking lady she had ever seen. Fully six feet tall and built along Rubenesque lines, she had glossy black hair topped with a modish hat whose single ostrich feather curved down from its brim to caress her cheek. Her blue velvet pelisse was obviously the creation of an expert modiste, and she'd had the wisdom to eschew the frills and furbelows that would have made her statuesque form appear ridiculous. In fact, she looked nothing like a lady who could be held against her will, and still less like one who had only just escaped such a captivity.

Her eyes, of so dark a blue that they appeared almost violet, held a glint of amusement that Julia could not quite like, as if the woman knew exactly what she was thinking, and enjoyed confounding her expectations.

"Miss Bonner," Julia said, approaching her caller with outstretched hands. "How kind of you to call."

"Mrs. John Pickett, I presume," the lady responded in kind, and it seemed to Julia as if her eyebrows rose slightly at the evidence of the coming blessed event. "I'm pleased to meet you."

"And I you," Julia returned. "Do, pray, sit down, and I shall ring for tea."

She suited the word to the deed, and soon both ladies were ensconced upon adjacent sofas and regarding one another somewhat warily, like combatants on the field of honor.

"It's good to see that you appear to be none the worse for your adventures," Julia observed.

"No, none the worse," agreed her guest. "In fact, I consider that I am a great deal better for knowing the truth, however unpleasant it may be."

Julia, all at sea, merely nodded, and waited for the lady to elaborate. Alas, her next words were no more illuminating.

"I'm sure Mr. Pickett knows what he is about, and I hate to complain when I am so very much obliged to him, but I don't know how much longer I can keep putting Edward off, and my aunt has begun to ask the most awkward questions!

Have you any idea when he intends to take some action?"

Julia could only stare at her, hardly knowing where to start. The fact that her visitor clearly expected her to understand this cryptic utterance only made it all the more incomprehensible.

"Miss Bonner," she said at last, "when did—how long, precisely, has it been since my husband—since Mr. Pickett—exactly how long has it been since you escaped from the Larches?"

Miss Bonner loosed a merry peal of laughter. "I would hardly call it an 'escape,' although I suppose the end result was the same."

"If it wasn't an escape, then how did you win free?"

"Has he not told you, then? A wise man, I'm sure! I'm hesitant to give him away, lest you make him sleep on the sofa."

"I wish you will stop being coy!" Julia said, her patience having very nearly reached its limit. "Pray tell me plainly: How long has it been since you left the Larches?"

"Why, more than a se'nnight—nine days, to be exact," she said, clearly puzzled by her hostess's vehemence. "But surely you must know; after all, Mr. Pickett—"

"Mr. Pickett"—Julia kept her voice steady with an effort—"has not yet returned home."

"He—he hasn't—" The smile was banished from Miss Bonner's face, but Julia took no pleasure in the sight. "He's still there?"

"So far as I know, he is still in residence at the Larches."

" 'So far as you know?' " Miss Bonner echoed in shocked

disbelief. "Do you mean to tell me you haven't called even once in the last week?"

"On the contrary," retorted Julia indignantly, "I have called there repeatedly, ever since I discovered his coat in the window of a secondhand clothing shop! But Mrs. Danvers steadfastly refused to let me see him, and then Kit got sick, and—but *nine days*, you said?"

"Mrs. Danvers banished me from the premises, so naturally I thought she must have done the same to him; after all, she caught us together."

"Caught you trying to escape together?" Julia asked, still struggling to make sense of it all.

"Not exactly. Oh, we would have escaped eventually, but we'd discovered some curious circumstances we wanted to investigate first."

Not so very long ago it had been she who had assisted her husband with his investigations, and now, hearing this self-possessed young woman refer to herself and John as "we" filled Julia with envy. The lady's next words, however, drove such petty jealousies from her mind.

"Mrs. Pickett, are you aware that Mrs. Danvers believes you are paying her to murder your husband?"

28

In Which Julia Is Spurred into Action

Miss Bonner, you cannot be serious!" exclaimed Julia, half laughing. "Mrs. Danvers and her husband help opium-eaters overcome their dependence on the poppy."

"That is certainly what they want outsiders to think," agreed Miss Bonner. "And it may be true that they do help certain individuals. Sir Anthony Moring, poor lamb, takes the cure quite regularly. And it seems to work for a time, at least until the siren song of laudanum becomes too much for him to resist. But aside from that, the establishment is a most convenient place to put inconvenient relatives, especially those with large fortunes to bestow who refuse to be so obliging as to cock up their toes in a timely fashion. If you doubt it, you need look no further than Mr. George Daniel Tomkins, who seemingly became so desperate for the substance that he fled the premises under cover of darkness. Depend upon it, we shall soon learn that he has met with a tragic accident, and that a distraught nephew or cousin has appeared just in time to inherit all the poor man's worldly goods. That is Mr. Pickett's prediction, and I think he is probably right."

As Miss Bonner expounded upon her extraordinary claim, every drop of color drained from Julia's face. It made a terrible sort of sense: the death of Mr. Tomkins as witnessed by her own husband, whose tailcoat had unexpectedly appeared "too soon" in a secondhand clothing store…

With an effort, she dragged her attention back to the matter at hand. "Are you saying that your aunt and uncle tried to—first your brother, and now you—"

"My aunt and uncle are two of the kindest people who ever lived," Miss Bonner assured her. "It is true that my aunt was the one who signed the papers admitting my brother—for Philip was underage, you know—but she did so on the recommendation of Edward Poole. And unless I much mistake my guess, it was he who introduced Philip to the pleasures of opium in the first place."

"But—but Mr. Poole engaged my husband to rescue you from that place!"

Miss Bonner gave her a pitying look. "I'm afraid Edward led Mr. Pickett straight up the garden path. Yes, he did indeed want me out of there, but it was because I admitted myself as a patient—unlike my brother, I am no longer a minor, you know—in order to discover what I could about poor Philip's death. And 'discover' we did, your husband and I—enough to make more than a few people swing."

"But even if what you say is true, how could Mrs. Danvers possibly think I wanted to do away with Mr. Pickett?

He has no fortune, so what could I possibly hope to gain?"

"No fortune, perhaps, but there are other reasons a woman might wish her husband out of the way." Her gaze dropped to the swell of Julia's abdomen. "If, for instance, a lady had a lover and was carrying his child—a child whose birth would almost certainly betray the fact that her husband was *not* its father—"

The very idea was absurd…and yet Julia did not feel like laughing. Certain of Mrs. Danvers's comments had been curious, to say the least, while a few of the provisos in the contract she'd been required to sign took on a sinister significance when viewed in the light of this new and terrible possibility.

She grabbed the arm of the sofa and levered herself to her feet. "Miss Bonner, I am deeply obliged to you, truly I am, but if what you say is true, then Mr. Pickett's life is in imminent danger. I know it is shockingly rude of me to ask you to leave, but I must go to the Larches without further delay. Pray forgive me, and let me tell you again how deeply I stand in your debt."

"Of course," Miss Bonner assured her warmly, as Julia accompanied her as far as the door. She stepped out onto the portico, then turned back to give her hostess a measuring look. "I've half a mind to take him away from you, you know. I feel it only fair to warn you."

And with this Parthian shot, she stepped off the portico, then turned and headed up Curzon Street toward Berkeley Square, leaving Julia staring after her in sputtering indignation.

* * *

She did not remain motionless for long. By the time Miss Bonner reached Curzon Street's northward bend, Julia had already rung for Andrew the footman, sent for the carriage to be brought 'round, and consigned her young patient to Rogers's care. Still, it seemed like an eternity before she reached Islington, and longer still before the brick wall that surrounded the Larches finally hove into view.

In the meantime, she dared not indulge in idle speculation as to her husband's health and safety, for that way lay madness. Instead, she focused her thoughts on what course of action to follow once she got there, and by the time she glimpsed the wall in the distance, she had formed a plan. Before bearding the lioness in her den, she would look for the signal Pickett had promised to leave if he should have need of her. If she discovered a conker or two where none could have occurred naturally, she would know how to deal with Mrs. Danvers.

"Set me down just before we reach the wall," she called to the coachman. "I want to walk a little distance down the road. No, Andrew, I shan't need you to accompany me. The road is a private one—it is part of the property—so there should be no other traffic."

She accepted Andrew's proffered hand and stepped down from the carriage, then set off alone down the dirt track that gave access to the rear of the property.

At first, she saw nothing in the lane but a thick carpet of leaves: dry, dead leaves of a reddish-brown hue. As she drew nearer, however, her steps grew slower and slower until at last she stopped, staring in sick dread at the road before her. What she had taken for dead leaves were in fact horse chestnuts. Dozens, perhaps even hundreds of them, in a place they could not possibly have fallen, not even in a strong wind…

She could not have said how long she stood there, motionless, staring dumbly at the horse chestnuts covering the ground, before her benumbed brain finally registered the need for action. Turning away with an effort, she hurried back up the lane with all the speed she could muster, pausing only long enough to utter two short words to the coachman.

"Bow Street!" she commanded, then grabbed Andrew's hand in a viselike grip, levered herself into the carriage, and collapsed upon the seat.

They reached Bow Street in very good time, the coachman having been urged by his passenger (several times) not to spare the horses. Even so, Julia flung open the door and leaped down before it had fully rolled to a stop, drawing a protest from Andrew, then burst through the door of Number Four without waiting for him to open it for her. Once inside, she headed straight for the magistrate's bench, all the while unburdening herself of a disjointed speech in which laudanum, horse chestnuts, coffee-stained tailcoats, ornamental pools, dead bodies, and John Pickett all strove for prominence.

"Easy, Mrs. Pickett," said the magistrate in soothing accents. "Step into my office, and you can sit down and tell me all about it. Mr. Yates," he called to someone beyond her left shoulder, "a cup of tea for Mrs. Pickett, if you please."

"I've no time for tea!" Julia insisted impatiently. "I'm sure I should choke on it!"

"Nevertheless, you shall sit down and catch your breath,"

he said in that tone of voice with which, as any of his men could have told her, it was useless to argue. "It can't be good for you to distress yourself like this."

"Oh, if it were only *myself*—!"

Still, there was something oddly reassuring about his authoritative manner, and Julia found herself sinking obediently onto the chair facing his desk, and even accepting a cup of tea from the fine-boned hands of a stripling who was surely not yet out of his teens.

"Close the door on your way out, Mr. Yates," ordered Mr. Colquhoun.

"Yes, sir," responded the youth, and did so.

"Now then, Mrs. Pickett," he said, once they were alone, "you may tell me what is troubling you. I gather it concerns your scapegrace of a husband."

Thus adjured, she took a deep breath and began. "Yes. I suppose you know about John's being engaged to extricate a young woman from an asylum for opium-eaters."

"Aye, he told me as much. I believe he had the fixed intention of entering the place himself under the pretense of taking the cure."

"He did," agreed Julia. "He has been there for the last fortnight, and it appears he may have got himself into a great deal more than he bargained for."

"Now why," Mr. Colquhoun wondered aloud, "does that not surprise me?"

"The last time I saw him, he told me he'd watched from his window as two men led a third down to the ornamental pool just inside the gates and threw him in. The man's lack of resistance, and the fact that he appeared to be wearing only his nightshirt, led John to think the man had been drugged—he had reason to believe that dinner the previous night had been laced with opium—and then murdered. But John had eaten some of that same dish, and so he wasn't certain if he'd really seen it, or if it had been a hallucination. When that same man was absent the next day, having purportedly run away during the night, he was almost certain he'd witnessed a murder."

The magistrate listened in silence, his only response being the gradual meeting of bushy white eyebrows over the bridge of his nose.

"Go on," he said, when she stopped to gauge his reaction.

"Yes, well," she continued, "he told me he intended to dive into the pool the next day, to see if the man's body was actually there. The pool has been shockingly neglected, so a body might lie there undetected for years, provided it was"—she shuddered at the mental image conjured by her own words—"was properly weighted, to prevent its bobbing back up to the surface,"

"And what did he find?"

"I don't know. I haven't been allowed to see him again, although I called there almost every day, at least until Kit had a reaction to his smallpox inoculation."

If it were possible, the magistrate's frown grew even more forbidding. "I won't lie to you, Mrs. Pickett; I don't like the sound of it."

"Nor do I, but as it turns out, that isn't the half of it." She took a fortifying sip of tea, then recounted, as nearly as she could remember it, Miss Bonner's astounding claims concerning the true nature of the business conducted at the Larches.

"And you say it's been nine days since Miss Bonner made her escape?"

"That is what she told me. Mrs. Danvers ordered her from the premises, and Miss Bonner assumed that John had been dismissed in the same fashion. As I understand it, they were discovered in the act of searching through Mrs. Danvers's files, and were obliged to—to feign an amorous intrigue."

Mr. Colquhoun's countenance lightened somewhat. "I daresay Mrs. Danvers isn't the only lady who'll have something to say about that."

Julia attempted a laugh, which turned halfway through into a sob. "I confess, that was my first reaction, but if only he is safe, I—I shan't utter a word of reproach!"

"Never fear, Mrs. Pickett, I believe he's still safe, at least for the nonce. They won't want too many deaths occurring too close together." The bushy brows drew together again. "In fact, I believe your husband may have suspected something of the kind already, given the number of tragic accidents and suicides amongst the residents, and that was why he wanted the records of the coroner's inquests. I'm afraid I didn't give his suspicions the consideration they deserved, but perhaps, being forewarned, he'll be on his guard against any attempt on his own life."

He had turned away to rummage through one of the desk drawers as he spoke, and Julia, fearful of being dismissed, pleaded, "Can't you at least go and get him out of there?"

Having found the paper he sought, he had dipped a quill in ink and begun to write, but at her plea, he paused and looked up. “I intend to do a great deal more than that, but not without a warrant. I don’t think Mr. and Mrs. Danvers would allow me to order a search of the pool without it, nor would they take kindly to one of my men taking a dip without permission. Now,” he added, with a twinkle in his blue eyes, “I wonder how well Mr. Carson can swim?”

29

In Which a Rescue Is Effected

Having taken the carriage, Julia and Mr. Colquhoun, drew up adjacent to the Larches' elaborately scrolled and sadly rusted front gates, where the magistrate spied out the lay of the land while he awaited the arrival of his men, who were following behind on foot.

"It's a fine old place, or once was," he remarked. "A pity it's fallen into such a state."

Julia recalled that this had been her own first impression; now she could happily watch it burn to the ground, provided John was got out of it first.

"I assume these gates are no longer used," the magistrate continued. Climbing down from the carriage, he strode over to the gates in question and rattled them ineffectually, confirming his assumption.

"There is a second gate, a tradesman's entrance at the rear," she called to him from the vehicle. "There had been a third, on the south side, but it has long since been bricked up."

"Very well, then." Mr. Colquhoun returned to the carriage and climbed in beside her. "Shall we go?"

"Let's!" Julia said with feeling, and gave the order.

The carriage started forward with a jolt, rolling slowly past the disused gate—through which Julia peered in vain for some glimpse of her husband—and turned in through the entrance on the back side of the house. They took the fork that curved around the end of the house to the front door, and within a very short time, Mr. Colquhoun was handing her down from the vehicle.

"I understand this lady has been asking to see her husband," he informed the stout, somewhat seedy-looking man who opened the door to their knock.

"Oh, er, you will want to speak to my wife, then," he said, darting an uneasy glance over his shoulder. "Come with me, and we'll see if she is in her office, shall we?"

The question was purely rhetorical, for he had already turned away, leading them to the small room to which, Julia felt, she could have by this time found her way blindfolded.

"Mr. Danvers," she murmured to Mr. Colquhoun, who nodded in understanding.

"My dear," their host called, scratching lightly on the closed door. "Here is Mrs. Pickett again. This time she's brought a—a friend," he added, glancing uncertainly toward the magistrate as if trying to ascertain the relationship between the two visitors.

"Very well, show them in." Her displeasure could be heard even through the wooden panel.

Mr. Danvers complied. Mr. Colquhoun ushered Julia into

the office before him, then strode boldly up to the woman's desk.

"I believe this lady has been trying to visit her husband, and has been repeatedly denied," he said in a voice that dared their hostess to do so again at her own risk.

Mrs. Danvers did not rise, but looked up from the open ledger on her desk with a little sigh of irritation. "Indeed, she has, and I have told her repeatedly that to disrupt his course of treatment at this point could have irretrievable consequences. Although exactly how this concerns you, Mr.—?"

"Colquhoun," said the magistrate, offering his hand. "Patrick Colquhoun, magistrate of the Bow Street Public Office."

"Mr. Colquhoun." She accepted the proffered handshake, but it seemed to Julia that her voice now contained a note of wariness that had not been there before.

"Ah, yes, his course of treatment. I would like to learn more about this treatment you offer."

"As I have told your…friend"—her gaze shifted from the magistrate to Julia and back again—"my methods have been carefully developed over years of experimentation. I cannot and will not divulge them for the sake of idle curiosity."

"Oh, but you misunderstand me, ma'am!" Mr. Colquhoun protested. "It isn't merely idle curiosity, but keen interest in a unique business practice. You seem to have hit upon a very unusual way of earning a living, Mrs. Danvers."

The woman bristled as if she'd been insulted. "Well, and what if I have? Can you wonder at it? My father's dependence upon opium, and the decisions he made—or rather, did *not* make—while under its influence cost me everything. *Everything*, do you hear? I was once an attractive young woman; I might have married a peer of the realm. But no! I was obliged to wed Father's steward—my hand in marriage in lieu of the wages he could no longer afford to pay. Not that Mr. Danvers profited much by it, for my dowry was long gone—and it was no more than he deserved, a man so weak-willed that he dared not gainsay my father, no matter how reckless or how negligent were the orders he was instructed to carry out! After Father died, it was not my husband, but *I* who contrived to save this house and most of its furnishings from the auctioneer's hammer, although it cost me every last farthing of what remained. Since I owed my near-penury to the seed of the poppy, why should I not repair Father's depredations on the estate by turning it into an asylum for those who are in thrall to it just as he was?"

"I can think of no reason at all," Mr. Colquhoun assured her, although the sympathy in his voice was underlain with steel. "In fact, I should call such a plan admirable, perhaps even noble. But I was speaking of your other, more lucrative source of income."

"I don't know what you're talking about!" sputtered Mrs. Danvers, but the note of fear that had crept into her voice suggested otherwise.

Mr. Colquhoun's gaze shifted to the wall at her back, where the large wooden cabinet (source of so much clandestine interest) was flanked by tall windows. The heavy brocade curtains had been drawn back, and through the window on the right he could see Harry Carson approaching the ornamental water with a length of toweling draped over his shoulder.

"Do you not?" the magistrate asked. "Perhaps my man will discover something in the pool that may refresh your memory."

She whirled toward the window and saw Carson, who had cast aside his towel and was now shucking off his coat. When she turned back to the magistrate, her eyes were wild, her face livid. "How dare you, sirrah?"

"Very easily." Mr. Colquhoun extracted a folded paper from the inside pocket of his coat and handed it across the desk. "This is a general warrant allowing my officer to search this house and its grounds, including the body of water beyond that window. Would you care to hazard any guesses as to what he might find there?"

"He will find nothing!" she rasped. "Nothing, do you hear me? I must insist that you put an end to this gross imposition at once, or I'll—I'll—"

"You'll what?" asked Mr. Colquhoun, his tone indicative of nothing more than mild interest. "Haul me before the magistrate, perhaps? Or dose me with laudanum and have your henchman—forgive me; your husband—toss me into the water with the poor blighter who disappeared a se'nnight past?"

"I tell you, I don't know what you're talking about!" she reiterated, although her restless hands, clenching and unclenching at nothing, gave the lie to this declaration.

Mr. Colquhoun ignored her, turning instead to address the two officers who had just entered the office, the wide-eyed Mr. Yates looking impossibly small next to Mr. Maxwell, fully twice the youth's age and with an erect military bearing into the bargain.

"Ah, there you are. This lady is going to take me to Mr. Pickett. Mr. Yates, stay here with Mrs. Pickett. Mr. Maxwell, if Mr. Danvers should return to this room, nab him. I shall be back directly. Mrs. Danvers?"

He made a sweeping gesture toward the door, inviting her to lead the way. The lady, however, had other ideas.

"I won't! I will not allow you to jeopardize a process that has taken almost a fortnight to achieve, all because this foolish young woman"—she darted an impatient glance at Julia—"is having second thoughts!"

Nor was she alone in her objections to this plan; she had a rather unexpected ally.

"I'm going with you," Julia insisted, clutching the magistrate's sleeve.

He patted her hand, and when he spoke, it was with unwonted gentleness. "You may not like what you find," he cautioned her.

Julia swallowed hard, and her throat worked. "Yes. I know."

He regarded her silently for a long moment. "Very well, then," he said at last, then turned his attention back to his men. "Mr. Maxwell, Mrs. Pickett and I are going to pay a long-delayed call on her husband. Since Mrs. Danvers has declined to accompany us, you will see that she waits here. Mr. Yates, you have your occurrence book on you, do you not? Good lad! Take down every word this woman utters, beginning with that fortnight-long 'process' she just mentioned."

Having given his orders, he turned to Julia and gestured for her to precede him. She needed no second invitation. She snatched up her skirts and, in spite of her delicate condition, hurried out of the office and up the stairs with a speed that left Mr. Colquhoun's older legs far behind.

"His room overlooks the front lawn," she called over her shoulder to him, "so we need not waste time on those facing the back." Unless, of course, Mrs. Danvers had moved him to another room, realizing that this location allowed him to see far too much. Should they have asked first? Would Mrs. Danvers have given them an answer—an honest one—even if they had?

Having reached the landing, she stopped at the first door she came to and pounded on the panel.

"John! John, are you in there? Can you hear me? John!"

Receiving no answer, she tried the door and, finding it unlocked, opened it a crack and peered inside. The room was empty. The bed had been stripped of its linens, and the curtains at the single window were tightly closed, casting the bare little chamber into stygian gloom. She closed the door and ran down the corridor. Mr. Colquhoun was pounding on the next door, so she passed him and stopped at the one after that.

"John! John, are you in there?"

They repeated this process up corridor and down, on both sides of the wide central staircase, Julia berating herself all the while for not asking John, on that occasion when they'd walked down the slope to the water, to point out the window of the room to which he'd been assigned.

And then, after closing the door on yet another vacant room, Julia drew abreast of the door the magistrate had just opened, from which a cloud of smoke billowed. This curious circumstance caught her attention, and she glanced toward the opening.

This room, unlike its fellows, was not unoccupied. A gaunt, bearded derelict in a filthy nightshirt lay sprawled upon the narrow bed with one arm hanging over the edge of the mattress, the fingers of his left hand—long, slender, and surprisingly beautiful—just grazing the carpet. Muttering a somewhat sheepish apology (to which the occupant appeared to be oblivious), Mr. Colquhoun began to pull the door closed.

"*John!*" Julia cried in a choked voice. Pushing past the magistrate, she fell to her knees beside the unprepossessing figure on the bed, then caught up the limp hand in both of her own and began covering it with kisses. "Oh, my darling, what have they done to you?"

"Good God!" exclaimed Mr. Colquhoun, entering the room in her wake. "I never would have known him!"

"John, can you hear me?" pleaded Julia, ignoring this interruption. "Wake up, darling, please! John!"

He rolled onto his back and his eyes fluttered open, dull, unseeing eyes of brown, the pupils scarcely larger than pin-points. His hand slipped from her grasp, and he covered his eyes with his forearm. "Oh, God, no!" he groaned, turning away.

She had been prepared for almost anything but this, and found it even more disturbing than the oblivion in which she'd found him. "John, do you not know me?" Cupping his bristly jaw in her hands, she very gently turned his head back to face her. "It's me—Julia," she said ungrammatically. "Your wife."

"Julia?" He blinked, trying to focus his contracted gaze upon her. "You—you're alive?"

"Very much so—although," she added darkly, "Mrs. Danvers won't be, not if I can get my hands on her."

"She said—she said—" His voice broke, his throat working as he fought for control.

"What did she say, darling?"

"She told me you were dead."

Julia put her arms around him and drew him to her until his head rested in the curve of her neck. "It was very wicked of her," she said soothingly, stroking his matted hair as she might have done Kit's during his recent illness, "but as you can see, I am very much alive. We—Mr. Colquhoun and I," she added, acknowledging the magistrate with a quick glance over her shoulder, "we've come to take you home, darling."

"And—and Miss Bonner?"

"She is perfectly safe," Julia assured him, although it struck her like a knife to the heart, to know that that brazen young woman occupied his thoughts even at such a time as this. But the query sprang from his sense of duty, she reminded herself, not from any more tender attachment. In any case, she owed Miss Bonner a considerable debt, she acknowledged, somewhat grudgingly giving credit where it was due. But her sense of obligation did *not* extend to sharing her husband with another woman, and if Miss Bonner thought otherwise, she would soon learn her mistake; Julia had fought far more threatening enemies for his sake, from her first husband's disapproving family to John's own sense of unworthiness. In the meantime, she would not imbue the question with more significance than it deserved.

"In fact," she continued, "it was she who told me what they actually do here at the Larches. It was very clever of you to have discovered it."

"Look here," put in Mr. Colquhoun, having tried and failed to open the window, "we've got to get you out of this confounded smoke. Can you walk, do you think, or shall I send Maxwell and Carson to fetch you down?"

Whether by happy coincidence or design, the magistrate could not have named any men more likely to inspire his young protégé to try his own legs.

"I can walk," Pickett said, although in a voice so feeble that Mr. Colquhoun might have been forgiven for doubting this declaration.

"Excellent!" he pronounced, adding, with rare tact, "Now, if you two will excuse me, I'll go downstairs and relieve Mr. Maxwell."

He suited the word to the deed, but neither of the Picketts displayed any eagerness to leave the smoke-filled room. Pickett sat somewhat gingerly upright, but only so that he might pull Julia onto his knee and bury his face once more in the curve of her neck, murmuring inane observations to the effect that she was, in fact, alive. Julia's actions were no more sensible, for she only held him close and crooned "oh, John…oh, John…" into his dirty hair.

At last, spurred, no doubt, by the prospect of Maxwell and Carson arriving to carry him bodily down the stairs,

Pickett reluctantly released her.

"Let's go home," he said, and although they were only three little words, they carried a world of meaning.

"Gladly," Julia agreed, leaving his side only long enough to remove his banyan from the back of a chair. "Ugh!" she grimaced, eyeing with disfavor this garment, whose appearance, like that of its owner, had not been improved by its stay at the Larches. "Do you suppose it will ever come clean?"

She held it open, and he slipped his arms into the sleeves. "If Thomas can do that, he deserves a rise in his wages." Pickett said over his shoulder, giving her a rather weak smile that made her heart turn over nonetheless.

They had taken two somewhat shaky steps toward the door when Pickett bethought himself of his hidden stash.

"Under the mattress," he said, turning back. "I've got a notebook—"

"Never mind, I'll get it," Julia said.

She looked beneath the mattress, and her eyes grew wide. Here was not only the familiar notebook in which he'd kept notes on his findings, but also the letter, never delivered, that he'd written for her to take to Mr. Colquhoun, along with two thick files, these last marked *Philip Henry Bonner* and *George Daniel Tomkins*. He would, of course, wish to turn these over to the magistrate, but in the meantime, she had matters of her own to attend to, matters no less important, and infinitely sweeter. And so she matched her steps to his as they quitted the room and made their painstaking way up the corridor and down the staircase, her arm wrapped about his waist and his draped across her shoulders.

"Julia?" he began, stopping just inside the wide double doors to catch his breath.

"Yes, darling?"

He looked down at her with his heart in his eyes. "I knew you wouldn't leave me here," he said, and together they stepped out onto the portico, leaving for the last time the dilapidated country house known as the Larches.

Epilogue

Which Concerns Itself with the Aftermath

The days that followed passed in a blur of court appearances, as Mr. and Mrs. Pickett were both called to the Old Bailey as witnesses in the trial of Mrs. Clarissa Huxley Danvers. (" 'Clarissa'?" had been Julia's reaction upon hearing for the first time that lady's Christian name, finding it jarringly unsuited to a woman willing to commit murder upon request.) Nor would their civic duty end there; Pickett, at least, would also be obliged to testify at the upcoming trial of her husband and co-conspirator, as well as those of Edward Poole and David Edwin Tomkins, seemingly distraught nephew and heir to the late George Daniel Tomkins, these last two on charges of soliciting a murder.

Pickett, Julia was relieved to see, appeared to have suffered no ill effects from his ordeal beyond a certain bruised look about his eyes that had not been there before. She trusted that this would fade with time; in spite of his slender, almost lanky frame, he appeared (as his magistrate had frequently observed) to have the constitution of a draft horse. She supposed it had been a necessity for any child of the rookery who hoped to survive to adulthood.

The recollection of his unenviable childhood led, not unnaturally, to thoughts of Kit, and she looked up from the newspaper account of the trial (which had ended with a verdict of guilty on all counts) to observe the brothers Pickett seated on the carpet, the two curly brown heads bent over the chessboard, where the elder was instructing the younger in the finer points of the game.

At least, that had been the plan.

"I'll thank you," Pickett said sternly, "to take my king out of your sleeve and put him back on the board."

With a huff of annoyance, Kit reached into his cuff and withdrew the small ivory figure. "*You're* the one who said I was supposed to capture him," he grumbled.

Pickett threw back his head and laughed aloud, to Kit's further (and vocal) indignation, and Julia wished she could bottle the sound and keep it forever.

For the painful truth was that, in spite of the brief interlude of a *cause célébre*, nothing had really changed. Before the chess lesson had commenced, Pickett had gone through the very same newspaper she now read, marking those advertisements that might hold some hope of a position for a former Bow Street principal officer turned unemployed clerk. He had no doubt that Mr. Ludlow had meant it when he'd told Pickett not to come back—and Julia, for her part, could not be entirely sorry.

There was no denying, however, that their finances were going to be stretched for a time. The arrest of Edward Poole had put an end to any hope of their being reimbursed for the expense of John's admission to the Larches, and although Miss Bonner had offered to cover the cost, as it was he who had discovered the answers for which she herself had gone there to seek, Julia could not bring herself to be any more beholden to that impertinent young woman than she already was.

A noise from the direction of the foyer interrupted her thoughts, and a moment later, Rogers entered the drawing room bearing a silver salver and wearing a mildly bemused expression.

Pickett, looking up and noticing the latter, asked, "What is it, Rogers?"

"The evening post, sir," the butler said.

He sounded more than a little dazed, and Pickett, his curiosity fully roused, rose onto his knees, from which vantage point he could see that the tray was piled high with correspondence. Since they were not—at least, not yet—in arrears as to any of their monthly expenditures, Pickett could not account for it. He took a letter from the top of the pile and broke the wax seal. As he scanned the lines, his expression changed to one so unreadable that Julia was moved to cast aside the newspaper and join him.

"John?" Laying a hand on his shoulder, she leaned down and tried to read the letter in his hand. "What is it?"

Pickett made no answer, for he had opened a second letter and then tore into a third with much the same reaction.

"John?"

Still receiving no reply, she snatched one of the letters

from his unresisting hand and read it for herself.

Dear Mr. Pickett,

Having followed with interest your testimony in the Danvers trial, I wonder if I might meet with you on a matter of some discretion...

She tore open another.

Dear Mr. Pickett,

After reading of your part in that business at the Larches, it occurs to me that I might do a good deal worse than to trust you with a matter of the utmost secrecy...

And another.

John Pickett, Esquire,

This is to request the honor of a meeting at whatever time you may find convenient, for the purpose of consultation on a subject of considerable delicacy...

She looked at Pickett, still ripping into letters and by this time looking frankly stunned.

"You've done it," she said, with a laugh that held more than a note of hysteria. "John, you've done it!"

He scrambled to his feet and, with a whoop of pure joy, snatched up a handful of letters off the pile and flung them into the air. Julia was quick to join in, and soon the air was filled with giddy laughter and fluttering sheets of foolscap.

"What? What?" pleaded Kit. Determined not to be left out, he scooped up a double handful of the letters littering the carpet and launched them once more into the air. "What did he do?"

By this time Pickett had pulled Julia as close as her condition would allow and was fully engaged in kissing her with an enthusiasm that lifted her quite off her feet. Kit, however, would not be ignored, and at last he was obliged to detach his mouth from his wife's and attend to his young half-brother.

"I'll tell you later," he said, and returned to his previous occupation.

About the Author

At the age of sixteen, Sheri Cobb South discovered Georgette Heyer, and came to the startling realization that she had been born into the wrong century. Although she probably would have been a chambermaid had she actually lived in Regency England, that didn't stop her from fantasizing about waltzing the night away in the arms of a handsome, wealthy, and titled gentleman.

Since Georgette Heyer died in 1974 and could not write any more Regencies, Ms. South came to the conclusion she would have to do it herself. In addition to the bestselling John Pickett mystery series (now an award-winning audiobook series!), she has also written several Regency romances, including the critically acclaimed *The Weaver Takes a Wife*.

A native and long-time resident of Alabama, Ms. South now lives in Loveland, Colorado.

She loves to hear from readers, and invites them to visit her website at www.shericobbsouth.com; follow her on social media through Facebook, Goodreads, Pinterest, Instagram, or Twitter; or email her at Cobbsouth@aol.com.

Made in United States
Orlando, FL
25 September 2022